Bon Bon Voyage

**Also by Nancy Fairbanks
in Large Print:**

Chocolate Quake
Death à l'Orange
Mozzarella Most Murderous
The Perils of Paella
Truffled Feathers

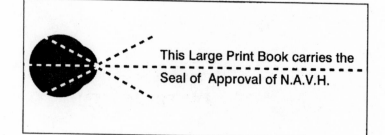

This Large Print Book carries the
Seal of Approval of N.A.V.H.

Bon Bon Voyage

Nancy Fairbanks

Published in 2006 by arrangement with The Berkley Publishing Group, a division of Penguin Group (USA) Inc.

Wheeler Large Print Cozy Mystery.

The text of this Large Print edition is unabridged.
Other aspects of the book may vary from the original edition.

Set in 16 pt. Plantin by Christina S. Huff.

Printed in the United States on permanent paper.

Library of Congress Cataloging-in-Publication Data

Fairbanks, Nancy, 1934–
    Bon bon voyage / by Nancy Fairbanks.
        p.   cm. — (Wheeler large print cozy mystery)
    "A culinary mystery with recipes."
    ISBN 1-59722-260-7 (lg. print : sc : alk. paper)
    1. Blue, Carolyn (Fictitious character) — Fiction.   2. Women food writers — Fiction.   3. Ocean travel — Fiction.   I. Title.
    II. Series.
    PS3606.A36B66 2006b
    813'.6—dc22
                                                                    2006009337

For my parents,
the late Robert S. and Ruth E. Fairbanks,
to whom I owe a wonderful childhood,
a good education
both at home and at school,
and an enduring love of
books, reading, and laughter.
I will love and remember them always.

Acknowledgments

I'd like to acknowledge all the delightful people we met on this cruise (which was not hijacked and actually stopped at all the fascinating places — well, almost all — on the itinerary), but especially Carolyn and Alvin Lipman from Queens, fellow opera lovers, knowledgeable cathedral visitors, wonderful storytellers. I wish I hadn't lost their address, and I thought of them often and fondly as I wrote this book.

Thanks also to my dear husband and travel companion; to my son Bill, who does my Web site; to Anne and Matthew, daughter-in-law and younger son, who tout my books to family and friends; to all those wonderful readers who e-mail me; to my good friends and members of my book clubs: Sisters in Crime, UTEP Women's Book Club, and Bookies. I'd never find so many terrific books and authors to read and pass on to Carolyn Blue if it weren't for the reading lists and discussions I attend monthly with these ladies. And finally, I'd like to thank Sandy Sechrest, who attended our Left Coast Crime Conference in El Paso in 2005 and for whom the ombudslady character was named.

Many thanks to my editor, Cindy Hwang, whose input on this book was particularly important. If it weren't for Cindy, *Bon Bon Voyage* would have been a much different, overly weird, and totally unbelievable book, although my readers may still think it's weird. But I can't help that; I have a weird imagination.

Last, I'd like to acknowledge the authors of the following books, which I used for reference: Ross A. Klein, *Cruise Ship Blues: The Underside of the Cruise Ship Industry*; Bob Dickinson, CTC, and Andy Vladimir, *Selling the Sea: An Inside Look at the Cruise Industry*; James Trager, *The Food Chronology*; Maguelonne Toussaint-Samat (translated by Anthea Bell), *History of Food*; edited by Andrew Eames, updated by Suzanne Lipps, *Insight Guide: Gran Canaria, Fuerteventura, Lanzarote*; Bradley Mayhew and Jan Dodd, *Lonely Planet: Morocco*; Editorial Director Katherine Marquet, *Eyewitness Travel Guides: Morocco*; Annette Solystz, *Timeless Places: Morocco*.

NFH

1

The Gift

Carolyn

I was sitting on my patio, enjoying a warm April day in El Paso and the sight of blooming spring flowers, whose bulbs had been planted by Hector, my recently acquired gardener. Hector had looked at my yard and announced, "*La señora* need Hector *mucho* much." He didn't approve of my gardening skills, which had been applied reluctantly at best. After all, what did I know about desert vegetation and keeping stickery, alien weeds out of rock beds? I'd only lived in El Paso a few years.

On the table beside me was the afternoon mail — seven catalogs for things I didn't want to buy; three offers of credit cards at 0 percent interest for short periods of time; *Chemical and Engineering News*, which was for Jason, who reads me interesting tid-bits at dinner; my electric bill, which I'd put off looking at because I'd already started using the refrigerated air-conditioning, which is so expensive; and — I couldn't be-lieve it — a letter from my children.

They always e-mailed. Why were they writing? Had one or both of them flunked something? Smashed up a car? Contracted a deadly disease? Accepted or made a pro-posal of marriage, and the letter was an in-vitation to the wedding? I fingered the envelope. It was quite thick and had several stamps on it. Warily, I pried up the flap.

HAPPY MOTHER'S DAY, MOM
WITH LOVE FROM
GWEN AND CHRIS

The message was pasted onto the first page with cutout newspaper letters and words, like a ransom note in a movie.

Isn't that sweet? I thought, my eyes misting. But why were they wishing me a happy Mother's Day in April? The event occurred in May. I scowled, remembering when Gwen had left school and flown off to meet me in Barcelona without my per-mission. They were up to something. That was clear.

I flipped to the second page and began to read.

Dear Mom,

We have the greatest Mother's Day surprise for you. We saw this ad for gourmet cruises, so we wrote the company and explained that our mother was a food critic with a syndicated newspaper column on eating in different cities and that we thought they might like to comp her a cruise so she could write columns about their tremendous cuisine. Chris said they wouldn't do it, but guess what? You and Daddy are to have the OWNER'S SUITE, all expenses paid, on the Lisbon-to-Barcelona cruise of their newest ship, the SS Bountiful Feast. *I added the "SS" part, but Chris says it's probably wrong.*

You leave before Mother's Day and get back afterward, visiting "exotic Spanish and North African ports," including the Canary Islands. (See included brochures and letter from the company.) You do have to pay your own airfare, but wait til you see the pictures of the food and rooms. And it's not one of those huge floating hotels, although it does have a spa and other stuff like that. Only 200 passengers with lots and lots of crewmembers to take care of your every need.

And don't worry about Chris and me. I'm staying here to do a summer play and will join you in New York when it's over.

Hi Mom. This is Chris. As you know, I'll be at MIT doing research with that friend of Dad's, but I'll be back to the New York apartment on weekends. You can just put up a cot for me. Gwen is promising me dates with glamorous actresses from that off-Broadway theater she's working for. Hope you and Dad like the surprise. It's for Father's Day, too. I think we got the deal because the "owner's suite" costs a fortune, and they couldn't find anyone rich enough to take it. It's got two bedrooms, two baths, and a sitting room where you can give parties. You should write them as soon as possible to accept, just in case someone actually offers to pay for it.

Love and happy parents' days,
Gwen and Chris

Marveling at the ingenuity and thought-fulness of my children, I looked over the pamphlets. The cruise looked absolutely wonderful — pretty bedrooms, small but nice bathrooms (one even had a tub), balconies, gorgeous public areas, a well-stocked library, and a computer room with Internet access (Jason would like that, and it would be convenient for me, too. I could send columns from the ship). The pictures of the dining room and the sample menus excited all my culinary taste buds. There was even a warm letter from the cruise company saying that they sincerely hoped I would accept their offer because they were very proud of their gourmet chef and his wonderful cuisine on the *Bountiful Feast.*

Next I looked at the itinerary. Lisbon, Gibraltar, Tangier, Casablanca, Gran Canaria, Tenerife, and a delightful assortment of Spanish ports on the way back to Barcelona — all kinds of lovely places to which I'd never been, except for Barcelona. Perhaps we could go early and spend some time in Lisbon, although, of course, we'd have to pay for that. But since the cruise itself was free, we could certainly afford to enjoy a stay in Lisbon.

The only problem I anticipated was the time constriction. April was drawing to a close, May almost upon me, and the cruise began in May, *before* Mother's Day. How would I ever finish the research I like to do for a trip? The history of so many cities. Places so diverse. And the culinary reading. I hated the idea of going on a wonderful trip quite unprepared. Not that I'd consider missing such an opportunity. The ship did have a library. And a computer room. The Internet would probably be a source of information, although time spent on the Internet would be time taken away from the adventures of the cruise. Oh, well, I'd worry about it later.

I picked up the telephone I'd brought out to the patio and speed-dialed Jason at the university. "You'll never guess what our wonderful children have given us for Mother's Day and Father's Day," I said, and went on to describe, with great enthusiasm, our virtually free vacation.

There was a moment of silence at Jason's end of the line, and then he said, "I can't go."

I was stunned. How could my husband even think of turning down such an opportunity? A *free* opportunity! Jason is so thrifty. Surely, he was teasing. "Of course you can," I retorted. "How could you not?"

"I have a meeting," he replied calmly.

"Well, surely you can skip one meeting, Jason." I fought down my disappointment with a dash of irritation. "When you have to go to a meeting, I don't tell you I have something else to do."

"You usually don't have anything else to do, Carolyn," he replied. "And I really can't skip this conference. I'm an invited speaker, and I'm responsible for one of the tracks."

"I haven't heard anything about a meeting," I muttered.

"Well, it's in Canada, out in the middle of the plains. It didn't occur to me that you'd be interested since it's probably not a place famed for its gourmet food. There aren't even any activities for accompanying persons."

"And you'd rather go there than on a wonderful cruise? What are the meeting dates?"

Jason told me and remarked that although he'd be free after the meeting, we couldn't very well try to catch the cruise out in the Atlantic Ocean, which was probably where the ship would be, coming or going from the Canary Islands.

"Fine," I said. "I'll have to go by myself."

There was another silence. Then Jason said, "I wish you wouldn't, Carolyn. Some of those places are in North Africa. Given the tumult in the Islamic world, I'd be worried about you all the time you were gone."

"Well, I'll be worried that you might get run over by a tractor out there on the great plains of Canada. We'll both just have to hope for the best."

And that was the way it ended. Jason would not go, and he didn't want me to go by myself. He probably thought I'd stumble across another corpse, and he wouldn't be there to urge me to mind my own business. I was really very peeved with him.

2

"A Frigging Cruise?"

Luz

I'd just returned from a visit to the rheumatologist, who gave me a repeat lecture on the stupidity of cutting back on my meds last fall. After that he said he was "very pleased" with my response to a new medication he'd prescribed. He would be! The self-satisfied prick. He didn't have to pay for the stuff. Pretty soon I'd need to go snag another scumbag criminal and turn him in for a reward to finance my frigging rheumatoid arthritis. I was just pouring some dog food into a bowl for Smack, a retired narc I took in when she was too old for service, when my phone rang.

Wouldn't you know? It was Carolyn Blue. Not that I don't like her. I'll never forget the time she slapped the hand of some jerk who decided to feel up one of the exotic dancers at Brazen Babes. Caro just hauled off and gave him a good whack right in the middle of a table dance. Still, I wasn't really in the mood for any girl talk at the moment. I'd been planning to sit down in my one comfortable chair and enjoy a shot of tequila, except the doctor had lectured me about drinking, too. I never should have told him that tequila was a better painkiller than any damn anti-inflammatory on the market.

"Yeah, Carolyn, hi. Listen, could we talk some other time? I just got in from —"

Whatever she had to say couldn't wait. In fact, she sounded so excited I'm not even sure she heard me. She went right on telling me about some cruise around Europe that she had free tickets for.

"Sounds great," I agreed, sitting down on a chair in my kitchen while Smack swallowed about a half-pound of dog food and then gave me a hopeful look. Right. Like I was going to let her get fat in her old age. Carolyn had just listed a bunch of places where the boat stopped. Most of them I'd never heard of. "Hey, you're gonna have a great time," I assured her, "but maybe you could tell me about it when you get back." I managed to get that in before she could describe every single detail about the room or cabin or whatever it was she'd be staying in.

"Not just me. Both of us," she corrected. "They've got a spa and a gym and fascinating shore excursions, and the food is supposed to be absolutely —"

"What's this *both of us* business?" I interrupted. "I couldn't afford to go on a cruise if I wanted to, which I don't." Smack came over and licked my hand, so I gave her an ear scratch while Carolyn told me that it wouldn't cost us a penny. The whole thing was complimentary, except for the airfare, because the cruise company wanted her to write columns about their fancy food. Jason couldn't go because he had a meeting, and he didn't want Carolyn to go alone because he was a weenie — she giggled at that — and was afraid of Muslim countries and stuff.

"Muslim, like terrorists?" I asked.

"Of course not!" Carolyn exclaimed. "These countries are in North Africa, and if anything dangerous happens, the State Department tells Americans not to go there, and the cruise company sends us to some other port. Don't you want to see Gibraltar? And the Spanish ports? And the Canary Islands? They're supposed to be so beautiful."

"Yeah, and what does the airplane cost?" I asked sarcastically. "You know all my money goes for meds."

"Surely you have some left from when we kidnapped that disgusting man in Juárez," she said. "After all, I gave you my half."

Oh, shit! She *had* given me her half, and actually I did have a lot of that money left, but I didn't want to spend it on some frigging cruise. When I told her it would be too expensive, she said Jason could pay for my ticket since he was being so mean about not going with her. "He'll be glad to," Carolyn declared. "Think of how much safer he'll feel if you're with me."

I doubted that. The first and last time I saw Jason Blue, Carolyn and I were half snockered on sangria, laughing and making toasts on her patio. He hadn't seemed that glad to meet me. Since then Carolyn and I met from time to time for lunch, but I finally had to take over picking the restaurants. She was into these cutesy places full of middle-aged, dressed-up women and food that had fancy sauce splashed on everything. I introduced her to some really great hole-in-the-wall Tex-Mex places where cops and workmen go to grab a bite. I even got her to try *menudo,* which is tripe soup, the local cure for hangovers. I have to admit she's game when it comes to food. Everything she puts in her mouth is something she might write about in a column. She's always asking some poor Spanish-only *abuelita* for a recipe, and I have to translate. Of course the places I like, they don't have recipes. They make stuff like their mamas did — a little of this, a little of that, and a hell of a lot of jalapeños.

All the time I was thinking about some of our weird lunch excursions, Carolyn was trying to convince me that I really did want to go on this cruise with her. "Why would I want to go on a frigging cruise?" I finally interrupted. "My knees would freeze up from sitting too long on the airplane, I wouldn't know the languages anywhere we got off, I'd hate all the snobbish passengers, I don't have any evening gowns to wear to the gourmet dinners, which I wouldn't like anyway, and I'd probably get seasick and spend the whole time barfing on their fancy carpets."

Carolyn said, "Nonsense."

"It's not like El Paso's really a seafaring section of the country," I put in before she could tell me why my reasons for not going were nonsense. "My only experience on a

21

boat was a trip to Elephant Butte, where we fished off the side of a rowboat with a put-put motor on the back. And someone drowned while we were up there. Think how many more people must drown in an ocean." Smack had dozed off sprawled across my feet, and my knees were starting to hurt.

Carolyn snorted. "It just so happens that I cut out an article about exercises one can do in an airplane seat that prevent frozen knees, not to mention those blood clots that scoot up to your brain or lungs and kill you."

"Blood clots?" That didn't sound good. "All the more reason for me —"

"And at all the ports except those in North Africa, people speak Spanish, even the Canary Islands, which are owned by Spain. Well, on Gibraltar they speak English because —"

"I can see that if I went, you'd want to tell me the history of every damn place the boat stopped."

"The guides will do that, and at the Spanish ports you can translate for *me*," Carolyn retorted. "I might even learn some Spanish if you'd take the trouble to teach me. I thought we were friends. I don't see why —"

"Look, I don't have a long dress, and I'm not going to buy one, so that's that."

"Luz, you don't have to. Just get a long skirt if you don't have one. You can find one for ten dollars at Ross. Then you pair it with different tops and some jewelry, and you're good to go. I know you've got some great jewelry. The night we went over to Juárez, I saw your grandmother's turquoise."

"My grandmother's turquoise isn't going to keep me from barfing up all the rich food I'd have to eat," I muttered.

"The cruise lines provide seasick pills," said Carolyn, "and I won't let you fall off the ship and drown."

So that's how it went, and guess who ended up getting talked into taking a cruise? I had to agree. Otherwise, Carolyn would have gone on and on about the history of the Canary Islands. My only consolation was that it would be my first and last cruise. And it wasn't going to cost me much. Not likely I'd get another offer for a free vacation. But my mom wasn't going to be happy when I missed Mother's Day because I was thousands of miles away, wandering around some country with a bunch of Arabs in it.

Well, if those terrorists tried anything

with Carolyn and me, I wouldn't mind kicking ass. A cousin of mine got about a pound of shrapnel in his leg over there in the Middle East. Poor Jaime's still limping, and he was a hell of a halfback on the Bowie football team before he joined the army.

3

"Not My
Mother-in-Law!"

Carolyn

I was in such a good mood after talking Luz into going with me that I decided to forgive Jason for ruining the children's plans and my Mother's Day gift. I'd make him something nice for dinner. Maybe lamb chops and twice-baked potatoes with both cheese and onions. And asparagus. I'd bought some lovely, thick asparagus at the market. I might even make hollandaise sauce to go on the asparagus. And I'd open a bottle of that French wine he liked, Carolus Magnus. I liked it myself. Who could resist a wine named after Charlemagne? Then, once I had him softened up, I'd tell him he didn't have to worry about me traveling alone to exotic foreign ports because Luz Vallejo had agreed to go with me. She was an ex–police lieutenant and a very tough woman, probably better protection than Jason, not that I'd mention that.

I wondered what we'd do about Smack, Luz's aging, retired police dog. I'd have to ask the cruise people if we could bring the dog along. No, that was a bad idea. What would we do with her on the plane? I certainly had no intention of buying a ticket for Smack and sitting with her all the way to Lisbon. And they probably wouldn't let Smack into foreign countries or on the boat. Luz would have to leave the dog with one of her sisters, but their children would love it. No one could say Smack wasn't well behaved. She spent most of her time napping and only got mean with people who were carrying drugs or irritating Luz.

It occurred to me that Luz and I should go shopping together. That would be fun, and it would soothe her worries about not having the right evening wear. How many dinners would be formal? I wondered. I might well have to buy myself something new.

While making all these happy plans, I began the dinner, potatoes first. As they were baking, I chopped the onions, grated the cheese, and seasoned the lamb chops. I even pared the asparagus stalks, not something I always bother to do. Usually I just break the ends off so the non-tip part will be reasonably tender. By the time Jason arrived at six, I had a relatively simple but very tasty dinner to serve him. I'd decided to skip the hollandaise sauce. Instead I put the asparagus under the broiler with pepper, butter, and cheese.

My dear husband arrived smiling cheerfully. He can smell a good dinner before he's even opened the door. When he looked at his plate, he beamed. Jason loves lamb chops. Who wouldn't? All that cholesterol! They're bound to be delicious. But we'd worry about cholesterol when we got into our fifties. For now . . .

"This looks wonderful," said Jason. He dropped a kiss on my cheek, pulled out my chair, and poured wine for me and then for himself. My, he is a handsome man, and so endearing when he's not lecturing me. I have to admit that the sight of Jason in an appreciative mood still, after twenty-odd years of marriage, causes my heart to do a little flip.

"Does the dinner mean you've forgiven me for having a meeting when you want to go on a cruise?" Jason asked.

Before I could assure him that I'd forgiven him, he added, "I was just worried about you going by yourself. Especially on Mother's Day."

"Oh, well, I —"

"But I've solved the problem." He looked so pleased with himself as he cut off a bite of his first lamb chop. Those delicious little rib chops only have about three bites on them. I always pan fry four chops for Jason and two or three for myself. "I called Mother this afternoon," he said, taking a sip of wine to complement the lamb.

"Oh?" I murmured, bemused. "How is she?" My mother-in-law, who is seventy-four, had a mild heart attack during the semester break. Her doctor advised her to stop teaching and rabble rousing for six months and take it easy, except for a planned exercise program at a senior citizens' gym. She was probably bored to tears and appallingly cranky.

"Fine," said Jason. "Good to go, according to her doctor. She talked to him and called me back with the news."

"That's wonderful. So she'll be teaching again in the fall?"

"Well, yes, that too. What I meant is that she can go on the cruise with you."

"*What?*" He couldn't have said that. He

28

couldn't have suggested that to her without telling me. Imagine sharing a suite with Gwenivere Blue for the duration of the cruise! For years she's never had a kind word to say to me. She thought I was a disgrace to the feminist movement, of which I'd never been a part, so her complaint was hardly fair. Then last year she'd sent me a size 16 dress. I wear a 10, and it was a frumpy dress, evidently her idea of appropriate clothing for a woman who spent most of her adult life taking care of a husband and children.

"For heaven's sake, Caro, what's that expression supposed to mean? Don't tell me you don't want to take my mother along with you."

"Well, I —"

"Mother can be very good company if she wants to."

But would she want to? And why was Jason being such a hypocrite? It's not as if he got along that well with her. He even complained if I expressed any opinion that sounded as if she might have put it into my head.

"And now that you and she —"

"What?" I demanded. "Vera and I what?"

"She invited you to call her Vera. That's certainly progress."

"That's because I asked her, when she was in jail, if she wanted me to call her Mother Blue."

"You didn't!" Jason started to laugh.

"This isn't funny, Jason. The only time that I can remember your mother being half civil to me was at that women's center party in San Francisco. Ten minutes of civility does not constitute a close relationship. She was probably just happy to be cleared of the murder charges and out of jail."

"And you cleared her," Jason pointed out.

I tried not to glare at him. He hadn't been all that happy about my running around San Francisco, trying to find the real murderer. Not when it was happening.

"I'm sure she's still grateful," said my husband.

I took a big gulp of wine, but it didn't help, so I dropped my head into my hands and wondered what I was going to do. Luz had already agreed to the trip. "Don't you think you should have told me before you invited her on *my* Mother's Day cruise?"

"It didn't occur to me that you'd object," said Jason stiffly. "I thought you'd appreciate the company, and after all, she *has*

30

had health problems. A cruise will be just the thing for her. Her doctor agreed. She can take walks around the decks and that sort of thing. She hates the gym so much, she quit."

So if I continued to object, I would be endangering Vera's health? That's what my husband was saying? And what about Luz? I really *wanted* to take the cruise with Luz. If the other passengers were snobbish, Luz would be the perfect antidote. And her reaction to cruise luxury and entertainment would be a source of entertainment in itself. Whereas Vera would probably try to talk the female crew into going on strike or wonder loudly why cruise captains were never women and organize a gender-discrimination campaign against the cruise line.

My mother-in-law caused all sorts of trouble in the women's section of the San Francisco jail before I found the real murderer and got her released. Feminism and female convicts, not to mention female guards, were not all that compatible. When I'd gone to visit her on family visiting day, something her *son* hadn't found time for, Vera had infuriated people on both sides of the glass visiting window and couldn't be bothered to give me information that

31

might have made my familial duty to exonerate her easier.

"If you don't want to take her with you, you'll have to call and tell her yourself," said Jason, looking grim as he forked creamy, oniony potatoes au gratin from the crispy potato skin I'd put on his plate.

Wasn't that just like a man? He got me into an embarrassing, hopeless situation and then refused to accept responsibility for his actions. And what was *I* to do? Refuse to take his mother along because of my invitation to Luz, whom he didn't even like? Choose one of my prospective roommates to disinvite? That's obviously what I had to do.

Or did I?

4

All Aboard

Carolyn

When our plane landed at the Lisbon airport, it was a beautiful May day, sun shining, with puffy, cotton-candy clouds bouncing across a baby blue sky. By contrast, we were bedraggled, exhausted, and cranky. A limping, cursing Luz had planted her cane on the toe of a man who made the serious mistake of trying to get in front of her in the passport line.

He, in turn, demanded that the handsomely uniformed Portuguese immigration officer arrest Luz for assault. I attempted to defuse the situation by telling the officer that any man who shoved a woman with a cane was no gentleman. Then Luz said something in Spanish, and the two got into a conversation characterized by smiling, misunderstanding, laughter, and even possibly flirting. I couldn't be sure because I didn't know what they were saying.

She introduced me to the officer, who raised our hands to his lips, but without actually kissing our fingers. I could hardly blame him for that. I, for one, felt absolutely grimy, although before landing, I had scrubbed my face and fingers with one of those smelly hand wipes the airline provides with breakfast.

The fuming American with the sore foot was marched away by another officer, who had been summoned to the booth by Luz's new friend. What did they mean to do to him? Give him a lesson in gentlemanly behavior? Subject his person and his luggage to an embarrassing search? Behind us in the line, people were complaining about the delay. Not a promising start to our vacation.

The cruise lines may consider the overnight flight from the United States part of the total vacation experience, but I certainly didn't. A very large man in front of us on the airplane had tilted his seat back into Luz's face. Then his girlfriend threw herself into his lap, setting both seats to shuddering and knocking my book onto the floor while jamming

Luz's left knee. That was the beginning of a very bad night.

"I don't know why I let you talk me into this," she muttered for the millionth time as, with hundreds of other sleep-deprived tourists, we waited at the carousel for our luggage.

"If we can just get to the ship, we can fall straight into real beds and have long naps," I promised. "By the time we wake up, we'll be at sea and ready for a memorable meal."

"I thought international flights were supposed to have good food," she groused. "That stuff was pig swill."

"I told you to order the beef. It's always safer to avoid the rubbery chicken and even the overcooked pasta unless you're in business or first class. Anyway, the food on the ship will be heavenly."

She grunted, hooked her cane through the handle of her suitcase — she'd only brought one, and it wasn't that big — and hauled it off the carousel, sending three or four people to either side of us stumbling into other people in order to escape Luz's flying luggage. When mine came along, I leaned forward and grasped the handle, only to be dragged along by the weight of my bag. A nice gentleman pulled both the

35

suitcase and me to safety and murmured, *"Da nada, señora,"* when I thanked him profusely. Then we wheeled our luggage into a cavernous room full of people arriving, people leaving, people waiting, and people standing in line. I felt like weeping when I saw the crowd. How were we ever to find the cruise representative in this mass of humanity?

While I was ready to give up, Luz looked around and spotted a smiling lady wearing a smart periwinkle uniform and holding a sign that said, ALL ABOARD THE *BOUNTIFUL FEAST*. Much relieved, we trundled our bags toward her. I had my huge suitcase and my carry-on, which contained my laptop and other important possessions I'd never pack into a suitcase from which some sticky-fingered Homeland Security person could filch appealing items. Luz was festooned with her handbag, a small wheeled suitcase, and her cane, which I fervently hoped didn't contain that pop-out knife she'd used in Juárez to terrify a criminal. What an adventure that had been!

We identified ourselves to the cruise representative, who had the most luscious, gleaming black hair I'd ever seen and more curves that one usually expects to see on a woman in uniform. She also had a three-part name, which I immediately forgot, and made an amazing show of delight over our arrival, as if we were long-lost sisters or childhood friends she had been pining to see for years. Her delight ratcheted up several notches when she checked for our names on her list and discovered that we were to be in the owner's suite. By this time Luz was scowling ferociously.

"Ladies," exclaimed our greeter, "a representative of the line will be with us momentarily to escort you to the van, which will take you to the harbor where our beautiful ship, the *Bountiful Feast*, awaits you."

"Get your hands off my bag," snapped Luz, and brought her cane down on the wrist of a burly fellow in a white sailor suit with periwinkle decorations on the hat and blouse. He yelped and staggered back while I pulled my suitcase closer lest someone try to steal it, too.

"Madam," cried the greeter, "this is Luis, who will take your suitcase to the ship's baggage disposal room, from which it will be delivered to your stateroom."

"I can take care of my own baggage," Luz snarled.

"Passengers on the *Bountiful Feast* never, never take care of their own baggages," said the greeter, horrified. "We are do everythings possible for the comforts of our guests."

I could see that her English, so perfect to begin with, was deteriorating rapidly under the stress of this unusual situation.

"Madam — ah — Blue, please show your companion what is proper to do by giving your baggages to Luis. Is his job to carry them away."

Actually, I didn't want to give him my carry-on. It had my computer, a change of underwear, a nightgown, a mini–cosmetic case, and my jewelry. What if these two weren't really from the cruise line? That hadn't occurred to me before Luz raised the specter by attacking Luis, if that was his real name.

A tall, wrinkled lady in an olive green pantsuit pushed between Luz and me and ordered us to stop being silly. "You, Luis, those are my bags." She pointed to a set of three bags that matched her clothing. "Take them away. My name is Gross," she announced to the greeter. "R. L. Gross. Check me off your list and show me the way to the van."

"Of course, Madam Gross." The greeter

was all smiles again. "Welcome to Lisbon. Only a few moments. The van will —"

"Young lady," interrupted Mrs. Gross, her facial wrinkles deepening as her mouth turned grim, "I know what *a few moments* means, and I won't put up with it. If I'm not taken to the ship immediately, I shall complain to your superior." Before the greeter could say a thing, Mrs. Gross had turned to Luz. "Don't be an ass, woman. Give your bag to the boy. You, too," she said to me. "Only an idiot would suspect people wearing such silly uniforms of being luggage thieves."

Not a very charming lady, but what could we do? She was probably right. Luis collected her three bags, my huge one, my carry-on, over which we had a brief tug-of-war, and Luz's suitcase. "That better turn up in my room," Luz muttered.

"*Qué?*" Luis evidently didn't understand English, but Luz shouted something in Spanish as he staggered away, and he broke into a trot, the luggage bouncing along with him.

Under the grim instructions of Mrs. Gross, the greeter left her post, reluctantly, and escorted us toward the doors, where she turned us over with great relief to a man in a chauffeur's hat. He took us to his double-parked van and settled us into comfy seats. Luz was still looking for Luis and the bags, but he was nowhere in sight. I was looking for a Portuguese landmark I'd read about on the plane so I could point it out to Luz.

"Oh look, Luz, I think that castle up on the hill might be St. George's." I longed to see it, but I wasn't going to get to because Luz had absolutely refused to come two days early for a tour of Lisbon.

"As if I care," she snapped. "I feel like shit, and some foreign thief just ran off with my suitcase. It could be the Vatican up there on the hill, and I wouldn't give a rat's ass."

A woman behind us gasped. Unfortunately, I was going to have to talk to Luz about her language, and I knew from experience that she wouldn't take it well. Then the male companion of the woman behind us said, "It isn't St. George."

After that the van pulled out, and we dozed off, so I never did get to see anything of Lisbon but the airport and the harbor.

5

The Owner's Suite

Carolyn

I was hoping to enter the suite first since I'd have some explaining to do, but Luz barged in ahead of me in search of her suitcase. "Well, it's not in the frigging living room, if that's what this is," she snarled.

I was about to follow her in, but another uniformed person came bouncing down the hall, saying, "Is me, Herkule Pipa. The steward of you."

"*Your* bag is here," said Luz from inside. "I knew it. Mine's lost. That's just frigging great! I'll have to wear these jeans for the next two weeks."

"Look in the bedroom," I called through the open door. "I'm Carolyn Blue," I said to the steward, a funny little man about my height, which is to say five-six. He had a round, rosy face topped by sparse black hair that lay in silky strands on his forehead, the tops of his ears, and, presumably, around the back of his head. There was a bald spot like a monk's tonsure above the strands. His body was as thin as his face was round, and his smile was as welcoming as if I were already his favorite passenger. "It's very nice to meet you, Mr. Pipa."

"Herkule," he corrected. "Is me, Herkule. You think is comical name? Yes? Is Albania name. I am Albania. Handsome country, but very famished. Now I have steward employment with copious dollars and numerous food. Very fine for me."

"That's — ah — lovely." His English was peculiar, to say the least.

"Who are you?" demanded my mother-in-law from inside the suite.

Oh, dear. I had meant to be there when Luz and Vera discovered that they were sharing the suite with me. The cruise line knew and had agreed to the additional passenger when I explained my problem, but I had neglected to explain the situation to my mother-in-law and my friend. "I'm needed inside, Mr. — Herkule."

"No, no," he cried.

"I'm one of the occupants of this suite," said Luz. "And you're not the other one,

42

so would you get out of the way so I can see if my bag is in that room?"

"Oh, dear, if you'll excuse me, Mr. — Herkule —"

"No Mr. Is Herkule."

"The other occupant is Carolyn Blue," said my mother-in-law. "You're in the wrong suite."

"Very well. Herkule," I agreed in order to pacify the steward. "And now I really need to intervene —"

"Intervene? New word!" exclaimed Herkule. "I put on roster for tomorrow. Ten new words every day. Is my end to become mistress of English."

"Master," I corrected. "Very commendable."

"Carolyn Blue is *my* roommate," snapped Luz.

I shut the door in Herkule's face and cried cheerfully, "Well, I see you two have met — more or less. Vera, this is my friend, Luz Vallejo. Luz, my mother-in-law, Vera Blue." They both frowned at me.

"There's plenty of room," I assured them. "You and I can share the room with twin beds, Luz, and Vera can have the one with — whatever it has."

"I haven't shared a room since I got divorced," said Luz. "No way you want to sleep in a room with me. I groan when my meds wear off."

"You're not getting my room that way," said Vera. "I snore, and I'd like to know how this happened, Carolyn. Jason didn't say anything about there being three of us."

My mother-in-law was enveloped in a huge terry robe that dragged on the floor and wrapped all the way around her. She'd bundled it together with the belt and looked like a small, angry polar bear.

"And I didn't even want to come on this frigging cruise," said Luz. "You talked me into it, Caro, by telling me Jason didn't want you to go by yourself."

"Oh, for heaven's sake, Jason invited his mother the same day I invited you, Luz, so I just called the cruise line to see if a third person could come. What was I supposed to do? Tell one of you you were disinvited?"

"Since we haven't sailed, I'll just make them find my bag so I can go home," said Luz.

"Don't be ridiculous, young woman," Vera retorted. "Just because my son is an idiot, as most men are, and invited me without consulting his wife, that shouldn't keep you from enjoying the cruise." Then my mother-in-law turned toward the door, at which someone had been knocking during most of the discussion, and shouted, "Come in."

The steward popped his head in, beamed at us, and said, "Is me, Herkule Pipa, with the baggages for Mrs. Blue."

"It's about time," said Vera. "I need a nap, and I'm not going to get it wearing this gigantic robe."

"And where's *my* bag?" Luz demanded.

"Not to agonize, towering lady," said Herkule. "Baggages always materialize within hour. Can Herkule convey appetizing small foods, feathery towels —"

"A suitcase of clothes for Luz Vallejo," she reminded him.

"Bar has many intoxicating beverages. No cost. See?" He bustled over to a small refrigerator that became accessible when he flipped up one side of a table with three chairs. "Have calming cocktail while wait for baggages."

"Go away," said Luz, "and don't come back until you have my bag."

"Instantly I go," said the steward, and went.

"You shouldn't be mean to him, Luz. He's trying to be helpful," I admonished.

"Bosh," said Vera. "He's looking for a big tip."

"Tips are part of the price of this cruise," I corrected.

"Which we're not paying for, so he probably expects a chunk of money at the end."

Since there's no winning an argument with my mother-in-law, I didn't try. Instead I looked in the bar, poured out a glass of red wine from a one-serving bottle, opened a bag of cashews, and, feeling very decadent to be drinking before noon, took a look around the suite. First, the room Luz and I would be sharing: The twin beds had cream-colored, fitted spreads piped in what was evidently the line's color, periwinkle. The ship itself, which was white, had periwinkle stripes and was quite pretty, as was our room with its periwinkle carpet and drapes and its built-in drawers, not to mention its blond nightstands, doors, desk, and desk chair, and its small flowered easy chairs.

The bathroom — well, the colors were pleasant, cream tiles, some with flowers, but it was very small — a miniature sink beside the toilet with the paper roll fastened to the side of the sink cabinet, shower on the other side with an outward opening door that barely cleared the sink and would require a stout person to edge in sideways. Evidently Vera had the bathtub.

6

"Bon Voyage and Happy Mother's Day"

Carolyn

I edged out of the bathroom in time to hear knocking at our door and a shaky voice calling, "Is me, Herkule Pipa."

"My suitcase," Luz cried. She had begun to undress but quickly zipped up her jeans and dashed into our sitting room with me close behind to protect poor Herkule in case he wasn't bringing her suitcase. My guess was better than hers. When she flung the door open, our steward stood cowering in the hall, holding two boxes elaborately wrapped in silver paper with gauzy periwinkle bows.

"Offerings," he quavered, backing up hastily. "For —"

"You idiot," she snarled. "No gift is going to replace my luggage, and don't come back until you've damn well found that suitcase."

"For ladies Blue," he finished hopefully, now standing with his back to the wall across from our door and his hands quivering so violently that his grip on the packages was slipping.

"Gifts!" I exclaimed. "How lovely!" I pushed Luz aside and rescued them from his custody. "Thank you, Herkule."

"Herkule thank *you*, merciful madam," he replied over his shoulder as he escaped around the nearest corner.

While I was examining the tiny envelopes on the packages, Vera came out of her room and demanded to know what the ruckus was about. She was rewrapped in her giant robe, her white hair already sleep-ravaged from the few minutes she'd managed to catch.

"Herkule delivered two gifts, one for you and one for me," I replied, holding them up.

"Wouldn't you know? The line gives the two of you presents and loses my luggage," Luz muttered.

Vera seized the gift I extended to her, ignored the pretty wrappings and the card, ripped her way into the box below, and eyed the contents askance. "What the devil are those?"

"Bonbons," I replied. "At least I think that's what they are."

"Bonbons?" With about as much enthusiasm as she might have accorded a box of miniature hand grenades, my mother-in-law stared at the candies with their variegated colors and coatings.

Assuming that my box contained the same thing, I set it on an end table and opened the envelope. If the bonbons — and any sane person would have preferred truffles — were a present from the line, why hadn't Luz been given a box, as well? If not from the cruise line, then who would be sending me bonbons and, even more puzzling, sending them to my mother-in-law?

Luz had tramped over to the refrigerator, yanked it open, and removed a small bottle of tequila, which she immediately opened and drained. Vera said, "What a stupid gift," and handed the box to Luz. "Try one. You'll probably hate it, but if not, they're yours." Luz popped a mint green confection into her mouth; it must have tasted awful after the straight tequila she'd just gulped down, but maybe she was thinking *margarita.* Margaritas are green.

Meanwhile, I was taking the card from the envelope. It read:

BON VOYAGE AND
HAPPY MOTHER'S DAY
FROM YOUR
LOVING HUSBAND, JASON.

"Mine are from Jason," I said to Vera. "Yours probably are, too." I picked the card up off the floor where Vera had tossed it with the torn silver paper and fancy bow.

"My God," said Vera, "where did I go wrong raising that boy?" She headed back to her room, muttering, "Bonbons. Next he'll be giving me lace underwear."

"They're just candy," Luz announced. "What's the big deal?" She helped herself to another from Vera's box before heading for our bedroom.

I unwrapped my box, hoping for truffles. *Bon voyage and happy Mother's Day,* indeed! Jason had to know, after all these years, that I like truffles or anything chocolate, which the gift did not appear to include. Unless there was a second layer filled with chocolate-covered bonbons. And if he really wanted me to have a good trip and a happy Mother's Day, he'd be here. I left his gift on the end table and headed to my room for a shower and some much-needed sleep. I'd no sooner opened the door than I discovered Luz stripping off her jeans. "I can lend you a nightgown," I offered hastily.

"Jesus Christ, Carolyn, I can sleep naked. Just call me when the little guy gets here with my stuff."

I agreed and left hurriedly before she got all her clothes off. Because Vera had gone into her room and closed the door, I didn't get to see either her room or the advertised bathtub. Hadn't the brochure said something about waterspouts in the tub? It seemed unfair that Luz and I were stuck with a closet bath while my mother-in-law had the luxurious one.

Feeling put upon, probably as a result of sleep deprivation, I examined the sitting room more closely than I had while trying to mediate the initial meeting between my two roommates and during the arrival of the unappreciated bonbons. As well as the table and chairs, there was a sitting area with two loveseats edging a coffee table and one armchair on the third side, all of which faced a television set that folded down from the ceiling, according to the TV booklet on an end table. The color scheme was rose and gray. Beyond a large draped area were sliding doors that led to a balcony with white metal chairs and a low table. The outside chairs had rose cushions on the seats. If I hadn't been so exhausted, I'd have sat there with my abandoned wine and nuts and gazed at the harbor.

Instead, assuming that Luz was under the sheets by now, I put the unfinished goblet and half-eaten packet on the table, took a nightgown and toiletries out of my carry-on, and tiptoed through to the mini-bath. Luz was fast asleep while I struggled out of my clothes and into the shower, where the water ran hot immediately and I luxuriated in a thorough soaping and spraying, not to mention the scrubbing of my face and ears. The *Bountiful Feast* may have been sailing from a European port, but unlike European hotels, it provided washcloths. Of course, I'd brought my own, but I wouldn't have to use them.

I didn't even have to use my own toiletries. The mirrored door above the sink revealed a full array of lotions, shampoos, perfumed soaps, toothbrushes, and toothpastes. I brushed my teeth vigorously, slipped out of the bathroom, dropped my travel clothes into the laundry bag provided by the ship, and fell into bed. I doubt that I've ever fallen asleep faster in my life. I barely had time to realize that Luz did groan in her sleep, although I doubted that my mother-in-law snored. She just wanted the room to herself, which was fine with me. I didn't want to share with her anyway. She had an uncanny talent for hurting my feelings.

The first time I ever had bonbons, they came decoratively wrapped as a "bon voyage" gift. Granted, they looked pretty when I opened the box, but there wasn't a dollop of chocolate in the lot. Now, truffles are heavenly. I love truffles, which have chocolate on the outside or the inside or both. Imagine a truffle with dark chocolate coating, a crispy inner layer of chocolate beneath that, and then liqueur spurting into your mouth when you've bitten through. Godiva makes those. Then compare that to a bonbon.

My box contained a lot of coconut, which is very unhealthy. It shoots your cholesterol right up into the stratosphere, whereas dark chocolate lowers your cholesterol. Some of the bonbons were fruity or nutty, which is nice, but it's not chocolate. I'd swear that several had mashed sweet potato inside with hard frosting outside. How disgusting is that?

If for some reason you decide to make bonbons — and there are bonbon recipes — here is a strawberry version, since May is not only Mother's Day month, but also National Strawberry Month. Also, the recipe has a bit of chocolate in it to perk you up. For added perkiness, I've included a coffee bonbon recipe.

However, the ultimate candy to produce happiness is the truffle, so I've provided a simple truffle recipe that you can fix in any number of flavors.

Strawberry Bonbons

Blend well *8 ounces softened cream cheese* and *6 ounces melted semi-sweet chocolate chips.*

Stir in *3/4 cup vanilla wafer crumbs* and *1/4 cup seedless strawberry preserves.*

Shape into 1-inch balls and roll in *chopped hazelnuts.* (30 bonbons)

Coffee Bonbons

Mix the following ingredients: *1 cup finely rolled vanilla wafer crumbs; 1/2 cup confectioner's sugar; 3/4 cup finely chopped pecans; 1 tablespoon instant coffee powder; 2 tablespoons melted butter; 1 1/2 tablespoons light corn syrup;* and *1/4 cup coffee liqueur.*

Roll into 1-inch balls, dust with more *confectioner's sugar,* and refrigerate for several days.

Various Truffles

For raspberry truffles, defrost *3/4 cup frozen or fresh raspberries* and strain through a fine mesh sieve. Set 1/4 cup aside.

Chop finely *8 ounces good semisweet chocolate such as Lindt* and put in a bowl.

Bring *3/4 cup heavy cream* almost to a boil and pour it over chocolate. Whisk to blend.

Stir in raspberry puree and a nip of salt (or for a different truffle flavor, *3 tablespoons brandy, cognac, Grand Marnier, rum, or other favorite liqueur*).

Cover and refrigerate until very cold, one hour or more.

Make 1-inch balls with a melon baller or small ice-cream scoop and put on a baking sheet. Return to refrigerator.

Pour sifted *Dutch-process cocoa powder* or *favorite sugar* or *finely chopped nuts* on a plate or plates and roll cold truffles in them, coating thoroughly.

Move truffles to an airtight container with waxed paper between layers.

Can be stored for one week in fridge or frozen for a month.

Truffles can also be coated with a hard layer of chocolate, but the process, which involves tempering the coating chocolate, is more complicated (i.e., melting the chocolate, cooling, and re-melting before dipping and rolling the truffles and refrigerating again).

Carolyn Blue,
"Have Fork, Will Travel,"
Phoenix Sun

7

The Captain's Champagne Reception

Luz

I woke up feeling pretty good, taking notice of my mood and my physical condition, as I always do before I open my eyes. Some days it's not worth getting out of bed. That day it seemed safe: I didn't feel like biting anyone's head off or yelling at my dog, and my knees didn't ache. Then I did open my eyes and got a high-voltage jolt.

Where the hell was I? Oh, Christ! Carolyn's frigging cruise. Narrow bed, like I was a nun or some damn thing. Fussy boat colors. We were probably already at sea since I felt a weird vibration I never noticed in my condo at home. So I checked for seasickness. Nope. I didn't feel like puking, but I did look around wildly for the bathroom and, spotting a door, grabbed a terry robe someone had left on the bed, not the weird little steward I hoped, and sprang out from under the covers.

Whoops! I slammed the door to the living room shut and tried another. *Hijo de puta!* If this was the luxurious john with water-spouting tub Carolyn had told me about, the *Bountiful Feast* people were going to be really sorry they lied to us! To take a piss, I had to put one elbow in the sink. To take a shower, I was wedged between a tile wall and a glass door, on which I scraped my butt trying to get in. At least the water was hot, and the soap, which smelled like a whorehouse full of perfume, made suds. I felt better, except for a second scrape getting out, and scrambled into the robe. If I showed up naked in the living room, Carolyn would faint. No telling what her mother-in-law would do. The woman had a personality like broken glass.

I padded barefoot into the living room and spotted Carolyn and Vera sitting on a balcony, all dressed up, with a million miles of water in the background. What I didn't see was my suitcase, and when I glanced over my shoulder into the bedroom, it wasn't there either. The only things of mine in there were my traveling jeans and denim shirt, neatly draped over a chair (not by me; I'd dropped them in a heap on the floor when we got in) and my sling bag sitting on the carpet by the chair.

They'd lost my suitcase, the bastards. Or that Luis at the airport had stolen it. If the ship had been returning to Lisbon when this mess was over, I'd have torn the city apart looking for him and wrung his thieving neck. When I stomped over to the sliding glass doors and glared at Carolyn in her comfy deck chair, she jumped up, looking really surprised.

"Luz!"

"Right!" I snarled. "Where's my bag?"

"The Albanian can't find it," said her mother-in-law. "Silly man was in tears when he came to tell us."

Carolyn thought I might as well go back to bed while she tried to find a solution to my problem. "What? And miss the champagne party?" I snarled. "And the great hors d'oeuvres, and getting my picture taken with the captain, not to mention our first gourmet dinner at sea? No way."

I left Carolyn stuttering and her mother-in-law grinning like an ancient *bruja;* she lacked only the pointy hat and broomstick. Once back in the bedroom with the door closed, I climbed into my second-day-dirty clothes and considered how to make myself glamorous. My sorority sisters, nitwits all, used to say, if you had only a plain dress for a special occasion, dress it up with a scarf or jewelry. They probably read that in some woman's magazine that told how to charm a man or lose weight or find a good hairdresser.

Showing a little skin was recommended, so I unbuttoned the shirt down to my bra, tied the tails in a knot under my boobs, pushed my underpants down so they didn't show above my jeans, checked my belly button for lint, put on my grandmother's turquoise jewelry, and added lipstick. Now I had to choose between sneakers and bare feet. I remembered little bows stuck to the stuff in the bathroom medicine chest, so I rescued two of those and taped them on my big toes. Maybe people would think I had on see-through sandals. Or that I was just some nutcase. Satisfied, I sashayed out to startle my roommates with my new look.

Carolyn gaped. Her mother-in-law laughed out loud and said, "I like a woman with a sense of humor."

Carolyn

I'd been hoping Luz would want to order room service and go back to bed. No such luck. Obviously she planned to spend the whole tour wearing those jeans unless I could figure something out, but she was too tall to wear *my* clothes. We took the elevator down to the reception with people staring at us — well, at Luz, who smiled back and pointed a toe occasionally to admire the bow she'd attached to it. I couldn't help but feel that she was getting even with me for talking her into this trip.

My mother-in-law actually whispered to some woman on the elevator that she thought Luz was a famous designer from Madrid. Luz played right along by speaking in Spanish to a man next to her. He obviously had no idea what she was saying, but he was so flattered by her attention that he trailed us into the reception and stuck close, handing her glasses of champagne and snatching canapé trays from waiters to offer her while we were standing in line to be introduced to the captain.

The hors d'oeuvres were lovely: caviar on toast, tiny tempura shrimp, pork dumplings with a lovely soy and rice-wine vinegar dipping sauce, salty, red-brown cracked olives, and little puff pastries filled with everything from brandied fruit to tuna bits in a mild horseradish cream. I'm afraid I made a pig of myself, but then I was here to write about their food, so I had to taste it. The champagne waiters were followed by waitresses carrying trays with tiny portions of Chambord and a peach liqueur, which they would pour into your champagne to make Bellinis if you indicated an interest. I'd had two by the time Luz reached the captain.

Captain Gennaro Marbella was a very handsome man in his perfectly ironed white uniform with periwinkle trim and gold epaulettes, his black hair handsomely streaked with white, a tanned face, and a melting smile. He seemed to prefer to have his picture taken while each lady, looking bemused by his charm, was encircled in his arm and her male escort, if any, stood beside them looking awkward. After the introductory handshake, Luz snuggled up against him for the picture while he smiled down at her cleavage. Then she whispered to him, loudly enough for me to hear, "If you people don't find my luggage, I'm going to sue your asses off."

I groaned and helped myself to a third glass of champagne. The captain stared at her in astonishment. "No luggage?" he asked.

"You lost it," she replied.

"Get Patek!" he roared. Crewmembers scrambled, and in no time at all, a slender man with dark hair and skin and an officer's uniform, but with less decoration than the captain's, presented himself. "This lovely lady says she has no luggage," the captain growled. "You lost it."

"I am aware one passenger —"

"What do you intend to do about it?" demanded the captain.

"I have already been in touch with Lisbon, Captain."

"Not good enough," snapped Gennaro. "Passengers on my ship do not sail without their luggage." He turned to Luz. "My most lovely signora, tomorrow morning the ship's boutique will outfit you for your passage. With our compliments. Choose what you will, and accept my apologies. Even without your clothes, you look beautiful." He scanned her cleavage and belly button. "Most enchanting."

"Gee, thanks," said Luz.

I was up next, horribly embarrassed. My hand was perspiring when he shook it. At a loss for conversation while the photographer was aiming at us, I asked the captain if he came from Naples. "Holy Blessed Virgin!" he exclaimed with delight as he embraced me with both arms and asked how I knew.

"San Gennaro, the–the patron saint of Naples," I stammered.

"You have been there?" he asked. When I nodded, he kissed me on both cheeks, and the photographer took our picture. I wouldn't be able to take that one home to Jason. On second thought, maybe I should.

When the last of the two hundred passengers had been embraced and photographed — no one else got kissed — the captain introduced his staff to the crowd: Martin Froder, ship's engineer, a wiry fellow with short blond hair and a sour expression coupled with a German accent; Bruce Hartwig, chief security officer, American, burly, ugly, and sort of scary looking, although he had a nice smile and aimed it at the guests; the ship's doctor, Beaufort E. Lee, whose gray hair hung in untidy curls on his forehead; Umar Patek, the chief steward, who seemed unruffled after his brief tongue-lashing from the captain; Chef Demetrios Kostas el Greco, round, flushed, and sporting a two-foot, cylindrical chef's hat set slightly askew;

and Hanna Fredriksen, the blonde, Amazonian hotel manager, who gave the captain a killing look when he asked us to note what a luscious figure she had. Although the woman was standing, like a good soldier, straight with shoulders back, feet braced apart, and hands behind her back, I think the captain tried to pat her on the fanny.

"Ha!" said my mother-in-law. "That woman needs to be told she doesn't have to put up with sexual harassment even if he is the captain. And why was he kissing *you,* Carolyn? Obviously, I'm going to have to keep an eye on you."

I tried to rush Vera and Luz toward the dining room before Vera could make a feminist scene, but we were waylaid by a couple who could have been brother and sister with their light brown hair, suntanned faces, and matching greenish suits. "Kev Crossways," said the man, and offered me his right hand to shake and, in his left hand, a small tray of fried cheese balls speared with toothpicks. He must have snatched them from a waiter.

"Bev Crossways," said the woman, shaking all our hands before tossing back a flute of champagne, unadulterated with any of the colorful liquors being offered.

"Adjunct professors at the Scripps Institution of Oceanography."

"Did you notice how many pictures they took at this party?" Kev demanded. "Over four hundred. Four hundred! Now they'll develop them in their photo shop, sell them to you at outrageous prices, and pour the developing chemicals overboard."

"Those chemicals are toxic," said Bev. "Dangerous pollutants."

"Really?" *Too bad Jason isn't here,* I thought. *He'd be interested. In fact, he'd probably know more about the toxicity than she did.*

"Take a picture. Kill a fish," said Kev, looking outraged.

"A whole school of fish," Bev predicted.

"Well, let's hope we won't be eating any of them tonight," said Vera. "And speaking of eating —"

"A pleasure to meet you," I said politely to the Crosswayses and let myself be shepherded away by my sour-faced mother-in-law.

"Heads up, Luz," Vera called over her shoulder to Luz, who had bent over to readjust the bow on her left foot.

8

At the Doctor's Table

Luz

People actually believed that I was a fashion designer from Madrid wearing one of my own outfits. How dumb was that? I got stopped and gushed over by women who probably *were* wearing designer stuff, so I played along by answering in Spanish while Carolyn squirmed and her mother-in-law had a great time translating my remarks. I found out after the first translation that Vera didn't know a word of Spanish. She just improvised. For instance, she told some blue-haired snob from Connecticut that high heels were definitely out now that everyone knew heels were the result of a plot by the patriarchy.

The woman looked pretty surprised and seemed to think the "patriarchy" had a connection to terrorism.

The dining room was something else — big framed panels of silver and light purple silk and velvet stuck up on the walls, crystal chandeliers, silver carpet so soft the stuff inched up between my toes and knocked my toe bows cockeyed. I got my feet under the table as fast as I could because I kind of enjoyed playing Spanish designer. The tables seated eight, with velvet armchairs, white tablecloths, candles, china, place cards with our names written in old-fashioned script, and waiters who directed us to our seats.

We got the doctor's table. I had a sneaking feeling that wasn't a plum assignment. The captain's table had the blue-hairs and their well-fed husbands. I was next to the doctor, and on his other side were a really tall, busty, middle-aged black lady and her large, black husband — Randolph and Harriet Barber. He owned a string of funeral homes. How the hell he got so big is a mystery, because he had a video camera and took pictures of everything and everybody, pretty much ignoring dinner, while his wife talked about the Republican Party and her years at some fancy eastern girl's university where she was one of the first African-American students.

Carolyn was squeezed between the black mortician and a bald guy named Greg Marshand, the VP of a cereal company in Iowa. He'd retired to Florida to play golf and wanted to tell her in excruciating detail about every hole he'd played at the Boca Raton Club in the last five years. That was until he found out that she was a food critic. Then he told her more than she ever wanted to know about what kind of corn made the best dry cereal. Jesus Christ! If I'd had to sit next to him, I'd probably have slumped headfirst into my soup, which was pretty good. Pumpkin with flowers floating on it. Carolyn said they were edible, so I ate mine, but they didn't taste like much.

The mother-in-law sat next to Mr. Cereal and wouldn't even talk to him beyond giving him a lecture on some famous golf club that wouldn't let women join. Between her and me was a short, stocky guy named Commander Bernard Levinson, ex-*jefe* on a nuclear submarine and Mr. Cereal's golf partner. They were both Florida widowers, and Barney was seriously pissed off that after all those long tours underwater, with his wife at home raising the kids and taking care of everything else, she died on him when he finally retired so they could take cruises *above* water together. He seemed like a pretty good guy.

I wasn't sure what to make of the doctor. Beaufort E. Lee? What kind of name was that? He said he was from Atlanta, Georgia, and went cruising for a month each year, free of charge because he took over as ship's doctor. This was his first time on the *Bountiful Feast*, and he liked it — fewer people and a newer ship meant less chance of stomach viruses flattening all the passengers and ruining his vacation. If that was his bedside manner, I planned to stay well on my own.

Vera asked him if he knew what to do for someone who'd had a heart attack, which she'd had before Christmas. He told her she didn't have to worry because he'd seen hundreds of dead heart attack victims. "Young man," she said, "if I have a heart attack on this ship, I expect you to keep me alive, not add me to your list of dead heart patients." Then she waved a Caesar salad crouton at him and demanded to know what he'd do if she had a second heart attack.

"Why, ma'am," he said, "Ah'd try to keep you alive until the helicopter showed up to take you to the nearest hospital."

That's when he asked me to dance. Evidently he was expected to dance with all the ladies at the table. He'd asked Harriet Barber first, before the soup. They didn't seem to do too well until she started leading. I got asked during the salad and tried to get out of it, but he wasn't having any of that. So I let him step on my bare toes once, but when he gave me a twirl and knocked his knee into mine, that was it. "Doctor, you're one hell of a bad dancer, and I've got rheumatoid arthritis. You're doing me some serious damage here."

He stopped dancing and looked me over. "Sorry about that, ma'am. At least you are a very good lookin' cripple. What prescriptions are you on?"

So we sort of swayed in place to the music and talked about my meds. Turns out he was a pathologist, and he said I wouldn't be wanting him to give me any shots unless I was desperate. Medical examiner for the city of Atlanta. When I told him I'd been a cop, we got on just fine. I did warn him it might be a bad idea to mention his specialty to other people. After all, Vera hadn't taken it very well when he'd brought up all the heart attack corpses he'd seen.

Carolyn

My first dinner aboard the *Bountiful Feast*, and it was very good. An excellent pumpkin soup to start, flavored with ginger, if I was not mistaken. Then a Caesar salad that was a little heavy on the anchovy paste in my opinion, but Mr. Barber, who sat next to me, liked it a lot. He told me that he'd kept jars of anchovies in his room when he was a literature student at Howard University and had loved to snack on the anchovies while reading Milton. He sounded rather sad about the whole thing, although he had met his future wife there. I asked how he happened to get into the mortuary business after he'd majored in English.

It was a sad story. He'd received a Rhodes scholarship and gone on to Oxford while his future wife attended graduate school at Radcliffe. Then while he was enjoying his second year in England, his father and brother were killed in a collision with an eighteen-wheeler on the beltway around Washington, D.C. With no one left alive to take over the business his father had founded, he'd been forced to leave England and run the chain himself.

"Randolph had a duty to our people,"

his wife Harriet informed me. "We provide affordable, dignified, Christian funerals for African-Americans in ten of the major metropolitan areas, and we are expanding our services every year."

Naturally I expressed my admiration for their good works and then studied my entrée, a lovely piece of medium-rare New York strip steak edged by garlic mashed potatoes decorated with thin fried onion straws, broiled tomatoes, and crispy green beans.

"We do not do Muslim funerals," said Mrs. Barber decisively. "I feel that compassionate conservatism should not extend to Muslims, and I'm sure the president and the Party would agree with me."

Mr. Barber sighed and said, "I rather imagine, Harriet, that we bury the odd atheist from time to time."

My steak had been seared with spicy herbs and was absolutely mouth-watering. I'd have to visit the chef tomorrow to talk food and recipes for my column, "Have Fork, Will Travel." I'd only managed two or three bites when the doctor, a rather peculiar man with a pronounced Southern drawl, a distant relationship to Robert E. Lee, and waves of dark and silver hair falling over his forehead, asked me to dance. I really did want to finish my entrée, but dancing with the ship's representative seemed to be obligatory, so I accepted. He was a dreadful dancer, and after having my toes stepped on three times, I became very worried, not only about the safety of my own feet, but also that of my barefooted friend, Luz.

The doctor told me to watch my purse in Tangier, where purse-snatchers thronged the crowded streets, and also in Gibraltar, where the so-called Barbary apes were prone to snatching handbags, hats, jewelry, food, souvenir bags, and anything they could run off with. I did not find our conversation particularly reassuring. I had been looking forward to North Africa and Gibraltar. Thank goodness Dr. Lee had no warnings about the Canary Islands or the Spanish ports we'd visit on the return to Barcelona. Or perhaps he was saving those for another dance. If so, I might be forced to take over any future conversations.

Also, he was very tall, perfect for Luz, except for the damage he might do her feet; my nose was below his shoulder, and I don't consider myself a short woman. Goodness, I'm just about Jason's height. We dance very well together.

When the doctor and I returned to the

table, my mother-in-law was demanding to know whether the Navy had female sailors on their submarines. Commander Levin- son said not when he was captaining nuclear submarines, but he thought women would be less likely to come back to port pregnant from submarine duty than, say, aircraft-carrier duty, since it would be very hard to have sex on a submarine without an audience. Much to my astonishment, Vera laughed. They both laughed.

While I was finishing my entrée and making notes on the spicy surface of the meat, I could hear a woman behind me at another table complaining loudly to the waiter that her wine glass had dishwasher spots on it, which had ruined the flavor of the wine. She demanded not only a new glass, but also a different bottle of wine, although the waiter pointed out that she'd already drunk most of her first bottle. I managed to turn enough to catch a glance at her. It was Mrs. Gross from the Lisbon airport, the lady who had insisted that Luz give up her luggage to the cruise representative. She was wearing a strange brown evening gown that sort of glittered, and I wondered if sequins came in brown. I couldn't really get a good look at her dress without turning completely around. And why did she want a new bottle of wine? Ours was excellent, a bold cabernet, dry with a fine fruity finish.

Luz heard Mrs. Gross, too, and Luz did turn completely around to tell the lady that her advice had led to the loss of Luz's suitcase. "Excellent," said Mrs. Gross. "You should be able to get a free cruise if you play your cards right."

As dessert was being served, my mother-in-law refused to dance with Dr. Lee, and Mrs. Barber leaned across her husband to tell me that Vera had sound judgment. "Our poor doctor is as bad a dancer as I've ever come across. A woman as frail as your mother-in-law could end up with broken bones if she danced with him. Thin white women are prone to osteoporosis, you know. They die of broken hips every day."

I glanced over quickly to see if Vera had heard this grim outlook on her lifespan, but she and the commander were having a rousing argument about whether or not women were up to the rigors of work in shipyards.

"I'm a very good dancer myself," said Mrs. Barber. "I'll have to take the poor man in hand. That is, unless, being a

Southerner, he thinks he's too white to learn anything from an African-American woman."

"Now Harriet," said Mr. Barber, putting down his video camera, with which he'd been zooming in on an elaborate piece of strawberry pie with whipped cream and nuts. "You don't know that the man is a bigot. After all, you were the first woman he asked to dance."

"Humph," said Mrs. Barber.

What a wonderful pie! I thought. It had definitely been made with fresh strawberries, very sweet, very flavorful. And the crust was superb! I'd never have thought of adding nuts to strawberry pie, but it worked. And the cream had a slight fruity flavor. Even if I had to glue my purse to my hand in the various ports we visited, the prospect of dinner when we got back to the ship would be worth the stress.

"Of course I'm taking the bottle back to my room," said a sharp voice behind me. "It's my bottle, and I haven't finished it." Then I caught sight of a skeletal figure in sparkling brown passing behind me, her wrinkled hand clutching a bottle of red wine. She wore an emerald necklace with matching earrings and bracelet, more emeralds than I'd ever seen on one person, even in one room. Although she wasn't pleasant, she certainly must be rich.

I do love strawberries. Not only do they smell wonderful — in fact, the aroma accounts for their historic reputation as an aphrodisiac — but the flavor is heavenly. For centuries, only wild strawberries were available, growing at the edge of forests. But then, of course, people who could afford to, like the kings of France, cultivated them.

Strawberries were served at a sumptuous banquet in Ferrara to honor the recent marriage of Ercole d'Este, eldest son of the famous (infamous?) Lucrezia Borgia, to Renée, daughter of Louis XII of France, in 1528. Since the feast took place in January, one wonders where they got the strawberries (indoor strawberry beds?), which may well have passed unnoticed, what with the peacocks in plumage and other amazingly exotic dishes.

Louis XIV was forbidden strawberries by his physician because of a serious digestive problem, but he paid no attention and continued to eat them with wine (the masculine recipe;

ladies had to eat theirs with cream). However, my cruise took place in May, when strawberries are abundant and were served in a pie with pecans one night at our table. Pecans were discovered in America by Cabeza de Vaca (whose name means head of the cow — poor man). I ordered champagne to go with my strawberry pie, as a salute to the freedom from stupid sex discrimination in our time. Take that Louis XIV!

Strawberry-Pecan Pie with Whipped Cream

Mix in a bowl *1½ cups sugar, ⅛ cup all-purpose flour, 1 teaspoon ground nutmeg,* and *1 teaspoon ground cinnamon.*

Add *2 cups fresh chopped strawberries* and *1¼ cups chopped pecans* and toss lightly.

Line a 9-inch pie plate with the *bottom crust of a pie* (make your own or buy at the market). Fill with strawberry-pecan mixture. Top with *lattice crust* and bake on middle oven shelf at 375°F for 50 minutes or until browned.

Allow to cool, and top with *whipped cream* and *3 strawberries, quartered and dipped in powdered sugar,* at edges of the cream and *more chopped pecans* in the middle. (Quartered strawberries and added chopped pecans are optional.)

Carolyn Blue,
"Have Fork, Will Travel,"
Boston Bay Bugle

9

In Crew Quarters

The five of them sprawled on couches and chairs in the officer's lounge, which was otherwise deserted because of the late hour. "You get the pills on board without any problems?" Hartwig asked Hanna Fredriksen.

"Of course." She nodded. "They're perfect. They look just like the standard seasick pills we hand out, and I've got enough to knock out all the passengers and as many of the crew as we need to put under."

Patrick O'Brien grinned playfully and asked, "Did I see a wee bit of fanny patting at the cocktail party, me darlin' Hanna?"

Hanna's mouth tightened, and her perfectly tanned Scandinavian brow furrowed with anger. "I am not your darling, Patrick," she snapped, "and as for Marbella, I'm going to handcuff his balls to the bars in the brig once we've taken over. I'll make him sorry he ever thought he could get away with groping me!"

"Ja," said Martin Froder. "Fräulein Sechrest knows better how to handle our captain than you, Hanna. A little squeak, a gasp, a wild look around with blushes, *und der* captain is embarrassed at being exposed *und* keeps his wandering Italian paws to himself."

"What do we do when the passengers start complaining to Sechrest?" Patrick asked.

Hanna shrugged. "I'll take care of Sandy. You just make sure no one gets a message to the outside."

"We'll have their cell phones and computers, and I'll have the computer room and the communications room locked up. No one will be talking to the owners or the press. Just us." Patrick's elfin face wrinkled into a delighted smile that raised his orange eyebrows and his pale forehead right up to the carrot curls atop his head.

"These are the small problems," said Umar Patek. "What about the helicopter?"

His black eyes turned coldly toward Hartwig.

"It's covered," said Hartwig brusquely. "It will lift off south of Casablanca and pick us up whenever we're ready. I'll be reconnecting with my people to make the final arrangements once we put into port. After that, I give the owners two days to cave to our demands. Then we're out of here."

"So you think you can trust Muslims in Morocco? They do what you say?" Patek asked.

"You know something about my contacts I don't know?" Hartwig demanded. "Didn't you say you were a Hindu from Malaysia? Do I need to run another check on you, Umar? Just to be sure I can trust you?"

Patek shrugged. "You got the guns on board? More important than pills."

"We'll be well armed," snapped Hartwig.

"Too late to be not trusting each other," warned Froder, the engineering officer. "Hanna has pills, Hartwig has guns, we have *der* plan, I sail *der* ship, *und* you get us off, Bruce. Then the money makes us all happy in Zurich, *und* we never see each other again. *Ja?*"

"Aye, the money," said Patrick softly. "That's the thing."

10

A Visit from the Ombudslady

Carolyn

My mother-in-law and I were having a cup of coffee on our balcony the next morning, I listening enviously to her description of her bath in the tub with waterspouts, when the first problem of the day erupted.

"For God's sake! First they lose my luggage. Now my jeans and shirt are gone. Even my underwear's disappeared," shouted Luz, who had just stormed out of our bedroom, clad in a *Bountiful Feast* bathrobe, with its embroidered cornucopia on the lapel.

"Calm down," said Vera. "Have some coffee. That weird little Albanian came by last night after you finished flirting with the doctor and took your clothes away for washing. He'll get them back."

"Me flirting? What do you call your huddle with the submarine guy?" Luz demanded.

"Short," said my mother-in-law. "Carolyn was fast asleep before *you* ever came back to the suite. If you did. Maybe you spent the night with Robert E. Lee."

"Beaufort E. Lee," Luz corrected. "Beau for short. And how could I be sleeping with Beau if my clothes were here for Herkule to pick up? Anyway, you were on the sofa reading when I got in."

"I have to warn you, Luz," Vera continued, paying no attention to the interruption. "Southern men want to put a woman on a pedestal and pour corn syrup all over her. You won't like it."

"What I don't like is losing my last outfit to this damned cruise line. So fine. I'll go to breakfast in the bathrobe."

"Now Luz, I'm sure —" Before I could remind her that the captain had promised her a new wardrobe, she cut me off by sitting down and pouring herself a cup of coffee. I could see that she was about to begin another tirade about her clothes, so I said, "Did you know that coffee came from Ethiopia, or maybe it was Abyssinia. It's

86

said that it got to Yemen because the Queen of Sheba came to visit Solomon and had a son by him, Menelik, who brought the coffee bush from his mother's homeland and planted it in Yemen."

"Look, Carolyn, I couldn't care less where the coffee came from," Luz began.

"You haven't let me finish my story. Centuries later a goatherd from an isolated monastery in Yemen complained to a learned monk that the goats were frisking around at night when they were supposed to be asleep. The monk was fascinated and investigated what the goats had been eating, which was these little beans from some scraggly bushes, so he picked the beans and experimented with them, but without much success. Finally he threw them in the fire, where they released a delicious aroma. Because of the odor, he retrieved the roasted beans, ground them, and made a drink from them, but it was too bitter, so he added honey and drank some. As a result he, too, stayed wide awake and felt amazingly alert and intelligent."

"Sounds like a bunch of bullshit to me," said Luz, and poured more coffee.

"I don't see why," I protested. "Doesn't coffee make you feel alert and intelligent?

Anyway, he then noticed that the bushes were planted in rows and traced them back to the Queen of Sheba by reading old writings. Isn't that interesting? Oh, and the Turks say that the first coffee was given to the Prophet Muhammad by the Angel Gabriel when Muhammad was all tired out from his religious devotions. Since the Arabs can't drink alcohol, they really like coffee and tea."

"And I'd like some clean clothes," snapped Luz.

"And sugar. The Arabs like sugar. They even refined cane sugar on Crete as early at A.D. 1000. It's said the Crusaders were lured there by the sweet smell, and —"

"Holy crap! If you're planning to tell me the whole history of the Crusades, don't. Pope John Paul apologized for them, so let's just forget it. We Catholics — Hey, you!"

Herkule Pipa had crept into our sitting room with her clothes over his arm, looking terrified when she spotted him.

"I bring s-s-sanitary pantaloons and sh-shirt," he stammered. "Fresh from machine for sponging of lady's wardrobes. Yes?" He flung them on our sofa and sprinted out the door while Luz shouted after him that she didn't see her underwear.

It was, however, neatly and demurely folded between the shirt and jeans. She went off to put her clothes on, muttering that if they hadn't shown up, she'd have gone to breakfast and to the ship's store in the bathrobe. "What the hell do they sell, anyway? Sailor suits? I'm not wearing some stupid sailor suit with pale purple stripes. They'll just have to keep washing my stuff overnight."

"Not a morning person?" my mother-in-law murmured, hiding a grin in her coffee cup.

"Her knees probably hurt," I replied. Waves were slapping against the ship, but not, fortunately, splashing us since we were on an upper deck.

When Luz reappeared with her denim shirt hanging loosely over her jeans, she stuck a flower from the bouquet on the table into her bra. "Got to keep up my Madrid designer image. You going to keep translating for me, Vera?"

"I'd be delighted to," said my mother-in-law cheerfully. Obviously she liked Luz better than she did me. So much for Jason's idea that his mother and I had bonded in San Francisco. All during breakfast, women kept dropping by our table to get the latest fashion news from my sometime friend, the retired lieutenant, who spoke Spanish exclusively while Vera told them that Luz was displaying how a woman could wear the same clothes for all occasions with the impetus of a little imagination. "The male designers hate her," said my mother-in-law solemnly. "Just another plot of the patriarchy."

I had eggs Benedict, a small bowl of fresh grapes glazed with sugar, and a mimosa. Vera asked if I'd become an alcoholic since she last saw me. "Champagne with breakfast? I'm sure my son wouldn't approve." This trip wasn't working out at all as I had anticipated. I felt that my mother-in-law and my friend were ganging up on me. Maybe neither one of them had wanted to come on the cruise. I shouldn't have forced Luz into it, and Jason shouldn't have forced his mother on me. I could have spent Mother's Day by myself, enjoying the good food and being bored speechless by a retired breakfast cereal executive. Why he'd think that I cared what kind of corn made the best boxed cereal was beyond me. Maybe I could get moved to a table away from all of them.

"Is one of you ladies Ms. Vallejo, the famous Spanish fashion designer?" asked a short young woman with blond curls and round cheeks. Luz nodded regally, and the newcomer, after asking permission, plopped down in the fourth seat at our table out on the deck and introduced herself. "Sandy Sechrest. I'm the ship's ombudsman."

"Woman," said Vera, sounding huffy. "You're not a man, and you don't have to put up with male gender endings."

Sandy's blue eyes widened. "How super. Thank you so much. That would make me an ombuds*lady*. I like that much better." She beamed around our little circle. "Now, as ombudslady, I've come to commiserate with Ms. Vallejo over the loss of her baggage and to escort her to our fine boutique for the fitting of a new wardrobe."

"You go, girl," said a loud voice over near the railing. Mrs. Gross, in a dreadful khaki pants suit, was in our midst. She looked none the worse for her two bottles of wine, just similarly wrinkled and skinny.

"Which one of you ladies is Ms. Vallejo?" asked Sandy, looking eagerly from one to the other of us.

"Yo soy Señorita Luz Vallejo," said Luz.

"Oh, dear. You don't speak English. Well, never mind. Picking out clothes doesn't require a mutual language. Maybe one of you ladies could —"

"I'm going to meet the chef," I said hastily.

"Was something wrong with your breakfast?" asked the accommodating Ms. Sechrest, looking alarmed. "I can certainly relay any complaints you might have. That's my job. He's really somewhat — er — volatile."

"I'm used to volatile men," I replied, remembering the chairman of the music department at UT El Paso; he had shouted at me repeatedly. "I'm a food columnist. I'm sure we'll get along beautifully."

"Of course you will," agreed the ombudslady. "As long as you liked your breakfast, and your dinner last night, and —"

"I did," I assured her. "And he knows I'm here." With that I scurried away without any idea whatever of how to find the chef. I was *not* accompanying Luz to the boutique. No telling what she'd do there. We were much better friends, I mused sadly, when we'd each had a few drinks, but obviously my mother-in-law wasn't going to allow that.

11

Boutique Clothes — Culinary Miscues

Luz

Like I'm going to find anything I want to wear in a frigging ship's boutique, I thought, as Vera and I followed the Sechrest woman to the elevator. Carolyn had certainly bustled her proper butt away before she could be shanghaied into this useless expedition. Maybe I should snap up everything in their shop to replace my missing "wardrobe," which hadn't been that much to begin with. Why not? Then they wouldn't have anything left to sell.

There was one salesgirl in the boutique. Babette. I'd have felt sorry for her, having a name like that, if she hadn't been such an idiot. First, I had to sit down in a chair so

93

soft I'd probably ruin my knees trying to get out of it. Then I had to watch while Babette tottered around on four-inch heels bringing in dresses for me to look at. She even held them up in front of herself and twirled, for Christ's sake. Of course, Ombudslady Sandy thought they were all "gorgeous," while Vera pointed out which ones she thought had been created solely to make the wearer uncomfortable. More male patriarchy crap, I figured. Actually, some of them looked okay. Nothing I'd ever wear, of course. Nothing I could ever afford.

"Ha. Here you are. You may remember me from the Lisbon airport. I certainly remember you from last night. Since you made it quite clear that you blame me for the loss of your clothes, I thought supervising this expedition was the least I could do. I'm here to make sure that the cruise line doesn't try to cheat you on the replacements."

It was the withered old lady who always wore ugly colors — camouflage green in Lisbon, brown with sparkles last night, khaki today. She started flipping through the clothes Babette had draped everywhere, checking the price tags.

"Madam," cried Babette. "I am helping this lady."

"And being the ombudslady," Sandy admonished, "I can assure you that Ms. Vallejo will not be cheated. She is, after all, a famous designer from Madrid."

"My ass," muttered the old lady, and tossed an evening dress into my lap. Deep blue. I would have picked it out myself if she hadn't butted in. "Go try it on," ordered the woman.

So that's how it went. Mrs. Gross — that was her name — kept sending me into the dressing room with the most expensive stuff in the store. Babette kept cooing, in what I took to be a fake French accent, about "Madam's" excellent taste, and I had to climb in and out of all these clothes — day dresses, evening dresses, nightgowns, slacks with fancy shirts and sweaters, shoes, scarves, handbags. She expected the ship to provide me with more stuff than I owned, not just in my missing suitcase, but in my closet at home as well. She even wanted to get me into shorts and a swimsuit, but I said I didn't swim. The truth is that I've got a bullet scar on my left thigh that isn't all that pleasant to look at.

I found out something interesting about expensive clothes: They feel great against your skin. All that silk. A black evening gown Mrs. Gross insisted on was as good as having a massage. I had a massage about ten years ago when this big prostitute from Juárez, built like a tank, pushed me off a downtown fire escape and sprained my shoulder. Of course I got right up and broke her arm, she went to jail for attacking a police officer, and I got a commendation and the massage. Not bad for a night's work.

While I was trying stuff on, with Babette's help, Vera was telling Mrs. Gross and Ombudslady Sandy about a policeman she'd slugged in downtown Chicago for trying to arrest some little Chicano girl who was begging on the street, trying to get bus fare home. Generally speaking, I wouldn't approve of hitting a cop, but the one Vera smacked sounded like an asshole. Probably hated Chicanos. Good thing I live in El Paso, where we're mostly all Chicanos or illegal Mexicans. If I lived somewhere else, I might be slugging bigoted cops instead of having been a cop myself.

So I ended up with all these clothes in "boutique bags," lavender and white with a picture of the ship, and Herkule Pipa was called to carry them to the suite for me. Sandy helped him while Vera and I led the parade. Mrs. Gross, who figured she had done enough damage to the ship's bottom line, hustled off in the other direction, probably looking for another bottle of wine.

I had more clothes to hang in my closet than Carolyn had to hang in hers and wondered how she'd feel about that. Turns out she was delighted on the grounds that, looking so classy in my new stuff, I'd naturally give up foul language. Like that was going to happen!

I was wearing slacks and a silk blouse, both of which had to be dry-cleaned, for Christ's sake, because Vera insisted that I change out of my "tatty jeans." Considering how old she was, she probably never wore jeans, so I forgave her, although my jeans were very comfortable. Pipa, the Albanian, had managed not to shrink them.

Carolyn

The executive chef, Demetrios Kostas el Greco, was volatile, as advertised, but he never shouted at me, only at his underlings. In fact, he greeted me with a hug, the result of which was that his tall hat fell off, spraying the pins that had held it in place hither and yon. He roared, and a female sous-chef dashed over to scoop up the hat and pins and return him to his previous chefly glory. Then he and I paced up and down the aisles of his huge, modern kitchen while he shouted in Greek what I took to be foul language at his employees and chatted with me in English of a sort. The kitchen was a veritable Tower of Babel, different languages assaulting me from every side as they prepared lunch, which I certainly didn't intend to miss.

I was offered a sip of a wonderful melon soup, the melons for which had been flown to Lisbon from Israel; a smidgen of chicken in dill sauce; and a fingerful of frosting for an orange cake, the finger belonging to Demetrios. I can't say that I appreciated having his sticky finger thrust in my face with the demand that I open my mouth, but the frosting, which was red-orange, tasted so smooth and so very orangey with just a touch of brandy, that I forgave him. After all, he probably washed his hands often.

"Blood oranges?" I asked when I had savored the forecast of a dessert to come. "I've read that they were a natural mutation in Sicily."

"Yes, yes. Absolute. We boil down the

orange with the fine brandy, and then fold it by the hands with spoons into the sweet whipped cream."

"Wonderful," I exclaimed. "Do you know the myth about the naming of oranges? It's said that in the very distant past in Malaysia, where oranges originated, an elephant discovered an orange tree and ate so many oranges that he exploded and died. Centuries later a human found the bones of the elephant with a grove of orange trees growing from the elephant's former stomach. The man said, 'What a fine *naga ranga!*' In Sanskrit that meant *fatal indigestion of elephants.* Thus the name."

Demetrios gave me a puzzled look; perhaps he wasn't interested in culinary history and myth. He kissed my hand, then scooped it into his and whisked me off to his office to discuss the spicy coating on the steaks the night before. Evidently, his minions were forced to beat the chili powder and other ingredients into the steak with special mallets, a process he demonstrated by pounding his desk in between rushes to the door to shout at people in the kitchen. His office was glass, and he didn't miss a thing that happened beyond his windows. Cooking under his direction had to be very stressful for his workers.

Having discussed his steak recipe, he rushed me back out and "let" me wield the wooden spoon with which the brandy was stirred into the orange frosting. Unfortunately, the brandy fumes made me rather dizzy and nauseated. It's a problem I have when making fondue at home. When Demetrios noticed that I had become pale and begun to perspire, he snatched the spoon from my hand, passed it to a waiting pastry chef, and lifted me bodily with both hands around my waist. From the pot to the kitchen door, he hoisted me several inches off the floor and carried me. "Come to visit once more when you are not to vomit. Vomiting in my kitchen is not good." I was extremely embarrassed as he pushed me — not violently, mind you — out the door.

So much for impressing the chef with my expertise in the kitchen. I took deep breaths all the way to the elevator and was feeling much better by the time I reached our suite, where I found a Luz I hardly recognized. "You look absolutely gorgeous!" I exclaimed.

"Thanks," she muttered. "Now, will you tell your mother-in-law that I do not want to round up female cops to march in some demonstration in Chicago?"

"Vera," I said cheerily, "Luz doesn't want to." I was pleased to note that not only did my friend look very chic, but also she hadn't used foul language. It had to be the clothes. I now wished that I'd given Luis, the inept handler of baggage in Lisbon, a more generous tip.

Out in the hall we could hear Herkule calling, "Is now serving yum-yum lunch in dining room. Chef not likes laggard tardies. He comes from kitchen and barks loudly."

12

Touring the "Onboard Amenities"

Luz

Lunch was pretty good, great if you took Carolyn's word for it. She actually ate two desserts. She was starting on the second and talking about paying a visit to the pastry chef when the fire alarms went off and gave everyone but Carolyn indigestion. She wrapped the piece of cake in her napkin and took it with her when the crew people hustled us off for the fire drill. The worst of it was wearing these Styrofoam life jackets, sitting around listening to a safety lecture, and then answering a roll call while standing under a huge rubber lifeboat. Some computer guy from Silicon Valley said it was like standing under the sword of Damocles, whatever that meant.

The damn Styrofoam was hot as hell and made me sweat on my new clothes. I figured they did it on purpose so we'd have to send our stuff to the ship's dry cleaners, a service that was not free. Carolyn's mother-in-law couldn't even see over the collar of her life jacket and raised a big ruckus about having to walk down stairs as good as blind because we weren't allowed to use the elevators for the fire drill. A steward showed up to help her. Poor guy got an earful about life jackets that might be all right for men, but were dangerous for women, especially older women with fragile bones and hearts that might seize up at any minute. During the lecture, Carolyn scarfed down the whole piece of cake.

After that we had to take the rotten life jackets up to our rooms and stow them before we met for a ladies' tour of the ship so we'd know all the great things it had to offer, especially the ones that would cost us money, "onboard amenities" they called them. I'd have settled for a bigger bathroom. At least I'd managed to make a deal with Vera to use her tub when my knees got bad. The thing has water swishing out holes in the sides and water whirling around in the tub. Pull the plug, and you'd probably wash down the drain. Well, maybe not me, but Vera for sure. In return I promised to walk around the deck with her twice a day so her doctor wouldn't bitch at her when she got back. She said she didn't think Carolyn was much on exercise. I could have told her that.

First — big surprise — we looked at the casino. Very fancy. I don't mind gambling once in a while. The Tiguas used to have a casino, Speaking Rock, in El Paso until all the tight-assed, Republican born-again Protestants in the legislature got together in Austin and closed it down. In the old days, you could have a great birthday party with margaritas and cake at Speaking Rock and then shoot some craps.

Carolyn wasn't much impressed. She said, "I have never been able to see the fun in feeding money into a noisy slot machine, or attempting to remember all the cards that have been played in a series of blackjack games — although at least you get to sit on a chair for that — or pretending that you know what is going on at the craps table, which is truly a dreadful name for a game of any sort."

I offered to teach her to shoot craps, since it's the one thing you're likely to break even on if you know what you're doing, but she wasn't interested, even when I told her that reading a book on the math and stuff was pretty interesting. She said she'd never liked math, and some years back Jason had given her a long, boring mathematical lecture on shooting craps that put her to sleep. She'd gone straight to bed in their Las Vegas hotel room and refused to join him in the casino. Poor guy. He may not have liked me much the one time we met, but I felt sort of sorry for him.

While we were in the casino, that Mrs. Gross, who'd horned in on my clothes giveaway, said, "Don't ever gamble on a ship. The games are crooked." Our guide was really insulted and looked like she might burst out crying.

The gym really pissed me off — all those extra-fit, good-looking kids supervising senior citizens, who were sweating it out on a bunch of machines that would have crippled me for the rest of the trip. Vera said that she'd had enough of gyms to last a lifetime since her heart attack and had no intention of ever visiting this one again. Of course, Carolyn reminded her that she was supposed to take regular exercise. That went over like finding a scorpion in your shower. Vera reminded her that she was going to get her exercise walking the decks in the fresh air with me. I think Carolyn was hurt not to be invited along.

Then Miss Perky in formfitting spandex bounced over and asked if I'd like to try out a machine. I gave her the Spanish designer routine, and Vera translated it, "She says no woman of fashion would sweat on fine clothes." Perky girl turned red, and twelve sweating blue-hairs jumped off bicycles and treadmills to prove that they, too, were "women of fashion" with "fine clothes." Vera added, "Señorita Vallejo wants to know what exercise you recommend." Actually, I used to like working out at Central Regional Command with my fellow cops, mostly guys, but those days were long gone.

Then the trainer, who had bigger boobs than you'd expect of someone who worked out, came up with the idea that I could lie on a mat raising my arms and legs in a leisurely fashion and avoiding unfashionable sweat. "I can do that in my own living room," I muttered.

"Señorita Vallejo says you should consider breast reduction so that you can wear fashionable clothing," Vera translated.

That woman was a hoot.

"Large breasts are only attractive to infantile men who still long for the mother's nipple," Vera added for good measure. Blushing down to her cleavage, the kid claimed someone needed her advice and rushed off to encourage a fat guy who was puffing away on a stair-stepper.

Carolyn asked if I'd really said that, because she didn't think it was a kind thing to say. "Hell, no," I told her. "Would I embarrass a girl who probably has a bra size bigger than her IQ?" But I had to wonder whether Carolyn thought her mother-in-law was translating comments that I'd actually made. Good thing Carolyn didn't understand Spanish. She wouldn't have liked what I said in Spanish any better than what I said in English.

After that we headed for the library, which was full of soft leather chairs I'd never be able to get out of and way too many books. "Who-oa," I murmured to Carolyn, "not much like the library downtown, is it? No smelly homeless guys coming in out of the heat."

Carolyn whispered back, "Luz, homelessness is a tragedy and a terrible social problem in our society." She was scanning the fiction section and yanked out a book, which she handed to me. "You should read this. It narrates the lives of three women, one of whom is a formerly middle-class lady who ended up homeless in Boston, working as a maid and sleeping wherever she could, often in the homes of employers who were out of town. It's a terrifying situation into which any woman could fall if her husband divorced her and she had no particular skills. Until I began writing my column, it could have been me, had Jason and I fallen out."

"Which is just why you should have been working instead of staying home cleaning house and cooking," said Vera, who had been looking over another section of books. "I don't think they've got a single feminist publication in here."

I looked at the book in my hand. Marge Piercy. *The Longings of Women.* Reading about a homeless woman sounded like a downer to me. I could have been homeless if I hadn't had my police pension. Of course my family would have taken me in, and we'd have driven each other crazy. I put the book back on the shelf while Carolyn was off looking for a book on Morocco.

After the library, we visited the spa, where I was kind of interested in a capsule where you were supposed to lie down and stretch out. The top part closed over you, like a coffin, only rounded, and then some spa woman turned it on so the capsule could do God knows what to you and pop you out in twenty minutes feeling as if you'd had a "refreshing, full night's sleep." The full night's sleep bit sounded good to me, but Carolyn told me that spa services weren't free and were undoubtedly extremely expensive. When Vera asked, "What if you got stuck in there?" the spa attendant showed her the release latch inside.

Too bad they don't have more release latches in Juárez, I thought. *Then all those* maquila *girls who get thrown in trunks, driven out of town to the desert, raped, strangled, and dumped would have a fighting chance to get away. Wouldn't matter, though. The drug dealers, gangs, rich guys' sons, or whoever was doing it would just tear the latches out.*

"Carolyn, don't take that copy of the price list," Vera ordered when the attendant offered one. "Just because you put it on your account and it gets charged to your credit card doesn't mean Jason won't have to pay for it next month."

"I know that," said Carolyn, looking indignant. "And I can pay my own bills, thank you, Vera. I make money writing my column. If I want to give myself a Mother's Day spa treatment while my husband is attending expensive scientific conferences on the plains of Canada . . ."

They argued all the way to the lecture hall where we were reunited with the guys. Their tour included looking at the ship's engines and navigational stuff. Commander Levinson gave us a sarcastic description of the bridge and the captain in his pretty uniform and his fancy *Star Wars* captain's chair. After that, Barney had insisted on seeing the real engines and not some movie, and Froder, the engineering officer, complained about having passengers wandering around his engine room.

Barney summarized the tour by announcing that we were paying big money to ride around on a fancy, oceangoing barge, not a ship. Thank God I wasn't paying big money. In fact, I figured I might be making a profit. Food and drink free and all these clothes. As long as I didn't sweat on them and have to pay dry-cleaning bills, it was a pretty good deal.

Then we all sat down, for which my knees gave thanks, and listened to a really boring lecture and slide show on Tangier, the Arab place we were going tomorrow. They'd have done better to give self-defense lessons to all those clueless millionaires.

13

Dinner with Embarrassing Friends

Carolyn

Once our tour was over, I planned to write a column. Several of the dishes at lunch were certainly worth my attention, especially the desserts. I don't know what got into me. I ate two. It was probably the stress. I never knew what Vera and Luz were going to say next. I did get a few paragraphs completed, sitting on the balcony with the laptop on my knees. However, the sound of people chatting on the balcony next to ours, which was separated only by a sort of plastic divider, was distracting, not to mention the smoke from their cigarettes. The *Bountiful Feast* was supposed to be a nonsmoking ship with only a few areas reserved for smokers. Maybe balconies were among those areas, although I didn't see why they should be since the smoke drifted in my direction into my nonsmoking space.

Finally I gave up on writing and went in to take a nap. Luz had had the right idea. She was fast asleep in her underwear. I noticed that she'd even hung up her new clothes, but surely they'd provided her with a nightgown she could have worn. I also noticed a dreadful scar on her thigh and her puffy knees. Was that the arthritis? Vera had gone off to take a walk around the deck with the submariner. I'd heard him saying as they departed that it was nice, in some ways, to be on a ship that had enough room to walk around, unlike a submarine, where you couldn't walk three feet without ducking to miss a pipe or a hatch frame.

"Probably doesn't smell too good on a submarine either," said my mother-in-law. "Bunch of men sweating in an enclosed space. Now that I think of it, no woman would want to be assigned to a submarine."

"You're right," replied the commander. "My wife always complained that my clothes came home smelling like a men's locker room. Made me throw them in the shed with the lawnmowers until I got a chance to take them to one of those Laundromats that do the washing for you. Can't say that I blamed her." And that was the last I heard as I drifted into a nice nap.

Vera woke us both up and told us to get ready for dinner — formal. Luz looked very stylish in an amazing blue gown and silver heels that must have been very uncomfortable. Vera and I were less stylish. She had on a long skirt and a jacket she probably wore to teach, and although my low-heeled sandals were more dressy than her flats, my long skirt and top were dress-down formal, chosen so I wouldn't make Luz feel uncomfortable in the clothes she'd bought at Ross, all now lost in Lisbon. I have to admit that I felt a bit peeved. I could have packed fancier evening wear if I'd known Luz was going to reap a fashion bonanza because of that thieving Luis at the Lisbon airport. Well, at least my feet didn't hurt. Luz would be sorry about those high-heeled sandals when she had to dance with the left-footed doctor.

Luz

I'll swear that Dr. Beau's mouth dropped open when he saw me in my blue dress.

Babette had insisted that I take this bra that pushed my boobs up above the neckline. The damn thing was so frigging uncomfortable I was expecting to feel a rib give way when I sat down to dinner, and then there were the shoes. I'd have been better off in work boots with steel toes. I noticed that Mrs. Gross, wearing that ugly brown sparkle outfit again, didn't put up with high heels or exposed toes. She'd been the one to insist on these silver heels; I'd only stood up in them for about a minute in front of a mirror. Walking in the suckers was hell.

And dancing? I'd never make it, but the way the medical examiner was looking at me, I figured he was going to insist on more dancing. Problem was I liked him well enough, but I sure as hell didn't want to dance with him again. Lucky me. Harriet Barber took him in hand for the first dance and gave him some lessons — prefaced by, "If you step on my feet, young man, I'm going to step on yours. How do you like that?" I had to admire her determination.

By the time he got to me, he wasn't very good, but he didn't mash my toes. I'd threatened to knee him if he did. He laughed heartily and said, "An' after that, what, sugah? You gonna shoot me?" Then he pulled me in real close and didn't make any dangerous foot moves. Kind of nice. It had been a while since I'd been pressed flat up against a man, especially one that was taller than me, even in those frigging shoes.

Dinner was pretty good too — except I was beginning to have jalapeño withdrawal symptoms. Should have had my mother pack me up some emergency Tex-Mex to take along.

Carolyn

I had an excellent tilapia dish with a black-bean, corn, and mild-chili relish for dinner while Mr. Marshand told me about the wonderful motorized golf cart he'd given his late wife for her seventieth birthday. "Right," said the commander. "Greg took it out one day when his was in the shop and damned if it didn't run away with him. He jumped ship, and the cart ended up in the lake."

"I had it fixed," protested the cereal king.

"Oh sure," Commander Levinson retorted, "but it never was the same. Alicia was furious. I always figured the stroke that killed her was brought on by that golf cart that kept stalling."

"Alicia died of pure frustration after she three-putted on a par-four hole," snapped Marshand. "She was a very excitable woman, and she took her golf seriously."

Commander Levinson then asked my mother-in-law to dance, and she said, "I don't know. Probably not if you're the kind of Jew who expects women to wear wigs and spend all their time washing multiple sets of dishes."

I was so embarrassed that I accepted a second dessert when it was offered, a lovely chocolate cup filled with lemon curd and drizzled with raspberry coulis. *I'll never maintain my size 10 figure if I keep on like this,* I thought, but with less regret than I should have felt about my own gluttony. Still, it was hard to feel regret when the chocolate and lemon curd had been so tasty.

Much as I like chocolate, I came to the conclusion on the cruise that any dessert provided relief from stress. This recipe is delicious and easy to prepare if you don't insist on making all the ingredients from scratch when you can buy them in a supermarket. Also, it does have some chocolate.

Lemon Curd in Chocolate Cups with Raspberry Coulis

Buy jars of *lemon curd* and packaged *cups made of dark chocolate* in your supermarket. Fill cups with lemon curd, assigning as many cups to each guest as you think proper.

In your food processor or blender, puree *2 1/2 cups fresh raspberries; 1/4 cup sugar (10 to 1 if you need more coulis)*; and *1 teaspoon fresh lemon juice* (or more to taste). Pour mixture through a fine sieve (pressing on the solids) into a bowl.

Drizzle coulis on and around the individual servings for a pretty and flavorful dessert.

Carolyn Blue,
"Have Fork, Will Travel,"
Madison, WI, State Courier

14

Entertainment at Sea

Carolyn

What I needed was to head straight back to the room and complete my column, but everyone else at the table insisted that we watch the evening's entertainment. Since they weren't intending to visit the casino, I let myself be persuaded and ended up stuck between the cereal king and an executive from a Silicon Valley computer company.

The first act, a comedian making jokes about his wife, set Vera off again. She listened to about three minutes of his routine and then said, loudly, "That man's a sexist pig."

The comedian stopped talking, cupped his hand to his ear, then leapt over to our half-circle, shouting, "Granny. I love you."

119

He tried to kiss my mother-in-law, which was a serious mistake because when she jerked away from him, she spilled her martini on the fly of his baggy trousers and snapped, "What happened to you, you moron? Your mother tried to abort you, and it didn't work? I have to give the woman credit for trying."

The comedian, who was billed as Russell Bustle, grasped his fly and yelled, "Look. I came. This is one sexy old babe." Commander Levinson, grimfaced, stood up and gave the man a shove that sent him staggering backward. I tried to scoot down in my seat, embarrassed to death, and that ugly security officer, who was wearing a tux instead of his white uniform, came over to intervene.

"I intend to file a sexual harassment charge against this oaf," said Vera, and ordered another martini since her glass was empty after the drink landed on Russell Bustle.

Mrs. Gross could be heard croaking, "Way to go, Granny!" Luz and the doctor from Atlanta were laughing their heads off, and Randolph Barber got the whole incident on video while the security man and the comedian had words, most of them interrupted by feminist threats from my mother-in-law and Luz's remarks in Spanish, which Vera translated.

"Our friend, the famous designer from Madrid, says that your comedian should be put off at the next stop for — not sure of what that means — perhaps abuse of respectable women."

The comedian, who *was* unquestionably disgusting, was marched away by Mr. Hartwig, and the dancing girls came on. Still, the thought that they might actually put Russell Bustle off the ship in Tangier worried me since I doubted that Tangier was a friendly place for an American to be stranded.

While Vera stared angrily at the chorus line of skimpily clad dancers, gritting her teeth and muttering about women being seen only as sexual objects by chauvinist cruise lines, Commander Levinson ignored the dancers completely and took it upon himself to talk Vera into a moonlight stroll on the deck. He thought the walk would be good for her heart and her blood pressure. Although I'd expected her to insist on staying to harass the rest of the entertainers, she surprised me by agreeing and stood up, leaving me wondering what exactly he'd meant by a moonlight walk being good for her heart.

He had a surprise coming if he was imagining a romantic interlude.

The chorus girls were followed by a second round of drinks for the rest of us — including Mrs. Gross, who, carrying her own bottle of wine, invited herself to join our party — and a pianist playing and singing romantic songs from Kurt Weill's Broadway period. Luz listened to two rounds of what she called "sentimental crap" and then left as well, accompanied by Dr. Beaufort E. Lee, who was obviously enchanted by her or her new dress.

I felt quite melancholy, having been deserted by my roommates and left with the cereal king; the computer executive, who looked about twenty, but claimed to be thirty-six; and Mrs. Gross, who declared over the music that she had found a cockroach in her raspberry crème brûlée at dinner and planned to sue the cruise line. Raspberry crème brûlée sounded good to me. If it turned up again, I'd certainly try it. Then Mrs. Gross advised us to do as she planned to do — not sign up for any of the shore excursions, which were overpriced and boring.

"But I want to see Tangier," I protested.

"Get off the ship, flag down a taxi, and

take your own tour," said Mrs. Gross. "You can come with me if you want to."

"Isn't that dangerous?" I asked, thinking a woman her age shouldn't be wandering around an Arab city in a taxicab. Still, for me the tour was free, and I intended to get the most out of it. I doubted that a Moroccan cab driver would make a very knowledgeable tour guide.

When I explained, she shrugged and said, "Suit yourself," and she left.

"She's one of those people who spend their lives cruising and getting freebies from the cruise lines with a lot of loud complaining," said Greg Marshand, interrupting his own monologue about successful putting on wet greens. "She probably brought the cockroach with her."

"That's not a very nice thing to say," I retorted.

"Well, she better watch out. The companies keep lists of those people, and they share the lists. I saw a guy get put ashore at the next port for posting a newsletter about the high price of drinks at the bars. He wanted to organize a buy-no-alcohol boycott, so they charged him with mutiny. His wife was furious and yelled at him all the way down the gangway."

I found that a truly astonishing story and

wasn't sure that I believed it, but my thoughts were interrupted by the computer man, John Killington, who said, "That lady is really asking for trouble if she hops a taxicab in Tangier. That's not something you do in third-world countries. The first thing I was told when I went to Russia on business was to avoid taxis you hadn't called yourself. The gypsy cabbies will take you out into the country, rob you, and toss you out of the car."

"You're right," I agreed morosely. "Almost that very thing happened to me in Barcelona." Then the pianist began singing "September Song." That was really too much. Here were Jason and I, getting older — certainly not November old, but perhaps October, which the song skipped, and free to enjoy traveling in each other's company before we reached December and were *too* old — and what was Jason doing? Talking toxins in the middle of the Canadian wheat fields. I could have wept. Instead I excused myself and went to my room. My *empty* room.

As I passed out of the nightclub, I heard Mrs. Gross, who had joined another table, saying that she'd found hair, not her own, in her shower, and she intended to lodge a complaint. Now that was really disgusting, if true, I thought, so I stopped and advised her to talk to Ombudslady Sandy Sechrest.

"I'd say that's a made-up name," muttered Mrs. Gross. "She probably picked it out to make herself seem more nautical and less like all the other perky cheerleader types."

I thought of warning Mrs. Gross about her chances of being charged with mutiny by the cruise line and put off the ship or robbed and dumped by a third-world cabbie, but I doubted that she'd listen since she'd paid no attention to my advice about seeing the ombudslady.

Once back in our suite, I put on my nightgown, ate a package of chocolate-covered macadamia nuts from the room bar, and finished my column — there's nothing like chocolate to chase away the blues — but still my friend and my mother-in-law hadn't returned. Feeling very lonely because they both seemed to have acquired male companions, and I was all by myself, I went to bed. This was *not* turning out to be as much fun as I had expected. But tomorrow was Tangier, which sounded so exotic. Probably the food would be, too, and having had much more sleep than my roommates would get, I'd be ready for the adventure instead of tired and grumpy.

I woke up only once, and that was when Commander Levinson and Jason's mother came in talking about Mrs. Gross, who had staggered off with a bottle in her hand and taken the elevator to the wrong floor. I buried my head under my pillow and went back to sleep.

15

Uninvited
Down Below

The Hijackers

Bruce Hartwig dropped into a chair in the officers' section of the crew dining room and blew out an angry breath. "We've got a goddamned old feminist crone on board. Raised a ruckus at the show tonight, and I had to drag the comedian out in the middle of his act. Marbella's on his high horse and laid into the show director, so she got pissy and said she'd pull all the entertainers if we dumped Russell."

"Russell is disgusting — not at all what's appropriate for this group," said Hanna. "I find him offensive myself."

Hartwig shrugged. "We've also got a thriller writer called the Wild Welshman

— Owen Griffith. Anyone ever heard of him?" No one had. "Well, let's hope he doesn't think he's some *Murder-She-Wrote* type who wants to solve real crimes."

Froder laughed. "So ve give him some thrills. Maybe he is never hijacked before. He can write a book, und ve sue him for some of der money."

"We've better things to worry about, me darlin's," said the Irishman. "Just received a bulletin. We've got a deadbeat on our passenger list. *Queen of the Southern Seas* passed the word. A woman named Gross, R. L. Gross, is suing them for poisoning her on a cruise from Singapore to Hong Kong. Their ship's doctor says there was nothing wrong with her."

"You call that a problem?" snapped Hartwig. "Let her sue the line. Won't make any difference to us once we're gone. But if the entertainers quit, we'll have a load of angry passengers before we ever hijack the ship. We need to keep them happy until we clear the Canaries. After that, we've got a day or two before they get really mad and think about making trouble."

"The guns will take care of that," said Hanna disdainfully. "It's not as if we're hijacking two hundred commandos. Don't tell me you're afraid of the passengers, Bruce."

"Well, he should be," said a croaking voice from the doorway, taking them all by surprise. "Because I intend not only to sue, but to tell the captain your plans."

"That's her. The deadbeat," said the Irishman. "*Southern Seas* sent a photo."

Bruce Hartwig stood up and walked toward Mrs. Gross, who had forgotten completely that she had come to complain about alien hairs in her shower. "Stay away from me," she said, "or I'll sue you personally and have you arrested as well." Her voice had climbed from a low croak to a high one and reminded Hartwig of a parakeet his mother had let loose in the house when he did something to irritate her. He'd hated, and still did hate, birds. He reached out for the woman's arm, thinking that there was no one in the brig. They could drug her and hide her in there until they took over the ship. Since he controlled the brig, it shouldn't be a problem.

"Look, Mrs. Gross," he said with the smile that always disarmed people, even on his admittedly ugly face. He could see Patek coming up on the other side of her.

"You must have misunderstood —" The old bitch kicked him in the knee.

Before Hartwig could get control of his temper, Patel slid between her and the door and wrapped his arm around her neck. When she struggled, they all heard the sharp crack of brittle bones breaking, and the old woman slumped, head askew, against the head steward.

"Dead?" asked Froder calmly.

"She better not be," snarled Hartwig.

"Alive, she is problem we can't solve. Dead she is no worry." Patek let her slide to the floor and rubbed his hands against the legs of his uniform as if disposing of any essence she might have left on him.

"Hell, all we had to do was drug her and hide her until —"

"No, Bruce. Better she is dead," said Patek as he locked the door to the dining room. "We dump her overboard and —"

"— risk her getting caught in the propellers?" asked Froder. "Then she vould be discovered. Broken neck und absence of vater in der lungs vould be necessary to explain."

"Well, we can't keep her on board dead," protested Hanna. "That's disgusting. She'll start to smell."

"Maybe not," said Hartwig thoughtfully.

"I can take care of it. But, Patek, I give the orders here. You've screwed things up, and I don't like it."

Patek said nothing. He sat down and resumed sipping his cup of tea.

"Don't know what you're planning, laddie," said the Irishman to Hartwig, "but people are going to notice she's missing."

Absently, Hartwig scratched the chest hair that showed above the open shirt of his tux. "So, you fix the computers, Patrick. I want them to show that she left the ship in the morning and never returned."

Hanna nodded. "Very good. She says to people in the club that she won't take our tours. She'll get a taxi to take her around Tangier. It's cheaper. Who knows what might happen to an old woman in an Arab taxi in an Arab country."

Hartwig nodded. "So after the tours return, we use the loudspeakers a couple of times to ask passenger Gross to call the desk, and then we leave."

"Will she be aboard or dumped in Tangier?" asked the Irishman. "*Southern Seas* will think we wouldn't let her back on, laddie."

"Cut the Irish crap," Hartwig replied. "The whereabouts of Mrs. Gross will be my business. Mine and Patek's."

131

"Just make sure she doesn't start to smell," murmured Hanna. "Housekeeping doesn't want to deal with a rotting corpse."

"We'll need some of those black plastic bags," said Hartwig when everyone but Patek had gone. "The heavy ones we use to get rid of medical waste."

16

Off the Coast of Morocco

Carolyn

Because I'd gone to bed early, I woke up early, or maybe it was jet lag still playing havoc with my internal clock. At any rate, I could see light through the drapes, and Luz was fast asleep, as well she might be. I'd never heard her come in. The ship was almost motionless in the water, so I assumed that we were off the coast of Morocco. After dressing quickly in the lightest, whitest outfit I had, I applied more sunscreen than makeup and tiptoed to the sliding balcony doors. And there it was: rippling blue water lightly shaded with pink from the rising sun, and the white, flat-roofed buildings of Tangier climbing away from the Strait of

Gibraltar — the Barbary Coast, pirates, souks. I tiptoed back for my wide sun hat and scuttled out of the suite. We were scheduled for the nine o'clock tour, but that didn't mean I had to sit around waiting for Vera and Luz to wake up. What if they decided to sleep in? Well, not me.

Herkule — Didn't the man ever sleep? — caught me on my way to the elevator and whispered conspiratorially, "You know lobster?" I had no idea what he meant. Was *Lobster* someone on the boat? If so, how unfortunate to be named for such a tasty but unattractive creature.

"Lunch is lobster. With pastas. I have snipples from kitchen once. Is many tasteful, so yummy." He sighed rapturously. "Not to miss."

Not that I didn't like lobster pasta, but I wasn't cutting short my time in Tangier to get back for it. I thanked Herkule for the tip about lunch — hoping we'd have lunch in Tangier — and took the elevator to the dining room, which was almost empty, only three or four people. During breakfast and lunch, we could sit wherever we pleased. I chose an empty table with a view of the city, shivering with delight at the exotic scene before me.

After glancing over my menu, I settled

134

on crab Benedict, which evidently substituted crab for the Canadian bacon in the traditional recipe. If Herkule asked me about lobster, I could talk about crab. After all, they're both shellfish. With the table to myself, I opened my *Eyewitness Travel Guide: Morocco.* I'd hardly ordered and read my way through the eighth-century Phoenician settlement at Tangier, the later Carthaginian and Roman towns, all B.C., and the A.D. 711 gathering of Arab and Berber forces to sail the Strait and conquer Spain, when the Crosswayses invited themselves to join me.

I'm sure they're very nice environmental types, but I really would have enjoyed my crab Benedict more if it hadn't been accompanied by their agitated descriptions of all the awful things that cruise ships dump into the sea — sewage full of fecal matter and dangerous bacteria, petroleum waste that leaves nasty slicks, dirty gray water from dishwashers and laundry facilities with the accompanying chemicals in the detergents, not to mention other toxic substances. Jason would have been enthralled.

"When we have vacation time, we cruise to see what they're up to," said Kev.

"But don't tell anyone," Bev added.

"They'd put us off the ship. All they care about is money."

I gulped down my last bite of crab Benedict, took the last sip of coffee, left the toast, although a luscious looking jam in a pretty periwinkle pot accompanied it, and promised to be circumspect about their mission, whatever it was, aboard the *Bountiful Feast.* Having escaped, I checked my watch, assured that I'd never again feel comfortable swimming in the sea, and just when I was beginning to recover from a terrifying experience of an aquatic nature in Northern France.

With an hour and a half before the tour left, I went back to the suite to see if anyone had awakened. Both Vera and Luz were gone, which made me a little sad, so I wrapped a few of Jason's bonbons in Kleenex and tucked them in my purse, unplugged my laptop, and left to find a nice deck chair on a nonsmoking deck.

I'd consumed a bonbon and written two paragraphs about crab Benedict when a somewhat ursine-looking man plopped himself down beside me and opened his own laptop. "You a writer?" he asked.

"Food columnist," I replied, peeking at him out of the corner of my eye as I continued to type so that he'd know I wasn't interested in conversation. He was stocky and muscular with rather dark skin, wild black hair, and an English accent. Actually a rather nice-looking man in a rough sort of way. His clothes certainly needed ironing. Perhaps he'd packed for himself. "The ship will iron your clothes if you like," I couldn't resist telling him.

"I never allow my clothes to be ironed," he replied. "It's against my principles as a thriller writer and international adventurer. Owen Griffith." He lifted a broad hand from his keyboard and shoved it in my direction.

Obviously I was meant to shake it, so I did. His grip and handshake were so vigorous I felt that he might have dislocated my elbow, so I withdrew my own hand hastily.

"Food columnist? Doesn't sound like much fun," he remarked.

"It's my first job, and I like it very much. I even get paid for it," I replied defensively. I'd heard of Owen Griffith and thought he was a best-selling author, although I'd never read any of his books. "If you're an international adventurer, perhaps you can tell me if a single, elderly woman hiring a taxi in a third-world country would be putting herself in danger."

137

"I wouldn't call you elderly," he replied. "In fact, you're bloody good-looking and younger than I am, I'd guess. What's your name?"

"I wasn't referring to myself as elderly. I'm worried about an acquaintance who plans to skip the tour and —"

"Right. Then she'd be an old fool. Tell her to forget it. It's a bloody stupid idea."

"Just what I thought," I replied as I mused on his use of the word *bloody* and came to the conclusion that it must derive from an ancient blasphemy such as *God's blood,* which morphed over time into *s'blud* and so forth. After frowning at Mr. Griffith, I saved my two paragraphs and closed my computer. Perhaps I could catch Mrs. Gross before she embarked on a foolish expedition.

"Where are you going?" he called after me. He sounded rather peeved at my abrupt departure. Ah well, I'd introduce myself properly and explain the history of the adjective *bloody* if I ever saw him again. Perhaps he'd want to excise it from his vocabulary. With only two hundred passengers on the ship, I'd no doubt see him one of these days.

I put a call through to Mrs. Gross's room since the perky young woman at the desk wouldn't give me her room number. However, no one answered. Then I searched for the gangway that led off the ship. There was a desk with a sign that advised passengers to have their personal identification cards swiped before leaving the *Bountiful Feast.* Besides the uniformed officer behind the desk, the ugly security chief was lounging against a wall. He seemed like the right person to talk to, so I approached, introduced myself, and explained my worries about Mrs. Gross.

"Gross? She's that tall, elderly lady who wears a brown dress to dinner?" I nodded. Mr. Hartwig said she hadn't left while he'd been there. "You got a Mrs. Gross signed up for any of the tours, Mark?" he then called out. Mark checked his computer and shook his head.

"Oh, dear," I murmured. "I've been told that it's dangerous for a single, elderly woman to hire a cab and go off sightseeing on her own. Perhaps you could keep an eye out for her and warn her of the possible consequences."

"Sure, but she strikes me as a cantankerous old lady," he said. "She's not likely to listen."

Remembering my few encounters with Mrs. Gross, I had to agree. Then I recalled

hearing my mother-in-law and Commander Levinson talking about how drunk
Mrs. Gross had appeared the night before.
Perhaps she'd been in her room sleeping
off a hangover when I called. She might
sleep right through the day and miss
Tangier entirely, which, for her, would certainly be the safest thing. How sad that a
woman her age, evidently a wealthy woman
who could afford anything she wanted, was
an alcoholic. "I do appreciate your con-
cern, Mr. Hartwig," I said politely, and
turned to make my way back upstairs. Did
one say "upstairs" on a ship? Or was there
some nautical term?

17

"Hitler in a White Dress"

Luz

Last night Dr. Beau and I had gone off to the outdoor bar to toss down a few drinks and swap stories about grisly corpses. I stayed up way too late, slept late, and would have missed the tour if Vera hadn't dragged me out of bed. I didn't catch up with Carolyn until we walked down to the gangway that put us on shore. From there, a bus picked us up and chugged off to a neighborhood that was really crowded — narrow, crooked streets stuffed with people. Tourists, guys in robes, women in tents. And it was hot. Damn. I was going to sweat on today's fancy — Babette called them casual — clothes.

Our guide was a little guy with a white beard, a white robe, leather shoes that curled up at the toes, and a fancy little hat — not one of those black-and-white checkered Yasser Arafat deals. This one was like a beanie that stuck up a couple of inches and had colored designs. Looked like something my *tia* Guadalupe might have crocheted. The guy's voice rattled and grated like my car the time some neighborhood kids loaded the hubcaps with gravel. Little bastards. That was when I was still married to my ex and still a cop.

The guide had a whistle around his neck and told us — I think; I couldn't understand him very well, although he mostly yelled — that we had to line up and stay in line so he wouldn't lose any of us in the alleys or the . . . *soup* is what it sounded like. Carolyn said it was *souk,* like market. Then he handed out scarves to all us women and said we had to put them over our hair. Vera, who was wearing this little cotton hat with a brim, griped about the scarf, and he blew his whistle in her face. Before she could tear the guide's head off, the commander grabbed her arm and told her not to make trouble in a Muslim country.

Carolyn said she, for one, was glad he

didn't want us to get lost, and she put on her scarf under this big sun hat and began asking people in our group if they'd seen Mrs. Gross that morning. No one had. The idea was that we should stay lined up, follow the guide when he blew the whistle, stop when he blew the whistle, and listen to what he had to say, all of which interfered with Carolyn's search for the old lady.

"Ex-military," said Barney, nodding toward our guide.

"Pig," said Vera.

"They don't eat pigs," Carolyn added helpfully, and off we went.

Everyone wanted to sell us something, but the guide drove them off and took us into stores from time to time — little, crowded, dusty places where you had to haggle over everything. I got to feel right at home, like I was in Juárez in the central market, the one that burns down every ten years or so. Carolyn took a fancy to this huge copper tray with elaborate designs all over it. She didn't even blink at the price, which was a hell of a lot of money. She told me it was a steal, but Vera said, "Nonsense," and haggled the guy down to about a fourth of the original price, which was still a lot of money.

Muhammad, or whatever his name was — everyone was named Muhammad or Ali or something like that — congratulated her on her purchase. I figured he probably got a cut on everything his tourists bought. Then he blew his whistle at me because my scarf had fallen off for about the fourth time. I told him if he liked the damn scarf so much, he should wear it himself, and Barney had to intervene. Poor guy probably wished he'd caught a different tour. Still, he really seemed taken with Vera. Go figure. Carolyn got in on that argument herself.

Then damned if she didn't get into trouble in the souk. She was looking at caftans and Berber rugs when she caught three teenagers pointing at us and making remarks that were pretty obviously insulting. Not that I actually knew what they were saying, but if we'd been in El Paso, I'd have expected them to be showing off gang T-shirts and tattoos — your usual teenage macho crap.

Carolyn took offense and demanded that the guide translate, and the dumb shit did: "They say lady with camel-piss hair must be concubine or other bad woman for not covering head." Whoops! Somehow or other Carolyn had lost her scarf completely, and her blond hair was hanging out

144

from under that big sun hat. Needless to say, she was not amused. In fact, she really lost it. I haven't seen her so mad since she went after Boris Ignatenko in the office at Brazen Babes and he blacked her eye.

She whirled on those kids and really tore into them. "Concubine? Is that how you treat respectable visitors to your country?" She grabbed Muhammad's arm and ordered him to translate what she had to say, and then she lectured the boys about how their mothers would be ashamed of their terrible manners, and her children would never do anything like that because she'd taught them better. She finished them off by saying, "And since you so charmingly commented on my 'camel-piss hair,' I'd like to say that I much prefer to have blond hair than a camel-piss personality like yours, you nasty little twerps."

Everyone was trying to shut her up; the guide stopped translating pretty quick and started blowing his whistle, but once Carolyn takes offense, she's bound and determined to have her say, and she did.

The kids turned tail and ran, Muhammad yelled at her, and Vera was so tickled that she gave Carolyn a hug and called her a "woman after my own heart." Then she called Muhammad "Hitler in a white dress." Evidently Carolyn didn't get many hugs or kind words from her mother-in-law, because she looked pretty shocked. Muhammad missed the Hitler comment; he just wanted to get us out of there before we caused any more trouble, but Carolyn insisted on staying to buy two caftans. Killington, the guy from Silicon Valley, offered to carry the heavy tray for her. He was lucky she hadn't decided on one of the bright red, wooly Berber rugs. He'd probably have got stuck with that, too.

Then Carolyn trotted off after Muhammad, who had forgiven her because she bought more stuff, and we continued sightseeing. The buildings may have been cracked and crumbly, like the adobe houses in the Segundo Barrio back home, but they had these colorful doors and shutters, pretty yellow and blue tiling, and elaborate scrollwork decorations made of what looked like plaster. Vera said at least the streets weren't full of dog shit like European streets, but then they probably ate the dogs in Morocco.

"Camel and donkey taste good, too," Muhammad told her with an evil grin. Christ! I hoped no one wanted me to eat any camel meat. They were really smelly animals.

After that, we got back on the bus and started into the countryside, which was dusty and scrubby and had the thinnest cows you've ever seen, not to mention the edible camels and donkeys. We were on our way to see a lighthouse. I suppose it was old or historic or something. I couldn't understand the guide.

After that the bus bumped along some more so we could visit this cave that had something to do with Hercules. At least I think that's what he said. Anyway, the sea washed up into a hole in the cave with a whoosh-boom. It was pretty spectacular, but I figured that if a really big wave came in there, it would drown a hell of a lot of tourists at one time. Then we got back on the bus and returned to visit a teahouse in Tangier.

It was a big, shabby room with draperies all over the place on the second floor of a building that looked like it had been hit by an earthquake and never repaired. After walking in all those alleys and climbing into the cave, my knees were killing me, and I was not happy to see pillows plopped around low tables. We were expected to sit cross-legged on the pillows while we sipped green mint tea, which I didn't like. It was too damn sweet, not to mention hot enough to cause blisters on your tongue.

A waiter, or whoever, made the tea at the table, while Carolyn, who was sitting beside me, provided a whispered, running commentary. It was worse than watching a golf match on TV. I didn't really care that tea, the ultimate expression of Arab hospitality to visitors, was served in glasses because glasses were more masculine than teacups, and always was made by the male head of the household or his eldest son, because Allah didn't approve of women making tea. Vera overheard and looked furious, but Barney on one side of her and Muhammad on the other cut her off every time she started to say something abrasively feminist.

Meanwhile, the tea-maker put a bunch of green tea in a big metal teapot (Carolyn whispered that if we were at a palace, the pot would be a fancy silver thing) and poured some hot water over it (to take away the bitterness, Carolyn said), then added a handful of mint leaves. After that he picked up this long blob of sugar and whacked off a piece with a copper hammer, poured in more boiling water, and stirred it around while he and Muhammad exchanged sneaky smiles and

148

nods, like we were all going to drink some and fall over dead because we were rotten infidels. After that the guy tasted it and added stuff and tasted and so forth.

Finally, for God's sake, he stood up and started pouring tea into our glasses, which were on the table below. If I could have gotten out of the way, I would have. Carolyn, Miss Know-It-All, told me that the sound of the tea, falling from a height, was "pleasing to the ears of Allah." Meanwhile, half our crowd was scrambling back in case the guy missed and poured hot tea in their laps. He gave us a contemptuous look and left to get the Moroccan desserts, which Carolyn *loved.*

First, she ate sliced oranges with cinnamon sprinkled all over them, while telling me that in the thirteenth and fourteenth centuries, the Venetians had a monopoly on the cinnamon trade, then the Portuguese beginning in the sixteenth century, and finally the Dutch — like I cared. At any rate, a lot of people died because cinnamon was popular and expensive in the old days and came from someplace far away — Ceylon? The oranges tasted pretty good.

Then, she ate these fried donuts, some with honey, some with sugar. They were okay, too, and by then I'd had enough. The tea was the eat-a-hole-in-your-stomach variety, for all the sugar in it, but I wasn't going to ask for water to dilute the stuff. They probably didn't have any that was drinkable, and I didn't need a bad case of Montezuma's revenge. Or maybe here it would be Muhammad's revenge. Anyway, I figured the heat might have killed the germs on the hands of the guy who made it. Obviously they didn't provide plastic gloves for the cooks and tea-makers in Morocco, like we do in restaurants at home.

Anyway, Carolyn wasn't satisfied with oranges and fried donuts. She wanted to know if they didn't have any chocolate desserts. She tried saying *chocolate* in several languages and ended up with a Moroccan torte, into which she bit, said "Ah!" and ate the whole thing. She was going to put on about fifty pounds before the cruise was over if she didn't quit that.

Vera said Carolyn was eating like she was pregnant, and Carolyn snapped that she *wasn't* pregnant, but she was certainly stressed, and she felt a lot better for having had something nice to eat. *Well, whatever bakes your cake,* I thought, and had to be pulled off the damn pillow for more sightseeing.

We started running into other tour groups from our boat, and Carolyn asked everyone she met if they'd seen Mrs. Gross. No one had. Most of them didn't know who Mrs. Gross was, lucky them. Why Carolyn wanted to locate her was beyond me, but I found out when we finally returned to the ship. We'd been in the suite about a half hour and were having drinks on our balcony — you can't get a real drink in an Islamic country, or I'd have skipped the tea — when the loudspeaker system came on. "Would passenger R. L. Gross please call the desk? Passenger R. L. Gross . . ."

"I knew it," said Carolyn. "She's been kidnapped by a cab driver."

"Would passengers Janet and Harold Wilcox please call the desk? Passengers Janet and Harold Wilcox." And so it went. About six people hadn't returned, and the ship was ready to leave for Gibraltar.

"She probably didn't even go into Tangier," said Vera. "What would an alcoholic woman want with a country that hates women and doesn't allow drinking?"

"I suppose you're right," Carolyn agreed. She finished her drink and went in for a nap while Vera and I fixed ourselves seconds and had a good laugh about Muhammad and his whistle and Carolyn driving off the teenagers.

"She's lucky they didn't try to stone her," I said. "She told me that's what they do to women who don't follow their damned rules."

"You wouldn't believe what a wimp my daughter-in-law was for years and years," Vera mused. "I have to say, I was proud of her today. Did you know she saved my neck when the idiot San Francisco police arrested me for murder?"

"Yeah, she mentioned that," I admitted, "but I thought —"

"Went right out and found the murderer. Almost got shot herself. Jason had a fit."

"I can believe that."

Traveling in a city like Tangier can be very stressful, and finding food and drink that relieves stress is not easy. No alcohol is allowed in Muslim countries, so relaxing with a cocktail is out unless you're invited to a foreign embassy. Sweets are popular, but they're not what we're used to — not what an American would consider "comfort food." Two Moroccan dessert recipes follow. The first is healthful but not particularly calming. The second, because it contains chocolate, is much more satisfying to the frazzled tourist weighted down with pur- chases that required haggling and be- deviled by Arab youths who feel free to make rude comments at the sight of fe- male curls uncovered in public.

Cinnamon-Dusted Oranges

Peel and slice particularly sweet and juicy oranges into rounds (*one orange per person*) and arrange on a plate. *Apple and/or pear slices* can be added, as well.

Dust each portion with *1/2 tablespoon cinnamon.*

Serve immediately.

Orange-Walnut Moroccan Torte

Preheat oven to 325°F and separate *6 eggs.*

Beat the egg whites with *1/2 cup sugar* in an electric mixer until the mixture holds stiff peaks.

Using the unwashed beaters and a small bowl, beat the yolks with another *1/2 cup sugar* until fluffy and light. Add the yolks to the whites and then *1 1/4 cups coarsely chopped walnuts* and fold in gently.

One cup at a time, fold in *2 cups shredded, unsweetened coconut.*

Pour the cake batter into a greased, 9-inch spring form pan and bake for 45 minutes until lightly browned on top.

Remove from oven; mix *1/2 cup orange juice* and *1/4 cup Grand Marnier (or other orange liqueur)* and pour over cake while still in pan.

Once cooled, place cake in refrigerator until time to serve.

Whip o*ne cup whipping cream* and shave *1 square semi- or bittersweet chocolate.*

Remove torte from fridge and from pan, top with cream, garnish with chocolate shavings, and serve.

Store any remaining cake in the refrigerator.

Carolyn Blue,
"Have Fork, Will Travel,"
Little Rock Post-Time

18

Where is Mrs. Gross?

Carolyn

Dinner was, again, excellent — braised duck breast in a sauce made of cherries, wine, and rich duck juice. Delicious, as was a salad with tomatoes, mozzarella, and eggplant (I skipped soup and pasta because it seemed to me that my waistband was getting a bit tight). On the downside, Mrs. Gross was not in the dining room. I looked for her while I was having the obligatory dance with Dr. Lee. After the entrée and the selection of my dessert, I actually got up and walked from table to table looking for her, although it probably wasn't necessary. If she'd been in the dining room, she'd have been on a second bottle of wine and getting loud.

Back in my own seat and very worried, I was not inclined to listen to Mr. Marshand going on about how good a high-fiber cereal, of which his former company had several tasty varieties, was for the bowels. Really! He'd obviously had a good deal of wine himself. I'd ordered a raspberry crème brûlée, which was so good that I decided to try the chocolate-Kahlúa ganache in puff pastry.

Then I excused myself and went off to call Mrs. Gross's room. She didn't answer. My next strategy was to return to the suite and search out Herkule, who always seemed to be on duty. First, I told him about the amazing cave with its forceful, booming tide bursting in through a large hole — a cave that bore his name. He responded that Herkule was a "legendful" name and then agreed to have a fellow steward check Mrs. Gross's room to see if she was ill and needed help. She wasn't there.

Now very worried, I asked that Mr. Hartwig be paged, and we had the following conversation standing near the desk downstairs:

ME: She wasn't at dinner, and she wasn't in her room. Were you able to warn her about the dangers of third-world taxicabs?

MR. HARTWIG: Actually, I never saw

her this morning, but then I wasn't able to monitor the whole morning disembarkation. Let me check the computer. [He went behind the desk, displaced one of the young women whom my mother-in-law referred to as "those cheerleader types," and tapped some computer keys.] She left the ship at ten thirty, Mrs. Blue, and we have no record of Mrs. Gross returning. Actually, I remember now that she was among several passengers that we had to page before leaving port. Perhaps you heard the pages.

ME: [*Alarmed.*] Were all those people left behind in Tangier? Don't you send someone out to find them?

MR. HARTWIG: [*Looking, I thought, somewhat condescending.*] Passengers are responsible for getting back an hour before the ship leaves port; two hours is recommended. You'll find that in the passenger instruction booklet, Mrs. Blue. Occasionally we do have to leave people behind. Some get separated from their tours and temporarily lost. Some, foolishly, decide they'd rather walk back to the ship than take the bus. And there are occasionally those who prefer to go out on their own, as Mrs. Gross evidently did, and forget the time.

ME: But — but you can't just leave her there. An old lady in a country that doesn't even respect women.

MR. HARTWIG: I'm sure she's just fine, Mrs. Blue. I believe that Mrs. Gross is a wealthy woman and one accustomed to getting her own way. She'll find an expensive hotel in which to spend the night, then take a ferry to Gibraltar and reconnect with the cruise there, none the worse for her adventure.

I was somewhat calmed by his reassurances. After all, he obviously knew more about these things than I, although I did think that an old woman with an alcohol problem might not be able to take care of herself. *And what about those dangerous cab drivers?* I reminded myself as I made my way to the elevators. *And in a country where she can't get a drink, she might have serious withdrawal symptoms — delirium tremens.*

"Hi there. You never did tell me your name."

It was Mr. Griffith, the thriller writer, joining me on the elevator. "Carolyn Blue," I replied. "Tell me, have you, in your travels, ever heard of an elderly female passenger being left behind when the ship sails?"

159

"Again, we're not talking about you, are we?"

I frowned at him. "Do I look as if I've been left behind?"

"No, love, you look smashing. Why don't we have a drink, and we can talk about your friend, who's obviously gone missing."

"Well, she's not really my friend, just an acquaintance, and I *should* return to the dining room to see if my mother-in-law is still there."

"You're married, then?"

"Yes, I am."

"Right. Well, off we go." And he took my arm and led me out of the elevator at the dining-room level.

Of course, Vera wasn't there, or Luz, or anyone at our table, except Mr. Barber, who was taking videos of the waiters clearing the dishes and wine glasses. I had to wonder if he subjected friends at home to all these video memoirs of his trips. My roommates weren't at the evening's show, either. They were probably out taking romantic walks on deck with their new male friends.

"We don't want to stay for this," said Mr. Griffith, waving his hand toward some acrobats in turbans. "It's just the usual cruise crap."

I didn't appreciate his language, but I did accept his invitation to have a drink at one of the ship's many bars. In fact, Mr. Griffith had three to my one. He was very interested in the fate of Mrs. Gross. "Smashing," he said when I'd told the story. "We'll have to find out what happened to the old girl."

Finally, someone who had the common humanity to worry about the poor woman, even if she was an unpleasant drunk. We discussed strategies for locating her.

"But then she may show up tomorrow at Gibraltar as Hartwig said. Ugly sod, isn't he?" Mr. Griffith waved to the bartender for a refill. "I put a description of him into my computer," he continued. "Probably use him as the villain in my next book."

"Yes, everything's an inspiration to a writer, isn't it?" I agreed. "I've been entering notes on the meals, especially the desserts. They really are marvelous. Would you like a bonbon? I have some in my purse, although they may be a bit soft after all that heat in Tangier."

"Why don't I order you a nice, sweet liqueur?" suggested Mr. Griffith. "How about Galliano?"

"Too sticky. But I wouldn't mind a Baileys Irish Cream. And after that I really must get to bed. I want to be fresh for the tour of Gibraltar tomorrow. Did you know that they have apes running free there? I find that interesting, but quite possibly dangerous. On the other hand, I was warned that I'd have my purse snatched in Tangier, and nothing of the sort happened. The warnings for tourists are often quite overstated. Except for Barcelona. I was almost entangled in a sailor's brawl there, and a taxi driver tried to kill me. And then there was Mont-Saint-Michel. I got caught in the tide off the beach. Very frightening. And the dead people — I'm amazed at how many murdered people I've come across since I started traveling."

"Good God, woman," he exclaimed with a truly delighted smile. "You'll have to tell me all about your adventures."

"Well, I'd love to," I replied, flattered, "but there's Gibraltar tomorrow. I really should get to bed."

"Those apes aren't all they're cracked up to be," said Mr. Griffith. "More a nuisance than anything."

I've written about crème brûlée before in this column, but the raspberry crème brûlée I had on the cruise ship after a difficult day in Tangier is really worth a mention and a recipe. However, if your day has been doubly difficult, chocolate is always the answer to stress. For those particularly bad days, try the second recipe: Kahlúa Ganache in Puff Pastry. You can buy the puff pastries at the supermarket. For all I know, you can buy the ganache, as well, but this is a tasty version.

You'll note that the second recipe has two feel-good food stuffs in it, chocolate being my favorite. Chocolate was first made from the seeds of "the Tree" of the Mayan gods, who allowed their worshippers to imbibe the drink of the gods until the whole civilization mysteriously disappeared around A.D. 900. Then the Toltecs and Aztecs found the Tree, provided by Quetzalcoatl, the bearded god of the forest. The worshippers loved the gift, but the god deserted them by climbing on a raft and setting out to sea. The appearance of Cortés, unfortunately for the Aztecs, was taken to be the return of Quetzalcoatl. When Cortés asked to see their treasure, they showed him the huge store of beans. However, the Spanish were more interested in gold than beans.

Later, missionary nuns to South America decided to convert chocolate to Christianity by eliminating the heathen spices used by the Indians and adding instead cream, sugar, and vanilla — so much more civilized than hot chili powder.

Raspberry Crème Brûlée

Heat oven to 300°F. Set a teakettle of water to boil.

For six servings of raspberry crème brûlée, divide *48 fresh raspberries* among 6 ramekins.

Bring to a simmer *2½ cups whipping cream.* Whisk *9 egg yolks* with *⅓ cup sugar* and a little *salt* until blended. Then, whisk in very slowly the hot cream and finally stir in *1 teaspoon vanilla extract.*

Pour the cream mixture over the raspberries in the six ramekins and set them in a baking pan. Pour boiling water into the pan until it comes halfway up the ramekins.

Bake in preheated oven until set (35 to 40 minutes). Remove ramekins from pan, cool, and chill thoroughly.

Before serving, sprinkle 2 teaspoons of *sugar* (*12 teaspoons total*) over each ramekin of brûlée and put under the broiler only long enough to caramelize the sugar. If you have a little brûlée blowtorch, use that.

(Optional: Decorate each custard with several raspberries.)

Kahlúa Ganache in Puff Pastry

Buy and prepare the number of *puff pastry sheets* you need. I suggest shaping cups from the pastry.

Estimate the amount of ganache you will need and provide equal amounts in ounces of a *fine semisweet dark chocolate, chopped,* and *heavy cream.*

Place the chopped chocolate in a stainless steel bowl.

Heat the cream in a medium saucepan

over medium heat until just boiling and pour over chocolate immediately. Allow to sit for 5 minutes.

Add *1 tablespoon Kahlúa* (*brandy* or *cognac* can be substituted) per 16 ounces of cream and chocolate and whisk until smooth. Refrigerate.

Fill the puff pastries with ganache before serving.

Leftover ganache can be rolled into small balls and then coated with *cocoa* or *chopped nuts* to make truffles, a nice snack for the home chef who has to clean the kitchen after the dinner party. Otherwise, refrigerate the truffles. They will last for several weeks.

Carolyn Blue,
"Have Fork, Will Travel,"
Boulder, CO, Times

19

Barbary Apes and Bad News

Jason

After a satisfying day of discussions on toxin research, spent in a small Canadian town surrounded by flat agricultural fields that stretched in every direction to distant horizons, I connected my laptop to the telephone jack in my room so that I could access my e-mail from home. I planned to glance through the messages and then go to bed. All were academic in nature and didn't require instant replies, except for the last, an e-mail and attachment from a colleague in El Paso.

Hey Jason,
Your wife's column debuted in the

Times *today. What'd you do to her? She seems really steamed up about bonbons for some reason, and I take it they were a present from you. . . .*

I groaned. I didn't want to read the attachment. Although I'd meant well in ordering the bon voyage gift for my wife, obviously she hadn't forgiven me for sending her on the cruise with my mother for company. God only knew how my mother had responded to the bonbons. Not her sort of thing, but the inspiration had hit me late, and I hadn't had time to think of something else for my mother.

Luz

Gibraltar is one hell of a big hunk of stone, I can tell you. They put us ashore right after breakfast, and this chunky woman, our guide for the tour, shoveled us onto the minibus and drove us around town, mostly higher and higher, while she pointed out views of Africa and Spain and told us Gibraltar stories. First, we had to hear about this big monster cannon the English had brought in to help defend the place. We were on our way to see the miles of siege tunnels they'd blasted into the rocks, and the cannon was in there, but it hadn't been the big success they'd expected.

First screwup: they couldn't get it off the ship. Every time they winched it up, the boat rose with it, which was not what they had in mind. Then they weighted down both ends of the boat, successfully got the cannon off, but the boat sank. Finally, they got the cannon into the tunnel with its snout stuck out of a cannon window or whatever and took a practice shot. Shattered every window in town, which was not real popular with the locals. At this point in the story, we were walking in the tunnels, Vera complaining about the dust, and Carolyn soaking up everything the guide had to say. She thought the whole thing was great, but frankly I pretty much tuned out when we got to some tale about a French submarine surfacing while the English were shooting their cannon. I'm not sure what happened there. They accidentally blew the French out of the water? Or the French thought they were being attacked and shot up the town or torpedoed some boats in the harbor? Whatever.

After the tunnels came a cave with stalag-somethings while the guide griped about the huge taxes people on Gibraltar had to pay and the crappy health insurance, which, if you used it, got taken out of your pension. Ha! She thought she had health insurance problems. She should try getting an insurance company to pay for rheumatoid arthritis meds.

Then we drove around some more until we found some Barbary apes to stare at. They weren't actually apes and were either brought here by the English or got over on their own before the rock split apart, leaving some in Africa and some here. You'd think the guide would know, or maybe I missed it because I was staring at them.

They were chunky monkeys (making me wish I had some of that Ben & Jerry's ice cream, because my throat was dry after the dusty siege tunnels), and they had sort of blond-brown hair and liked to scramble around on the rocks or sit on one with their knees flat on the surface and their privates on display. Nice. They also liked to steal stuff. One big male jumped up and grabbed Vera's purse. She was really pissed — you can't blame her — so I grabbed the ape and pulled out the plastic cuffs I always carry in my purse. Harriet Barber was a real champ. She sat on him while he screamed and I cuffed him and yanked the purse away from him. Randolph got the whole thing on video, and it took a while because that monkey was strong and put up a fight.

The guide told us I couldn't do that because the apes, although a real pain in the ass, were a protected species. No one was allowed to mess with them.

"He's a thief, and I made a citizen's arrest," I said, but I had to uncuff him. Then he took a poke at me, and I knocked him over on his hairy blond butt so we could get back on the bus in a hurry before the local cops arrived to arrest me for ape abuse. Our guide ground the gears and took off for the shop at the end of the continent or the world. Whatever. It was full of tourist crap, which the guide insisted was cheap because it wasn't taxed.

Last, we made another shopping stop. We were going to get to see the famous Gibraltar glassblowers, and by mentioning the guide's name, we could buy stuff at a discount and send it back free to the U.S. I stayed on the bus. Carolyn stopped worrying about the still-missing Mrs. Gross and raced off to the glass place with Vera in hot pursuit to see that her daughter-in-law didn't spend too much of Jason's money. Good thought, but it didn't do Vera any good, because Carolyn bought a tall pink and purple vase. At least she shipped that purchase. If she kept buying stuff, we weren't going to be able to get into the sitting room.

Vera said it cost $275, which was a ridiculous price, but Carolyn said it was "signed by the artist," which made it "priceless." I don't know why. She couldn't even remember the artist's name. She probably could have gotten the same thing for ten dollars in Juárez. They've got glassblowers.

On our way back to the ship, the guide admitted that she couldn't stand the Barbary apes because they stole wash off the clotheslines, and nobody on the rock had air-conditioning but they couldn't open their windows in the hundred-degree weather, because the apes climbed in and stole everything they could eat or carry off, besides which they screamed a lot and woke up the kids at night. I was glad to get back on the boat.

Carolyn

My hope was that Mrs. Gross had caught up with the *Bountiful Feast* here on

Gibraltar and was even now in her cabin, dressing for lunch. Not that I wanted to join her; I just wanted to stop worrying about her. As soon as I entered the ship, I spotted Mr. Hartwig and hurried over to him, bypassing the desk where my return should have been recorded. Two men marched after me, but I passed them my card and told them to swipe it for me. Of course they looked to Mr. Hartwig, who nodded.

"Did she arrive on board while we were gone?" I asked eagerly.

Mr. Hartwig sighed and shook his head. "I'm afraid we haven't heard from her."

"Then you must call the authorities in Tangier and have them institute a search. Surely there's an American embassy or consulate that can —"

"Ma'am, if Mrs. Gross doesn't want to rejoin the ship, that's her right. My investigation tells me that she was not happy with the cruise. Or she may have decided to meet us in Casablanca, which is her right."

"But what if she's been kidnapped, or she's ill and not receiving proper treatment in Morocco?"

His lips compressed. "Or she's planning to sue us for leaving her behind and for other imagined deficiencies in our service.

173

The truth is, Mrs. Blue, that your friend has a record of inveigling money, unpaid services, and entire free cruises from other cruise lines by —"

"You put her off, didn't you?" I cried. "You considered her a troublemaker or even a mutineer and told her she couldn't reboard. I've heard that cruise lines do that. There's a story about a man who was trying to organize a boycott of the bars on board a cruise ship because of the high prices, and the ship's officers —"

"We did not put Mrs. Gross off at Tangier," Mr. Hartwig snapped, either his patience with me at an end or, more likely, his anger taking over when I put my finger on what had happened to Mrs. Gross. He turned away and left me standing there, discouraged because her fate was now back in my hands.

20

The Duty to Investigate

Carolyn

Owen Griffith asked to join me at lunch. Naturally, I agreed, eager to tell him the bad news about Mrs. Gross and my suspicions that she might have been told to leave the ship at Tangier. He thought that possible, in which case, there was nothing we could do for her, although she might have herself a nice case against the cruise line, which could be just what she wanted. "Maybe cruising and putting one over on the cruise lines is her hobby," he suggested. "Sounds like good fun, doesn't it?"

I didn't think so. Furthermore, I suggested that he wasn't taking the problem seriously enough. He grinned at me and said, "Oh, I'm fascinated, but we'll have to wait for Casablanca to see if she shows up there. In the meantime, have you met a couple named Crossways? Bloody fascinating people."

Mr. Griffith seemed to feel everyone was fascinating, including me — fascinating, but not to be taken seriously. "They're adjunct professors at the Scripps Institute of Oceanography," I informed him frostily, after which I finished my lobster pasta, which I'd ordered to please our sweet steward, and asked about the desserts that were available. I felt a great need for a nice dessert to cheer me up after the stress of finding out that Mrs. Gross was still missing and that no one seemed to be in a hurry to find her. I told the waiter that I'd have a double portion of chocolate mousse cake. Just this once I'd eschew my duty to order something I'd never tasted and eat something I knew would make me happy.

"Adjunct professors? Not likely," said Mr. Griffith. "What do you want to bet?" I told him I didn't gamble. "Fine, but we'll still check it out. My take on those two is that they're SOTS."

"They haven't indulged in any excessive drinking that I've noticed," I replied. "You drink a lot more than the Crossways do. Do you consider yourself a sot?"

Mr. Griffith laughed heartily and admitted that some people might consider him a sot, but he certainly wasn't a member of SOTS, which was the acronym for Saviors of the Seas. "They cruise to catch the lines dumping prohibited stuff into the water and then make reports to environmental agencies. The lines hate them."

I immediately saw how this might apply to the disappearance of Mrs. Gross. "Goodness, if you're right, Mrs. Gross may have caught them investigating and threatened to turn them in."

"Interesting theory, love. Let's check them out."

"Maybe they kept her from getting on the boat, or even injured her," I suggested over my cake, which had already effected a lifting of my spirits. After dessert, I accompanied Mr. Griffith to the computer room, where we accessed the Web site of the oceanographic institute. His guess was quite correct. The Crosswayses were not listed as adjunct professors or anything else. What if they'd killed her?

Again insisting that I call him Owen, he suggested that we track the Crosswayses down and question them. A good idea, I thought, especially since he'd be along to protect me in case they turned out to be murderers. I postulated that a thriller writer might know all sorts of hand-to-hand combat techniques, not to mention the obvious fact that he was a somewhat burly man. Next, he suggested that we check out the exercise room, because the Crosswayses struck him as the kind of people who would exercise regularly. We checked, they weren't there, and somehow or other I found myself trying out one of the treadmills that faced the sea. I could look right back at Gibraltar from the machine, a spectacular sight, so the experience was rather nice as long as the machine was set on slow.

However, we never did find the Crosswayses. Instead Mr. — Owen urged me to speed the machine up to see how I liked it. I was not enthusiastic, but since he was on the treadmill beside me egging me on and I didn't want to seem lacking in a spirit of adventure, I gave the lever a push, and the mat began to race under my feet. Naturally, I shrieked in terror and fell off. Owen hopped off his treadmill without mishap and tried to help me up. Then an attendant rushed over to check on my well-being and offered me twenty free minutes in the white health capsule. I just wanted to go back to my suite and nurse my bruises, which I did. I did not, however, cry, although I felt like it. Falling off a racing treadmill is very painful.

Luz

Evidently some guy lured Carolyn onto a treadmill and damn near killed her. I lent her some of my capsaicin cream to rub in where it hurt and helped her into bed while she muttered about someone named Crossways being the undercover killer of Mrs. Gross. I figured she just needed some sleep, so I didn't wake her up until dinnertime.

Dinner was great, as usual, but we got some bad news over the loudspeaker system. At least Carolyn thought it was bad news. We wouldn't be stopping at Casablanca because there were fundamentalists rioting there, and the State Department had warned Americans off. Instead, we were heading for the Canary Islands, and if things calmed down, maybe we could stop at Casablanca on the way back. Fine with me. As soon as I heard I'd have to take my shoes off to get into this mosque Carolyn was so crazy to see, I lost interest in Casablanca. My first night barefoot on the boat was enough for me. I could just imagine a bunch of American-hating Arabs stepping on my toes to get even for me visiting their mosque.

Carolyn took the news badly. She really wanted to see the mosque, even if she had to take off her shoes. After all, she said, they had carpets all over the place. Arabs and Persians were famous for their carpets, which meant, I figured, that she wanted to buy herself a carpet in Casablanca. And then there was Mrs. Gross, who was still missing. If Mrs. Gross was figuring on catching the boat at Casablanca, what was she going to do? Carolyn wanted to know. On the other hand, if the woman wasn't getting on at Casablanca, she was probably dead — put off the boat by the cruise line or killed by this Crossways or a taxi driver.

Harriet Barber thought the last was likely because she and her husband had been warned about cab drivers when they visited Russia. Carolyn nodded vigorously over her first dessert. She'd heard about Russian cab drivers. Harriet said she'd taken care of that by photographing their driver with her cell phone and sending his picture to the hotel in case they didn't get back on time. Smart woman, Harriet. I had to like her because she'd pitched in and sat on the Barbary ape so I could handcuff him.

The other interesting thing that happened at dinner was between Barney and Vera. Marshand, the cereal guy, got on Vera's case because she was bitching about all the male stewards with not enough females to balance them off. That's when Barney said to Marshand, "I have to say, Greg, that I like a smart, assertive woman who knows her mind and speaks it — a woman who can take care of herself."

Vera gave him a nod and said, "Well, I like a man who doesn't try to comb his hair over a bald spot, which everybody knows looks ridiculous." The point of this was that Barney had a bald spot, but what hair he had left was buzz cut, military fashion. No comb-overs for him. Marshand tried the comb-over, but it didn't work and looked stupid. I wondered if Vera and Barney were sleeping together. And if they were, how Carolyn would react if she tumbled to it. Although I thought about asking her, just for the hell of it, she took off after her second dessert and only turned up a couple of hours later, really excited.

"Guess what the man from Silicon Valley, Mr. Killington, just found out for me? Mrs. Gross never left the ship at all in Tangier. Someone hacked into the computer and made it look like she'd checked off the ship, but the entry was put in the night *before* we got to Tangier."

"How did the Silicon Valley guy find that out? And what's with his ponytail?"

"It's probably the style in Silicon Valley. I've heard they don't even wear suits to work, although some of those companies are worth billions, and their people earn lots and lots of money. Mr. Killington — John, I think — is an executive, but when I asked if he could find out for me, he was so excited. He said, 'You mean hack into their system? Sure, I can. It'll be like the old days in college,' and I could hardly keep up with him when he headed for the computer room. It didn't take him that long, and while I waited for him to finish, I went on-line myself and ordered a pair of stained-glass dresser lamps from the Smithsonian site. They look like something that architect — from the prairie school — might have designed. What is his name? Ah! Frank Lloyd Wright. Anyway, the point is, if she didn't get off the boat, where is she?" Carolyn asked triumphantly.

"Good question," I had to agree, although I didn't want to think about it just then because my knees were aching from hiking around the ship with Dr. Beau. He kept telling me that exercise was good for what ailed me. Maybe, but after all, Beau was a pathologist. I wasn't dead yet, so what did he know?

The Hijackers

"So ve're here," said Froder. "Meeting so often is not gut idea. Look vat happened last time. So vat's the problem?"

"You mean besides the fact that I can't get in touch with the helicopter pilots because the fuckin' fundamentalists are keeping us from docking in Casablanca?" Hartwig snarled.

"I can put you in touch with them if they're online," Patrick offered.

"And leave footprints in the computer. Not unless we have to."

"Then, what?" asked Hanna.

"Gross. Patek, why the hell did you have to kill the woman? There's this food columnist the line gave a free ride in return for publicity. She's chasing me around insisting that I call the consulate in Morocco

183

to send out people looking for Gross. She even accused me of putting Gross off the boat at Tangier for causing trouble."

"I take care of her," said Patek. "What name?"

"Leave her alone," Hartwig retorted. "For now."

21

Searching by Telephone and Internet

Jason

I had slept badly in my room on the great plains of Canada, but I collected myself and gave an admirable paper, "A Theoretical Process for Using Toxic Mine Tailings," which was well received by my colleagues and prompted lively discussion. Having finished what *had* to be accomplished at the meeting, I resigned myself to doing something about my disgruntled wife, although I knew my plan was going to prove costly and time-consuming. First, I made a long-distance call to the cruise line to get her itinerary, dates and places, and permission to join her on the boat in time for Mother's Day, if that could be arranged.

After increasingly long waits, which were costing me staggering international long-distance fees, the person taking my call said that there were already three people in my wife's suite, a situation that made it unlikely that there would be room for me. Irritated and anxious to get to lunch, I informed the woman that she was mistaken; the only person in the suite with my wife was my mother.

"Well, you're wrong," she said, "although for some reason I don't have the other name. Still, we seem to have lost a passenger. If she doesn't catch up with the ship soon, I suppose you and Mrs. Blue could use that cabin, but unfortunately, you'll have to pay for the added accommodations. I see here that Mrs. Blue is sailing as a complimentary passenger and that the line has already agreed to add two other people to her status. I really have to say that one more would be asking too much of the company."

"Don't worry about it," I snapped. "There'll be a bed for me in the suite. Now where can I fly to get onto the ship before Mother's Day?"

"Ummm," said the woman, whose name

was Rhonda. "Well, you've waited a bit late to do this. I'd have suggested Casablanca, but we don't know that they'll be able to dock there. The first attempt had to be passed up because of the rioting."

"Rioting?" I felt like clutching my head and groaning. "My wife was caught in rioting?"

"Not that I know of," said Rhonda patiently. "The *Bountiful Feast* changed its itinerary and headed for the Canaries instead, hoping to stop at Casablanca on the way back to the Mediterranean, but only if it's safe. We do *not* let passengers disembark at ports about which the State Department has issued warnings."

"I'm relieved to hear it," I replied, thinking that if anyone disembarked during a riot, it would be my wife, whom trouble seemed to dog on her travels, with or without me.

"I think your best possibility would be Tenerife, the second stop in the Canary Islands. You say you're in Canada? The ship won't leave Tenerife until three p.m. the day after tomorrow. Of course, that's local time, but that's the only real chance of arriving by Mother's Day. On the other hand, Casablanca, the next day, is a possibility, but I can't assure you that the ship will actually be able to —"

"It has to be Mother's Day. Do airplanes fly to Tenerife?"

"I have no idea, sir. If passengers get off at Tenerife and don't reboard, they're more or less on their own."

"Wonderful," I snarled. "I'll pull up Orbitz. Maybe they can figure out how to get me there in time. And at least I won't have to pay long-distance rates."

"We have a Web site," said Rhonda defensively.

"I tried it."

"Well, most people don't want to catch a cruise on some island in the middle of the Atlantic Ocean. Our Web site may not be set up for such an unusual request. I think you should consider meeting your wife at one of the Spanish ports that finish the cruise. I'm sure she'll forgive you for missing Mother's Day. I don't see here that she has children along. Mostly people don't bring children on our cruises because of the expense. Not that our cruises aren't worth every penny. *Condé Nast Traveller* said — wait just a minute. I'll look up that quotation. It was very —"

I hung up.

Carolyn

We wouldn't reach our first stop in the Canary Islands until tomorrow. In the meantime, what, if anything, could I do to find out the fate of Mrs. Gross? Of course, I could just wait until we arrived in the Canary Islands and see if she turned up there, but that seemed so unlikely. The islands are in the Atlantic Ocean, which was, as I noticed, bumpier than the Mediterranean. I'd even felt a bit queasy at breakfast, but that had passed.

I consulted with Luz over waffles bathed in lingonberry sauce, but she said that ordinarily the thing to do would be to contact missing persons at the local police department after forty-eight hours had passed, or, possibly, the FBI, but since we were in the middle of the ocean and we didn't really know how long Mrs. Gross had been missing, the whole thing was a puzzle. Then Luz went off to visit Dr. Lee in his clinic.

I, having been given at least a few ideas, went to the computer room. There I accessed Google, where I got e-mail addresses for our state department in Washington, D.C., our embassy in Rabat, and our consulate, which was in Casablanca. Wouldn't you know? The rioters might well have cut off communication to the consulate. Then I searched for the Tangier police department without much luck. I did learn that Morocco was the first country to recognize U.S. independence, and I found some articles about people being beaten up by Moroccan police, a rather discouraging piece of information. Did I really want to set a violent police department on the trail of poor Mrs. Gross?

About then, an Irishman, who seemed to run the computer room, although he wasn't always there, stopped by to ask if I needed any help. Since he was eyeing the page I had on the screen, the one about police brutality in Tangier, I asked how to find information on Casablanca, which I wanted to read since I might not get to go there. He immediately lost interest and went away, and I sent e-mails off telling the various American diplomatic sites my concerns about Mrs. Gross. I really doubted that my e-mails would do much good.

After all, the government couldn't even keep up with all the spy information they collected. Consequently, there was no reason to think they'd get to my e-mail about Mrs. Gross before both of us were dead of old age. But at least I was doing the best I could, and lunch was about to be served.

22

The Lone Detective

Carolyn

I'm not sure which I found more discouraging, the realization that my morning of computer research and messaging was probably a waste of time or the realization that the waistline of my slacks was still tight. At least I could do something about the latter. At lunch I had water instead of wine and a nice leafy salad instead of an entrée. I even gathered an interesting piece of information. While I was trying to talk Luz into joining me in detecting, for old times' sake if nothing else, a lady interrupted us to say that she'd seen Mrs. Gross the night before she disappeared and that Mrs. Gross had announced her intention of going to find the ombudslady to complain about the alien hair in the shower.

A lead, I thought, *finally!* I'd track down Sandy Sechrest to see if she could provide a later sighting of Mrs. Gross, but earlier than the fake computer entry that had her leaving the ship at ten thirty the next morning. Unfortunately, Luz refused to go with me. She said she was going to our suite to relax in the silk "robe-thing" the boutique had provided. So attired, she planned to finish off the rest of Vera's bonbons and watch television. I tried to imagine my crusty friend devouring bonbons while reclining in a silk robe and watching some romantic movie, of which Herkule had mistakenly provided many.

Then I discovered that the chef was offering seven flavors of freshly made gelato. All my good intentions about waist control fled, and I ordered small helpings of all seven, the four fruit varieties with strawberries and cream, the three others with chocolate sauce and nuts. Our waiter gave me a peculiar look but produced the requested dessert, and I must say, eating it made me feel much better, even considering the defection of my friend.

Sandy was in her minuscule office, writing up a free facial for a customer whose silk sweater had been shrunk by the laundry service. When she heard my story about Mrs. Gross, she was, naturally, distressed, although she, too, thought Mrs. Gross would turn up sooner or later, even if it was in court bringing suit against the line for leaving her behind. "I do so try to keep everyone happy," said Sandy plaintively, "but sometimes nothing I can do works."

"I know you do," I replied consolingly. The poor girl looked on the verge of tears. "But did you see Mrs. Gross the night before we docked in Tangier?"

"Oh, yes," she said sadly. "She told me about some hair in her shower, which she insisted was not her own, and I offered to contact her steward the very next day, but that just wasn't good enough. To tell you the truth, she seemed to have had a bit too much to drink. She was very aggressive; she even cursed and demanded that I write up her complaint, so of course I did. Then she decided to look for her own steward and give him a tongue-lashing, and if she didn't find him, she said she'd find the head steward, Mr. Patek.

"I really didn't want her to do either. The poor stewards are, I'm sorry to say, badly overworked. If her steward had managed to finish for the night and get to bed, I hoped she wouldn't wake him up. As for

Mr. Patek, well, I don't even like to take complaints to him myself. He can be very — well — abrasive. Goodness knows what he'd have said to her, and I'm the one who'd have had to calm her down."

Now that was interesting. "Where would she have found Mr. Patek?" I remembered him from the champagne reception. A dark-skinned, sour-looking man.

"By that time, probably in crew quarters. He has his own stateroom — all to himself — but I didn't tell her how to find it. Actually, I was lucky. She didn't ask. She just went away, muttering to herself. Considering her condition, I imagine she went off to bed. I certainly would have, if I'd been that — well — inebriated."

I thanked Miss Sechrest again, was again urged to call her Sandy, and went in search of Mrs. Gross's steward, not an easy task since no one would tell me the deck and number of Mrs. Gross's room. I got that by asking Mr. John Killington to hack into the ship's computer for a second time. He was glad to do it. With the information Mr. Killington provided, I found the room and the steward, but he said he'd remade her bed about eight thirty in the evening and hadn't seen her since, although it looked as if someone had slept in the bed when he arrived to do the room the next morning. When I asked how late he'd been on duty that night, his face lit up, and he said he'd been in his own bed by midnight, and no one had paged him the whole night. Of course, I then asked how to find Mr. Patek, because John Killington hadn't been able to find the chief steward's office or cabin number. Mrs. Gross's steward looked terrified and said he wouldn't tell me if he knew.

Since I had no more ideas to pursue, I went to our suite, where I found Luz sprawled on the couch in her silk robe, eating bonbons and watching not a romantic movie, but something that involved a lot of gunfire and wrecked, burning cars. "I don't know what to do next," I said woefully over the sounds of shouts and machine guns.

"Sit down and watch the movie. It's an old Bruce Willis flick. And I've got a cop movie with that Australian guy and his black partner to watch next."

"At least you could suggest something," I said.

Luz picked up the remote and turned the DVD off. "Hell, I guess keep following her trail. If she ended up in her room that night, that ugly brown dress and her ton of green rocks would be there."

"Emeralds," I murmured. It was a good idea, if they'd let me into her room. However, if the steward was that afraid of Mr. Patek, he probably wouldn't open the door.

"If you're not back in time to dress for dinner, I'll come looking for you," said Luz, grinning, and she clicked her movie back on.

I decided to talk to my friend Herkule, thinking that perhaps he could help, and he did. As we took the elevator to Mrs. Gross's floor, we discussed the desserts, the raspberry brûlée, the gelato — Herkule loved food, and even when he didn't get to taste the exciting offerings prepared for the passengers, he always tried to slip into the kitchen to take a look. Not, he added, that the crew wasn't well fed. He never went hungry, but the food for the passengers, it looked so succulent, which was one of his new words, yesterday's actually. He mispronounced it, but I did admire his relentless pursuit of English.

Herkule was able to talk his fellow steward into opening Mrs. Gross's room, as long as all three of us stayed in the room while I was searching. The brown evening dress was not in her closet. Nor was it in her dry cleaning bag, and her steward insisted that he had never picked up any dry cleaning or laundry for her. Then I searched drawers and suitcases and found no emeralds.

"Is expensive — emeralds?" asked her steward.

"Very," I replied.

"Probably in safekeeping box."

"Is that behind the desk downstairs?"

"No, here." He revealed a small safe tucked under a night table beside her bed. Of course, it was locked.

"No trouble," said Herkule cheerfully. He punched a long series of numbers into the keypad, and the door swung open. "For when passenger forget own numbers," he explained, an explanation I didn't find all that reassuring.

Even less reassuring was the safe with several pieces of expensive jewelry but no emeralds. Mrs. Gross, her dress, and her emeralds were gone. I didn't know what it meant, but it couldn't be good news.

Luz

Before we went off to dinner, an announcement from the captain came over the loudspeakers; he warned us to expect gentle swells during the dinner hour and evening. I'd hate to find out what he called a big wave. Vera and Carolyn and I didn't have too much trouble wobbling in to dinner, but Harriet Barber damn near broke her neck. When she finally fell safely into her chair, she said, "The captain might change his mind about how gentle these swells are if he had to wear high heels."

"Why do you wear them?" Vera demanded. "You're old enough to have figured out that panty hose and high heels were devised by men. Before that it was corsets and Chinese foot binding. Keep the women hobbled so they can't assert themselves; that's the idea."

"I accomplish all sorts of good works wearing heels," snapped Harriet.

"And don't get paid for it would be my guess."

"Vera," murmured Carolyn, trying to shut her mother-in-law up. She hadn't said a word since she told me about the missing clothes and emeralds. Depressed, I suppose. Here I was supposed to be on vacation, and I was going to have to help her find the old lady.

"Ours is a family business," Randolph explained solemnly, "and Harriet brings in more customers than anyone. She's out in the community working for better social services and good schools, and in return all those people she helps bring their loved ones to us."

"That's not why I volunteer in the community, Randolph," said Harriet crisply. "I volunteer because I'm a good Christian woman."

"And everyone she brings in is a good Christian corpse," added Vera.

"I'd be willing to bet that no female sailor on a sub would wear high heels," Barney Levinson declared in support of Vera.

"Damn heels leave holes on the greens," said Greg Marshand. "I've seen it. The young folks get dressed up for the big parties and then stagger out onto the greens and tear them up."

"I didn't notice," murmured Carolyn sadly. "Did Mrs. Gross wear high heels? Maybe she fell down searching for Mr. Patek, hurt herself, and died."

"Holy crap, Carolyn. If that had happened, someone would have found the body," I said.

"I just *hate* nasty language," Carolyn exclaimed, bursting into tears, and she left her macadamia key lime pie only half finished.

"PMS," said Vera. "She'll be okay in a couple of days."

Macadamia Key Lime Pie

Heat oven to 400°F.

Allow a *deep-dish, frozen piecrust* to defrost and prick bottom with a fork.

Chop *5/8 cup macadamia nuts* coarsely in a food chopper and sprinkle 1/2 cup over crust bottom. Bake 10 to 15 minutes until golden.

Prepare *4 teaspoons lime zest* and *1/2 cup lime juice*.

Whisk together until smooth *one 8-ounce package cream cheese* and *one 14-ounce can sweetened condensed milk (not evaporated)*.

Stir in zest and juice. Then fold in *2 cups whipped cream*.

Pour into crust and refrigerate for 30 minutes.

Toast remaining nuts to golden brown in a small saucepan, stirring constantly.

Whip *4 ounces heavy cream* and garnish top of pie with cream and *lime slices* (*optional*).

Sprinkle with toasted nuts and serve.

Carolyn Blue,
"Have Fork, Will Travel,"
St. Petersburg Coast Times

23

Destination — the Canary Islands

Jason

The plane from the meeting site to Ottawa held six people, and the pilot occasionally turned on the autopilot so that he could offer passengers sodas, kept in an ice chest behind his seat. I was too nervous to accept. I had discovered, after many frustrating Internet searches, that I could fly to Ottawa from the little town in the wheat belt, then from Ottawa to Gatwick, outside London, and directly from Gatwick to Tenerife. The last leg of the journey cost me only the modest sum of 269 pounds, which, given the terrible exchange rate between the dollar and almost any currency, was a lot of money, especially considering what the other last-minute, one-way flights had cost. When the stewardess on my Ottawa-to-London flight offered me a drink, I ordered two, even though they cost me seven dollars apiece.

Carolyn

I woke up far too early and singularly embarrassed with myself for making a scene last night at the dinner table. When I turned toward Luz's bed, I saw, to my dismay, that she was not there and had not been there all night. Either she too had disappeared, or I had driven her into the arms of the ship's doctor. After a few more tears shed into my pillow, I dragged myself out of bed and into the claustrophobic shower and then into the clothes I had chosen to wear for the tour of Las Palmas de Gran Canaria.

Actually, it promised to be very interesting. Whereas I had expected to find delightful islands full of singing canaries, one book I read said that Canaria referred to the wild dogs that had populated the islands, that or some place name from Africa. When the first Europeans arrived in the fourteenth century, they found Neolithic, fair-skinned natives with waist-length, blond hair, brandishing fire-hardened wooden spears, eating goat, and living in caves. Later research determined that these natives had come from northern Africa during Roman times and were of Berber extraction. Spain took over the Canaries during the reign of Ferdinand and Isabella and so forth — sugar economy, wine economy, reprovisioning and repair of ships going to and from the Americas, tourism, and a cuisine that blended Spain, South America, and Africa.

These interesting thoughts took me out to our sitting room, where I heard sounds coming from my mother-in-law's bedroom. Incontestably, she was in there with Commander Bernard Levinson. My first thought was that it served Jason right if she was having a fling; he'd be horrified. My second, that it wasn't very nice of her to bring her lover back to the suite we shared, and at her age! My third, as I escaped into the hall, was the remembrance of my own astonishment when a lady in Sorrento told me that her mother-in-law was given to discreet affairs, something I would never, at that time, have expected of my own mother-in-law. In fact, I was surprised at

Luz. Of course, she'd been divorced for years, but I'd just never thought of her as having a lover.

It would seem that cruises had a very bad influence on people. Even I was over-eating, and not things that I could necessarily write about, because I'd neglected to get the recipes. I promised myself that I would have something sensible for break-fast — fruit and cottage cheese, for instance, black coffee, and *no* pastries. Which reminded me that I needed to get some recipes from the pastry chef. Since I'd been stuffing myself with desserts, I should at least collect information on the dishes that were ruining my waistline.

Accordingly, I went to the kitchen instead of the dining room and found the head chef, the frightening Demetrios, prowling around. He spotted me instantly and asked why I hadn't been by to talk to him. I murmured excuses, among them my anxiety about the missing passenger. "Ha!" cried Demetrios. "The one who drinks the wrong wines with her foods? Who drinks more than she eats? She is an embarrassment to fine eating."

"Well, she hasn't been eating in the last two days. She's been missing," I retorted.

"Ha! She is probably drinking in her

room. Such people have no true love of fine food."

"I wondered if I might have your recipe for the seared duck breast in cherry sauce," I interrupted. "It was exquisite."

"Of course it was. The best choice of that evening. I shall provide the recipe to you, dear lady."

"Wonderful. And in the meantime, might I speak to your pastry chef?" Demetrios's broad smile turned to a disapproving frown, and he commanded an underling to find and copy the duck-breast recipe for me. Then he left me without even summoning the pastry chef. I had to find the man myself, and he would not give me a recipe. An unpleasant little Frenchman, he had heard that I ordered seven varieties of gelato when I could have had his famous something or other. I couldn't even understand the name because it was in French and he didn't translate. What a shame. It was probably something I'd have loved, and if it came up again, I wouldn't be able to order it, even with the translation the menus provided for everything foreign. It does look so much more exotic when the dish is given its foreign name with the translation in smaller print beneath. Of course that small print is probably hard on the elderly.

Discouraged, I accepted the duck recipe and went away, afraid that I'd be unwelcome in the kitchen from now on. I pondered the problem and decided to send copies of my columns, all full of praise for the wonderful things I'd eaten, to Demetrios. How often had I mentioned desserts? I might have to do some editing.

Oh my goodness! There was Mr. Patek. What luck! I called out to him, but he continued down the corridor, oblivious, so I had to run after him. I caught him at the elevator and rushed, gasping, in behind him to introduce myself. "I do hope you can help me, Mr. Patek. I'm investigating the disappearance of Mrs. Gross, the lady who hasn't been seen since Tangier. Well, not then really. The last person to see her was Miss Sechrest, your ombudslady, the night before we reached Tangier. But I heard that Mrs. Gross was looking for you that night, and I wondered —"

"I do not know this lady," said Mr. Patek politely enough, although his eyes made me nervous. He stared at me as if — I don't know — as if I wasn't there.

"She's elderly, wrinkled, and was wearing a glittery brown dress and emerald jewelry. I'm sure you'd remember her."

"I don't."

"She was — well, she'd had too much to drink. She might even have been carrying a bottle of wine."

"Very colorful description, madam. If I had see her, I would have remember." And he got off the elevator. Discouraged, I went on to the dining room, where I was joined by Mr. Owen Griffith. Although I was rather peeved with him, at least he was interested in my activities and declared that the facts I'd amassed, however few, added up to "a fascinating conundrum," which we both pondered over breakfast, his a huge plate containing a wonderfully tempting omelet, a pile of crispy bacon, and a heap of French toast with various jams and syrups. I, on the other hand, was faced with low-fat cottage cheese and pineapple. I had to bite my tongue to keep from ordering something else.

Then Mr. Griffith accompanied me down to the gangway to catch the nine o'clock tour of Las Palmas. Neither Vera nor Luz had even come to breakfast, and they were not among the passengers waiting in line to sign off the ship. Were they deliberately avoiding me, thinking I might burst into tears again?

"Sorry, Mrs. Blue, but you're not signed

up for the tour of Las Palmas," said the man at the desk.

"I am, too," I insisted. He turned the computer screen toward me and invited me to scroll through the nine o'clock lists. I wasn't on any of them. "Maybe a later tour," I said, appalled at the idea of missing what promised to be a delightful experience. He shook his head and showed me other lists, none of which had my name on it.

"Bloody bad luck, Carolyn, but don't look so miserable. We'll just take a cab," said Mr. Griffith cheerfully.

"You're on the nine o'clock list, sir," said the security officer.

Mr. Griffith shrugged and told the man to delete his name. Of course I protested that he'd paid for the tour and certainly shouldn't miss it. He laughed and assured me that he could afford to forfeit the money and would much prefer to accompany me on an impromptu tour by taxi.

"But they're dangerous," I objected. "Mrs. Gross —"

"The lady evidently never got into a taxi, and Las Palmas, in fact the whole Canary chain, is much safer and more civilized that Morocco. I'd wager they haven't had a riot here in years. Right, officer?"

"A very quiet place," the security man agreed. "And beautiful. Weird food, though."

Weird food? Of course, the mixture of several cultures! I could write about fusion cuisine with a whole new meaning. So I agreed to accompany Owen Griffith. What did the Canarians have in the way of desserts? I wondered. My breakfast had left me quite unsatisfied.

24

Las Palmas

Carolyn

The port was huge with arms reaching out into the sea, ships and boats everywhere, and white, many-storied buildings — condos for tourists, I suppose — climbing the shallow rise from the water. Owen was very amusing about the choice of the taxi in which we would explore Las Palmas. He insisted that we peer at every available driver and select the least sinister. As it turned out, they all looked quite friendly and non-threatening, and I felt a bit foolish about my fears — until our driver headed out of town.

His English was so poor that we couldn't find out where he was going. To rob us, I thought unhappily. However, when the car stopped, after a bumpy ride up a side road, he pointed and said, "Nice garden." And it was. We walked around looking at plants and flowers, although I kept an eye on the car to make sure he didn't drive off.

Then we ventured farther into the countryside and began to wind up a large hill. "The caldera," said Owen. "It's an ancient volcano." I suppose that I had looked confused, having read nothing about volcanoes on Gran Canaria.

I hoped it was so ancient that it wouldn't erupt while we were here, but I couldn't help remembering my reading about Mount Vesuvius, whose destruction of Pompeii had been a complete surprise to people. They thought they were living near a large, green mountain. As we inspected the caldera, I kept my eyes and ears open for trembling underfoot, whiffs of smoke or steam, anything that would indicate that we should flee. Nothing like that occurred, and we returned uneventfully to the town. Evidently, our driver wanted to show us everything, but since his English was so terrible, Owen sent him away with a big tip and led me off to explore the town on foot in a casual sort of way.

The cathedral, dedicated to Saint Anne, I think, was very pretty, with some nice windows and paintings, and a lovely ceiling with carved beams. While we strolled inside, Owen entertained me with the story of the competing Virgins. Gran Canaria claimed the Virgin of the Pine Tree, while Tenerife said their Virgin of Candelaria ruled over the whole island chain. Both islands were jealous and wanted the right to cense their Virgins more often. "Cense means wave incense in her face more often," said Owen wryly. "Wait until you see Candelaria tomorrow. Huge and grand with lots of gold." I looked forward to it.

We explored the old town, walked up shallow stone steps and narrow streets lined with whitewashed houses bedecked with long windows and ornate balconies. Then we visited Casa de Colon, where Columbus had stayed. It had an ornate portal, lavishly carved, and rounded wooden doors at street level with a window on the floor above. Inside, the house was built around a courtyard with balcony bedrooms upstairs. We got to examine, under glass, copies of important historical documents; for instance, Columbus's journal and the agreement that divided the New World between Spain and Portugal, leaving the Canaries to Spain. However, Spain had to take it away from the reluctant and aggressive natives, who were only defeated when they made the mistake of coming out of their defensive positions to fight a battle.

What a pretty town! I took pictures of everything — gardens, government buildings, old town, until we came upon a restaurant that advertised Canarian dishes. Terribly hungry, I peered in the windows while a man in black sandals, shorts, baseball hat, and a lime green shirt began to harangue Owen with descriptions of all the wonderful dishes to be had inside. I knew that Owen wanted to move on. Didn't the man ever eat anything but breakfast? I couldn't recall seeing him at any other meal. I suppose I might have allowed myself to be dragged away, had I not spotted Luz, Vera, and other people I knew inside.

I dragged Owen in, pointing out my friends, exclaiming about how interesting the food sounded, and inviting the two of us to join them. Chairs were dragged over for us, and once we were seated, Vera said, "Well, I'm glad to see that you haven't disappeared as well, Carolyn. You weren't back yet when I got up this morning. You weren't on the tour. Have you been with Mr. Griffith here since you left dinner last night?"

I can't think of when I've been more embarrassed or indignant. "I spent the whole night in my own bed," I retorted angrily. "When I got up, you had company in *your* room, so I was discreet enough to leave immediately."

"I'm a consenting adult and unmarried," said my mother-in-law, "so don't be a prude, Carolyn."

Consenting adult? I had to assume that meant she was actually having an affair with her submariner. Good heavens.

"As for you, my girl, you *are* married, and to my son."

"I thought it was against the feminist credo to call women *girls*," I retorted, "and I doubt that Jason would be upset that I had breakfast in the dining room and toured Las Palmas with Mr. Griffith when they'd lost my registration for the tour."

"Christ, we're back to *Mr. Griffith*," said Owen. "For those of you who don't know me, I'm Owen Griffith. You can call me Owen. Everyone does but Carolyn here, who keeps forgetting. If I'd been so fortunate as to get her into bed, she'd probably have called me Mr. Griffith then, but you can rest easy, madam." This to Vera. "Because she hasn't cuckolded your son that I know of."

I sent him a frown and continued to my

mother-in-law, "Not as upset as Jason would be to hear that you and Commander Levinson —"

"So what did you think of Las Palmas?" Luz interrupted quickly. "And by the way, I did spend the night out, so I can't vouch for your presence in our room, Caro, but I believe you. You obviously don't know what a prissy lady —"

"I am not," I snapped.

"— your daughter-in-law is, Vera, so lay off her."

"So that's why you won't call me Owen," said my companion for the morning.

"I'm not prissy," I muttered.

Randolph Barber was filming the whole thing, and I thought, for the first time, that his equipment might record voices too. How embarrassing. The strange waiter in the lime green shirt arrived in time to break up the impending quarrel and introduce himself as Vladimir Putin. After insisting that he really was Vladimir Putin, asking if anyone was interested in buying a missile, and receiving negative answers all around the table, he proceeded to translate the menu.

I ordered a wonderful piece of tuna in a green sauce made of cilantro and garlic, among other things, and I convinced Owen to try *Ropa Vieja,* which translates into "old clothes." As I found out later, the dish was called that because some of the ingredients were taken from leftover chickpea stew — namely the carrots, chickpeas, and meat. It wasn't bad — spicy and red from the paprika. Because Owen didn't care much for it, I had to give him half of my tuna and eat the rest of his *Ropa Vieja.* Vera muttered something about trading food being very cozy.

Harriet Barber had been reading up on Canary cuisine and said we had to try the Canarians' favorite dessert, fig cake, which the locals liked so much that many took it to South America when they emigrated. Since I intended to write about my experience with the local cuisine, I could hardly object, but truthfully, I don't like figs, and this recipe is made with very, very ripe figs, nuts, and not much else. And as I later discovered, it sits around for eight days before it's ready to serve. The recipe does not mention refrigeration. It's a wonder we didn't all end up in our rooms, sick as dogs.

Incidentally, there were statues of those native dogs in the town, and they looked large and mean. Owen said he thought that was the breed that killed a lawyer in a hall outside her apartment in San Francisco. They'd escaped from their owners. Frankly, I'd just as soon the islanders kept their dogs and their fig cakes at home.

After lunch we had to hurry to take cabs to the port so as not to miss the boat and tomorrow in Tenerife. I was really looking forward to seeing the golden Virgin of Candelaria and the *guanche* mummies in a museum there. The Stone Age natives had actually mummified their dead. How very interesting!

For those of my readers who like figs, I include this recipe, which is the hands-down favorite dessert among Canary Islanders. They encircle the cake with a *pleita de palma,* a pretty plait of palm leaves, not always easy to come by in the United States.

Figs have always been an important crop (the food of athletes, according to Plato) around the Mediterranean and in ancient religions. African women made ointments of figs and used them to promote conception and lactation. Berbers, believing figs to be fertilized by the dead and a gift from the other world, placed them on rocks as offerings when it was time to plough the fields, a practice much criticized by strict Muslims. Figs were thought to symbolize everything from knowledge to fertility.

Whether you're hoping for a baby, a good crop, or a high IQ, perhaps the Canary Fig Cake will prove to be your remedy. If not, figs are, at the least, nutritious.

Canary Island Fig Cake

Remove the stalks and tips from *34 ounces very ripe black figs.*

Grind figs together with *9 ounces walnuts* and *17 ounces almonds.*

Sprinkle on and mix in thoroughly *1 ground clove.*

Encircle mixture with a brass strip or mold to give a cake shape.

Dust both sides of cake with flour and allow to stand for 8 days, turning now and then.

Remove the cake from the mold and

dust all sides with flour (*5 or 6 ounces of flour* should suffice for both dustings).

Eat.

Carolyn Blue,
"Have Fork, Will Travel,"
Olympia, WA, Bulletin

25

Not Lamb!

Hartwig and Patek

Deep in thought, Bruce Hartwig sat alone in his office, chair tilted back, feet on his utilitarian desk. After the unexpected detour away from Casablanca to the Canary Islands, things were working out again. The riots in Morocco had been controlled, which meant that the men he had hired in Casablanca should have no trouble getting the helicopter and themselves away from their army base to pick up the hijack team from the boat.

With several hours before the passengers began to return to the *Bountiful Feast*, Hartwig decided to go ashore and put through an untraceable call from a public telephone to his two pilots. If he didn't reach them today, he'd try again at

Tenerife. Only after two misses would he risk connecting with them from the ship. After Tenerife would be the big Mother's Day dinner. The liquor would flow, and the passengers would stagger back to their cabins, only to be warned of heavy seas and given the "seasick" pills. Then he'd take over the ship in the night and keep it out in the Atlantic until the third morning, when the money would be in the Swiss account and he and his cohorts gone.

He was rising to go ashore when Umar Patek entered the office, unannounced, saying, "We have two problems."

"Tell me later. I need to call Casablanca from the docks."

"I tell you now. One is bad. Other is worse."

"Well, what?" asked Hartwig impatiently, thinking everything was going well. He didn't need any late-breaking trouble.

"Your comp passenger, Mrs. Blue. She stop me this morning. Sechrest told her Mrs. Gross was looking for me the night she disappear."

"So? I hope you told her Mrs. Gross never found you."

"I told her, but she get closer. A persistent woman, I think. Maybe we should do something about her."

"Like what? Break her neck?" Hartwig asked sarcastically. "We're in this for the money, not dead bodies, even if you do have a hard-on for killing women."

"Women. Men." Patek shrugged. "I kill both in my time. Worse problem is chef. He decides lamb for Mother's Day. Goes in meat freezer."

"Christ! He didn't have lamb on the menu until after we took the ship."

"So he sees lamb tag, finds Mrs. Gross inside plastic bag. Runs out yelling for doctor."

Hartwig slammed his hands on the desk. "Let's hope the doctor's ashore. As security officer, I can take charge of the body."

"Doctor is nap in office. Had tiring night with roommate of troublemaker Mrs. Blue."

"Did he figure out what killed her? Like a broken neck? Administered by you?"

"Last he cannot know. Neck, probably. He is pathologist. Should be able to tell."

Hartwig swore again and dropped into his chair. Patek sat opposite, silent and expressionless while several minutes passed. "So we take the ship tonight instead of tomorrow night," Hartwig decided. "Now I *have* to get that call through to Casablanca. And you, you see if you can't get the body back in the freezer and out of the doctor's hands. Then pass the word to the others that we're moving up the schedule."

Luz

Nobody was very talkative at dinner. For one thing, the food tasted like something from a school cafeteria. And Beau, who usually kept the conversation from dying, hadn't said a word and hadn't even asked anyone to dance. Maybe all the jokes about his dancing had hurt his feelings. I could tell the others that he might not be a Fred Astaire, but he sure was good in bed. Then again, since he did look a little peaked, maybe I'd been better than he was. "So you think the chef's on strike or something?" I asked, pushing away a limp salad that had followed a soup so boring I couldn't tell what kind it was. He gave me a really shocked look, like the chef was his brother and I'd insulted the guy.

Down the table, Carolyn was telling Greg, the golfer, and Randolph Barber about some opera-loving, Metropolitan-Opera-ticket-holding couple she'd met in the bar. Now that was weird. She'd gone to the room when we got back to the ship, and instead of taking a nap or reading her book from the library, the one about Casablanca, she took a shower, got dressed for dinner, and left. Mad at Vera for the showdown they had at Vladimir Putin's restaurant? That guy was a character. Or maybe Carolyn was shocked at me for staying out all night. Christ! She wasn't my mother. She'd have to get over it.

"And then in the scene when Manrico walks out of the convent, the giant cross fell down and just missed him. They said it was the strangest performance of *Il Trovatore* they'd ever seen, and the tenor's voice wobbled for the rest of the scene."

"Don't care for opera myself," said Greg.

"Okay, Beau, what's bothering you?" I asked. I'd just been served a steak that was brown all the way through with some frigging sauce on it that tasted so bad I had to scrape it off.

My vacation lover sighed and put his fork down. "You can't blame poor ole Demetrios for the food. He had a shock this afternoon that would shake any man, an' he's on the hysterical side at the best of times. I've already had to give him anti-anxiety pills to keep the whole kitchen staff from walkin' out."

"Okay, so he's nuttier than ever. What happened to set him off? A soufflé fall or something?" I grinned at Beau, hoping to cheer him up.

"You can't tell anyone this," Beau all but whispered.

"Okay."

"He found a corpse in the meat locker."

I had to squelch the urge to say the locker was probably full of corpses, animal corpses, so no big deal, but Beau didn't look like he was in the mood for jokes.

"Mrs. Gross," he whispered.

Oh shit, I thought. "What happened? Did she get locked in and freeze to death?"

He sighed again. "She was wrapped in a full-length, plastic bag marked *lamb* and hung from a hook."

I gulped. Not that I hadn't seen some corpses in my time, and Beau must have seen ten times that many, but he looked pretty shook up, and I was too. "Any idea how she died?"

"Broken neck."

"Accident?"

"I doubt it."

Oh man. I was going to have to tell Carolyn, promise or no promise, and then the two of us were going to have to find out who broke Mrs. Gross's neck. As for why, it could have been anyone; it's not like the woman wasn't a royal pain in the ass. "Was she wearing anything besides the bag?" Carolyn would have questions. Might as well find out.

"That ugly brown dress, the one she always wore to dinner."

"Right. So she must have been killed, or at least died, between dinner and morning when she stopped showing up for anything. What about the green jewelry? Emeralds, Carolyn told me."

Beau shook his head and then invited me back to his cabin, but somehow I felt like I should stay with Carolyn that night. I didn't know when I was going to tell her — tonight, tomorrow morning, whenever — but she was going to be upset, and she was going to want to see justice done and all that idealistic crap. Some vacation! Here I'd found myself a nice man for the duration — it wasn't like I had any long-term designs on him — and instead I'd get to go after another murderer with Miss Prissy. That may sound like I don't like her, but to tell the truth, I kind of get a kick out of her, as long as she doesn't burst into tears about my language.

"Maybe tomorrow night, sweetie," I said

to Beau. "You just about wore me out last night." Of course, Beau liked that.

"Isn't that pretty," Carolyn was saying as she viewed a tall goblet thing with white, red, and dark brown layers of stuff inside.

"Double chocolate raspberry mousse, ma'am," said the waiter. "It's one of our best desserts."

About time we got something decent with this meal, I thought, and dug in. Obviously the chef, who'd found the corpse of Mrs. Gross, hadn't had a hand in this course; it actually tasted good. Carolyn sure thought so. She said it was "superb" and after finishing the mousse ordered the Marmalade Delight.

My favorite marmalade story involves Mary Queen of Scots, who had to return from Calais because the English wouldn't let her ashore. She was miserably seasick, so her doctor mixed up an orange and crushed-sugar tonic to ease her mal de mer. The word *marmalade* supposedly comes from the phrase "Marie est malade."

These days we can enjoy marmalade without making our own or becoming seasick to get some, and the Italians have a delightful dessert that incorporates ladyfingers and marmalade, both of which are available at your supermarket.

Marmalade Delight

Press *1 cup ricotta* through a fine sieve into a mixing bowl. (If the ricotta is already creamy, you can skip the sieve.)

With a fork, beat *4 tablespoons confectioner's sugar* into *2 tablespoons heavy cream* until the sugar dissolves.

Blend the cream mixture into the ricotta with a rubber spatula until spreadable but not runny. If not spreadable, stir in a bit more cream.

Measure *1/2 cup orange juice* and *2 tablespoons brandy* into a small, shallow bowl into which you can lay a ladyfinger flat.

Choose a plate or oval platter to serve the dessert. Take *18 ladyfingers* from a package (you can buy them in 7-ounce packages with 22 to 24 per package). One at a time, roll 6 ladyfingers quickly in the orange brandy mixture and arrange them snugly against each other on the plate.

With your rubber spatula, spread half the ricotta cream, after pouring down the middle of the ladyfingers, and leave about a half inch on either side without cream.

Melt *1/2 cup orange marmalade* on high for 15 to 30 seconds in the microwave, stirring once. Drizzle half evenly over the cream.

Dip 6 more ladyfingers in orange-brandy and arrange on top of the others, pressing each down slightly.

Again spread ricotta, and place the last 6 dipped ladyfingers on the cream and glaze with the last of the melted marmalade.

Refrigerate for 3 to 4 hours (will last 3 days in fridge).

Can be decorated with *whipped cream, shaved semisweet chocolate curls,* or both. Cut down between ladyfingers for a 3-piece serving. Each serving can be garnished with a *candied or chocolate-covered orange peel.*

Carolyn Blue,
"Have Fork, Will Travel,"
Sacramento Bee

26

The Influence of Superb "Mice"

Crew Dining Room

The stewards ate while the passengers were eating upstairs, so Hartwig and Patek chose that opportunity to visit the dining room with their cache of seasick pills. However, Hartwig came upon a scene that interested him, so he held the chief steward back in order to listen.

"You should have examine it," cried Herkule Pipa. "Is called double-chocolate and berry mice. So handsome. I almost whimper — Is good word, no? Mean cry — almost whimper I have no taste for me."

The other stewards, weary after a long day, with more hours to work before they would see their own beds, stared balefully at the dishes of Jell-O that they had picked up from the buffet line. "You'd think they'd give us some of the good stuff, considering how hard we work," said one. "In United States, workers get more money for more hours than eight." Rumbles of discontent rose around the table.

"Follow my lead," hissed Hartwig, and strode toward the stewards' table.

Herkule, spotting him first and, more important, Umar Patek with him, said, "But gelatins is very tasty."

"In my opinion, you guys have got it right. You're overworked, badly fed, and underpaid," said Hartwig.

Herkule wanted to object to *underpaid.* He thought his take-home pay was wonderful and wished he'd said nothing about the mice dessert. After all, he never went hungry aboard the ship, for which he said prayers of thanks every day. But he was afraid to say a word to either of the two men now standing at the table. What were they doing? Some trick to get the stewards fired so the line could hire cheaper stewards who didn't complain?

"You ought to declare a work stoppage. Just quit doing the rooms and running errands for the passengers until the line agrees to shorter hours and better food.

That's what American workers do, and the line is American owned, no matter what third-world flag we fly under. Don't you agree, Umar?"

The chief steward frowned but said nothing. The stewards looked confused and apprehensive. "Big ship men not listen to us," said Herkule hesitantly, while visions of sumptuous desserts "danced in his head," a phrase he'd read in an English language book about sugar plums and someone named Santaclots. A passenger had left it behind. Since many Albanians, Herkule included, were Muslims, he was unfamiliar with that tradition but liked it very much. Imagine some nice person coming down the chimney and leaving delicious things to eat. It would never happen in Albania.

"Sure they would," said Hartwig. "With two hundred passengers making their own beds and not getting their towels changed for a couple of days, the line would fall over its own feet to meet your demands."

"And who of us would make such demands? We don't even know how to telephone big ship men," said another naysayer.

Hartwig laughed. "So that's the problem. Well, Patek and I know how, and we'll do it. It's something that needs to be done."

"Like alms for poor?" asked Herkule, looking toward the head steward. Patek claimed to be a Hindu whose family had immigrated to an island, but Herkule was almost sure the chief steward was Muslim. Herkule had caught Patek once praying to Mecca in his office and had stolen away. If he was right, and Patek agreed, then it would really be done, the calls, the good food, and the shorter hours. It would be Patek's duty as a good, if mean, Muslim.

"Right, Umar?" said Hartwig, nudging his fellow officer.

"Yes," said the chief steward.

"So, you guys want to vote on the work stoppage?"

"I say yes," cried the first man. Others, excited at the prospect of asserting themselves in the American style, agreed, even Herkule.

"Okay, tonight's your last night on duty until they agree. Sleep in tomorrow. And by the way, we'll all want to sleep in tomorrow. Big storm coming tonight after midnight." Hartwig pulled out the containers of pills. "Warn them and give one to each of your passengers as they come back to their rooms. Tell them to be sure to take them. Doctor's orders." He laughed. "After all, you don't want them

235

puking all over themselves tonight. Americans support work stoppages, but they won't feel too happy about it if they have to clean up their own vomit." The stewards laughed appreciatively because they'd cleaned up plenty of vomit when the weather got rough. "Better take some yourselves," Hartwig continued. "You don't want to miss the good meals that are on their way."

So it was settled. The stewards were chatting happily over their Jell-O as Hartwig and Patek left the room. Once in the corridor, Patek's hand closed over his fellow officer's arm, hard enough to leave a bruise under the white cloth of the uniform. "What was that about?" he demanded. "If you stop service to passengers, they rebel."

Hartwig shrugged. "We're armed; they're not, and they'll blame the stewards, not us. We'll just be keeping the peace in a difficult situation."

"And we call line tomorrow morning and ask for money and perks for stewards? Miami won't take us as serious men."

"Who said we're going to mention the stewards? All we have to tell the stewards is that we did it, and that the executives are considering their demands. By the way, the entertainers jumped ship at Las Palmas. The company that sends them called them in because we cut Russell Bustle. Of course Marbella thinks he's getting a new bunch at Tenerife — local dancers and that sort of crap — but then he doesn't know we won't be putting in at Tenerife. So with no entertainment and the casino and bars closing at midnight because I'm going to alert them to the coming storm at the last minute, everyone will be in bed, dead to the world, by twelve thirty. That gives us plenty of time to round up my security people and the officers who aren't in on this and lock them in the brig. Then we search the passenger rooms for cell phones, computers, and weapons, if any."

"And why do the rest of us not know about these decisions?" Patek demanded angrily.

"Because I had to improvise, my friend. We didn't expect to take the ship until to-morrow night, and we wouldn't have had to if you hadn't killed the Gross woman."

They parted company at the end of the corridor, Patek returning to his own quarters to think out how these new plans would affect plans he himself had, he and the brothers in Malaysia. Soon he would be acting in the name of Allah and of the

Prophet Muhammad, doing things more important, more satisfying, than working undercover on a ship of infidels.

27

Hijacked by Night

Luz

Because the entertainers had taken off, mad about Russell Bustle was what I heard, I headed back to the room, following Carolyn. Might as well get it over with about Mrs. Gross. Vera and Barney had gone to the bar; guess the bartenders hadn't jumped ship at Las Palmas. "Hey, Carolyn, I need to talk to you," I called, catching up with her at the door to our suite. She shoved her key card into the door, and I chased her right in.

"I'm tired," she said. "I appreciate your breaking up my conversation with Vera — imagine her accusing me of being unfaithful to Jason. I may never speak to her again — but I don't feel like talking. I want to go to bed."

"This will only take a freaking minute,

Carolyn, and it's about Mrs. Gross. You'll want to know."

"What about Mrs. Gross?"

"She's dead."

Carolyn sniffed. "I imagined as much."

"And you don't care how I found out or what happened to her? Well, okay. I was going to say I'd help you chase down who killed her, but since you're not interested, I'll just to spend the night with Beau. He invited me, but I said —"

"Murdered?" Carolyn interrupted. "I'm sorry, Luz. Don't go. Sit down and tell me. Can I get you a drink?"

"No, but you might want one." She fixed one for both of us anyway. Some fruity thing that was pink. Tasted like Kool-Aid to me, but I didn't say so. "The chef was looking for lamb in the walk-in freezer. Instead he found Mrs. Gross in a plastic bag marked *lamb,* which explains why he wasn't cooking tonight and we got such crappy food."

"The dessert was nice," said Carolyn, sounding very subdued. "How do they know she was murdered?"

"You mean she wrapped herself up in a plastic bag and committed suicide in the freezer?"

"Don't be sarcastic, Luz. I'm — I'm upset."

"Yeah, sorry. Beau said her neck was broken, and it wasn't an accident, which is pretty obvious anyway, because why put her in the freezer if it was an accident?"

"Was she wearing her brown dress?" Carolyn asked.

"Right, brown dress, but no emeralds, so maybe someone killed her for jewelry."

"Maybe Mr. Patek. That's who she was looking for."

"Right. Well, we'll start nosing around tomorrow."

"I don't need your help, Luz, but I do thank you for the offer," she said, all prissy again. "Now that you've told me, you'll want to join Beau. Oh, poor Mrs. Gross!" She burst into tears and ran into our room, where she stripped off her clothes, dumped them on the floor, and crawled into bed.

At a guess, I'd say Carolyn *never* drops her clothes on the floor, which meant she was pretty upset. Guess I'd have to stay. Just about then there was knocking on the door and that voice: "Is me, Herkule Pipa." He had three pills on a little tray and the news that we were heading into a storm and really rough weather. "Is for keeping no vomit when ship is pitch back and forth. Take before bedtime for good night slumbering."

"Okay, but you'd better leave four in case Vera brings home a friend."

"Is very old, old Mrs. Blue," said Herkule dubiously, "but okay. Vomiting on sheets not good."

"Right. You'd have to clean it up."

He went away; I entered our room and fed the first pill to the sobbing Carolyn — maybe she really did have PMS like Vera said. She took it like a good little girl and reburied her head in the pillow. I then had a hell of a time staying awake to pass out the other two to Vera and Barney. Vera said thanks and took hers, and I took mine, but Barney said that, being a Navy man, he didn't get seasick. So I put the last one into a funny bowl on our table that looked like someone had smashed it and glued it back together. I figured one of us, like me, might wake up needing another pill, or even the commander might want to sneak out and get it when he started to feel like puking.

The Hijackers

Although Captain Marbella was loathe to be hauled away to the brig and put up a good fight, shouting oaths and threats about the penalties for mutiny until they taped his mouth shut, everything else went easily and as planned. The passengers had been drugged and notified of cruise changes with formal letters pushed under their doors. The chef, not yet recovered from his unexpected meeting with Mrs. Gross, had been afraid to protest when informed that all meals were to be served buffet style, passenger menus to the crew, crew menus to the passengers, until the work stoppage was resolved.

The crew, so excited to find that they'd be eating fine food, acquiesced easily to the new regime and began planning their own work stoppages. Officer Froder took over the captain's duties and changed the ship's course away from ports and crowded sea-lanes, while his subordinate took over the engine room, none the wiser. Cell phones and computers were confiscated and locked away, and the computer room closed to everyone but Patrick O'Brien. Then last, Patrick sent a message to the home office that caused great consternation and many anguished meetings.

It was decided by executives high in the line's pecking order that the hijacking of the *Bountiful Feast* was to be kept quiet. Considering the value of the ship itself and the terrible publicity, they had to get it back without trouble, but they did have several days to negotiate a ransom of less than fifty million dollars. Once the ship was retrieved, the passengers could probably be kept quiet with promises of free cruises in return for signed agreements to say nothing.

Then the line would quietly pursue, to the ends of the earth, the criminals who had stolen the ship, and mete out justice in a way that would attract no notice.

Jason

Exhausted and dismayed by the amount of money I had spent, I stumbled off my plane at Gatwick Airport in England, having been held up by an unexpected landing in Newfoundland, the result of some worrisome engine problem. Heaven only knew whether I'd be able to find and catch the flight to Tenerife, and in fact, after a search for the gate made at a dead run, the door was closing, and I had to beg a soft-hearted airline person to allow me aboard so that I could spend Mother's Day with my wife.

It had been a terribly embarrassing ploy, but I was put on a bus headed for some other plane and dropped off at the stair to the Tenerife plane with a cheery "Good luck, mate," from the bus driver. Since the last passenger was at the top of the stairs, I then had to leap upward, shouting at the astonished stewardess and waving my ticket. Even then there was no guarantee that this plane would get me to the Reina Sofia Airport on Tenerife in time to find the harbor at Santa Cruz de Tenerife before Carolyn's ship sailed.

I fell into my chair, heart pounding, gasping for air — yet another embarrassment for a man who ran almost every morning of his life — vowing that I would never again let my wife travel by herself, lest I find myself in another such situation. Of course, I could have stayed on in Canada to the end of the meeting and flown home to El Paso, but Carolyn, the love of my life, who evidently did not like bonbons, might never have forgiven me, which would have made the last thirty or forty years of our marriage exceedingly uncomfortable. A man not that far away from his fifties valued the prospect of a happy marriage that would accompany him into old age; such were my thoughts as I drifted into exhausted sleep.

28

A Groggy Awakening on a Bad Day

Carolyn

When I woke up the next morning, I was surprised to see through the curtains that the sun was up. I was even more surprised at how horrible I felt — groggy and nauseated when I opened my eyes, wobbly when I tried to stand. Then I vaguely remembered Luz giving me a pill because a bad storm was coming. Had we tossed about all night without my waking or throwing up? I glanced at Luz's bed and saw that she was fast asleep, snoring, in fact, something she hadn't done before. Even that hadn't awakened me. And she hadn't gone back to Beau's room, although I'd told her to. I also remembered about Mrs. Gross, dead in the freezer of a broken neck, wrapped in plastic and labeled *lamb.* As a native Texan, Mrs. Gross probably had hated lamb. And I had told Luz I didn't need her help finding the murderer. Stupid me.

Sighing, I showered, dressed, and left the room quietly to begin my investigation. Alone. I saw evidence that the commander had been here last night and probably still was. My mother-in-law, in my opinion, should be ashamed of herself. Maybe she did have a right to male companionship, being long unmarried, but she didn't have to carry on in the same suite with me, and she certainly had no right to accuse me of — what was that? I'd spotted a white envelope on the floor. The outside read:

IMPORTANT NOTICE
TO PASSENGERS

It had obviously been pushed under our door. What now?

I bent to pick it up and experienced a wave of dizziness. That must have been *some* pill, or a terribly rough night. The following message had been tucked into the envelope:

The officers of the Bountiful Feast *re-*

gret to inform passengers that, after a vote, the stewards have elected to unite in a work stoppage until such time as the line agrees to a new contract giving them higher pay, shorter hours, and better food. Until this labor dispute is settled (no doubt a matter of only a few days), passengers will not have linens changed or cabins tidied.

Well, that's no problem, I thought. *I only change the linens once a week at home.*

Nor will the ship put in to port.

What? No Tenerife? No mummies? No Virgin of Candelaria? I was very disappointed, unless they planned to sit out in the ocean negotiating by Morse code or whatever, and then proceed to Tenerife. I supposed I could wait a few days for the mummies and the Virgin.

Otherwise, little will change aboard, although meals will be served in a simpler fashion.

What did that mean?

And there will be no evening entertain-

ment, the entertainers having left the ship at Las Palmas.

No loss there, I thought, remembering Russell Bustle and the chorus girls. The abrupt departure of the entertainers was probably my mother-in-law's fault.

We regret the inconvenience and will strive to make your cruise as pleasant as possible. Passengers who wish to organize their own entertainments are welcome to use the Grand Salon. The Library will remain open.

I put the message back in the envelope, leaned it prominently against the pretty, cracked-glass bowl on the table, and tip-toed out. The hall was empty. Everyone sleeping in, I guessed, after a wild night that I couldn't even remember. At least we hadn't been thrown out of our beds. Before I could get on the elevator, a little voice scared me out of my wits. "Is me, Herkule."

"Good heavens, Herkule. What are you doing here? I thought you were on strike."

"Strike? As hit a person or not hit a ball?" he asked, obviously puzzled.

"Strike as in work stoppage," I replied.

"Ah." He took out his little notebook and wrote busily. "Many thank. I think this morning, Mrs. Blue. Your food writing. Herkule is very sorry, but I describe for you everything I eat. Hokay? You not gnashing teeth at Herkule?"

"No, of course not. Everyone has a right to decent working conditions. I hope your demands are met. I have to say, I wondered why you were always on duty."

"Oh, most magnimousy madam!" he exclaimed. He threw his arms around me, then backed off hastily. "Sorry. Arousing Albanian."

He wiped his eyes and dashed off, leaving me to wonder if *arousing* was really the word he wanted to use (surely he didn't find me arousing or expect me to find him attractive), and why had he offered to describe his food to me? *Food.* Food reminded me of Demetrios, poor man, traumatized by finding a body in his freezer. Perhaps I should call on him and sympathize. Maybe if I were sympathetic enough, he'd give me the recipe for the double chocolate raspberry mousse.

Accordingly, I pushed the elevator button to the kitchen rather than the dining room. Much to my astonishment, Officer Fredriksen got on at the next floor.

I hardly recognized her. She was wearing fatigues, instead of her pretty white uniform, and carrying a large gun, sort of midway between a rifle and a pistol, but with a fat barrel. I'd never seen anything like it. And she wasn't wearing her usual high heels. "Why are you carrying a gun and wearing those clothes?" I asked uneasily.

"We officers have to be on the alert for trouble," she replied.

"It's only a little strike," I protested.

"Strikes can be violent," said Officer Fredriksen, "and passengers may prove to be very resentful of the situation. We're ready to break up any standoff between the two sides."

Goodness, the woman was either crazy — perhaps as a result of having no sleep during the storm — or unduly excited at the thought of being charged with a military responsibility rather than her usual hotel duties. "The stewards have always seemed very peaceable and pleasant to me," I said soothingly, "and why would anyone be upset about having to sleep on the same sheets and use the same towels for a few days? I'm sure you have nothing to worry about, Miss Fredriksen."

"Speaking for my fellow officers, ma'am,

we appreciate your tolerant view of the situation." Then she actually saluted and stepped off on the dining room floor. As I continued to the kitchen, I wondered whether she had expected me to return her salute, the way the president does when wearing his civilian clothes and confronted with a general. Ah, the kitchen!

No one was on strike there. The place bustled as always. I spotted Demetrios and headed in his direction, hoping he wasn't still irritated with me, especially since I was going to ask for another dessert recipe. "Maestro," I called, "I'm so glad to see that you have recovered from your shock. How terrible to be expecting a nice spring lamb and instead find poor Mrs. Gross. I'm here to express my sympathy and to tell you that dinner wasn't the same without you at the helm. Señora Vallejo's medium-rare steak was well done, something that would never have happened under your direction."

The chef grasped my hand and shook it vigorously. Evidently he had forgiven me. "You are too kind, madam. No one but you has thought to express sympathy for the horror I underwent yesterday. As for your friend, Señora Vallejo, I would make up for that detestably overcooked steak if I could."

"Oh, I'm sure you will. Here." I removed the edited copies of my columns on his menus and turned them over. "I thought it might cheer you up to see some of the articles I have written on your superb cuisine."

Beaming, Demetrios accepted the printouts and flipped through them. "Ambrosial potatoes? Tilapia perfectly cooked with a salsa never to be forgotten for its delicate spicing. Ah, madam, you are too kind." He shook my hand again. "When the horror returns to me, I shall retire to my office and read these over to soothe my soul."

How interesting, I thought. *He's lost his accent.* I'd love to have asked him where he came from, since it obviously wasn't Greece, but I still wanted to get that mousse recipe. "You have been so kind to provide me recipes. My readers will all want to take your cruise to see for themselves what fine food really is. Unfortunately, last night the only superior thing we had was the mousse. I did enjoy it, but I couldn't help thinking that the pastry chef was not as sensitive a man as you. I could not have made a mousse after the horror of yesterday afternoon.

"But then, as he refused to give me dessert recipes, even when you told him to, I might have known nothing would bother him. A Frenchman, isn't he? They can be a cold lot unless they are actually born on the Mediterranean." As I said all this, I was praying that Demetrios had been showing dislike of the pastry chef rather than the fact that I asked for dessert recipes.

"Alas, you are correct, madam," said Demetrios. "Our Jean-Pierre produces a fine dessert, which is why I hired him, but he is a man of no sentiment, no sensitivity. I cannot believe that he refused you recipes. If I must, I will rip from his miserly hands the recipe for the mousse. If you will wait here just a moment."

Demetrios strode off, wearing a thunderous expression. I, meanwhile, saw that someone had abandoned a slender, very sharp knife, not large, on the counter beside me. Remembering the hotel manager with her dangerous-looking gun, it occurred to me that it might be a good idea for me to have a small weapon of my own. I glanced around furtively. There was no one at the table with the abandoned knife, and all eyes followed Demetrios's charge toward the other side of the room. My slacks had pockets, so I slipped the knife into one and covered its outline with my handbag. I pride myself that by the time Demetrios returned with the recipe held triumphantly aloft, I was looking quite innocent, and not at all like the thief of what I took to be a filleting knife, or possibly a long grapefruit knife, although it didn't have the usual beveled edge.

The chef bowed and presented the recipe, and I cried, "Ah, you are so kind, Maestro, a true conductor of haute cuisine." I wanted to be sure he understood why I was calling him Maestro. "The Giuseppe Verdi of enchanting gastronomy," I added for good measure.

"And you, dear madam, are the queen of cuisine reviewers."

So, that went well, I thought as I tripped off to the elevator. Maybe he'd send up something truly wonderful for breakfast.

29

Morning Discoveries of an Unfortunate Kind

Luz

"Holy crap!" I said to Vera. "You look like I feel." And I felt like I had the mother of all hangovers — headache, sloshing stomach, foggy eyes, and I was so dizzy I staggered into the table and knocked the broken bowl off. It must have been one hell of a storm, and I was really glad I slept through it.

Vera was wearing the twice-her-size robe and clinging to Barney's arm, but he was dressed and looked fine. Go figure. I could see the unused pill among the pieces of the bowl I'd broken. The guy had obviously slept through the storm with no pill to help, and awakened feeling fine.

"I better go check on Greg," he said. "See you at breakfast."

Vera groaned as he lowered her into a chair before he left. I bent for the envelope that had been in the bowl, stumbled into the chair across from her, and tried to focus on the flyer inside.

"Shit. I think I've gone cross-eyed. Can you read this?" I passed the paper across to her, and she read it.

"Says the stewards are out on strike, and we have to make our own beds and re-use our towels. Good for them! We should go out and support them, send e-mails to the line complaining about their rotten hours and food or whatever and how much we're being inconvenienced by the line's stingy, racist policies. Nothing like a good labor fight to make you feel better."

"So you say," I mumbled. "Just the idea of eating breakfast makes me feel like throwing up." Not that complaining did me any good. Vera made me drink a bottle of Bloody Mary mix from the refrigerator and had me out of there in ten minutes. We staggered into the dining room, hanging on to each other while Vera told me stories of labor disputes she'd supported —

she sounded like she was ready to go out and hit someone with a placard as soon as she got some breakfast in her stomach. The food was on a long table, and we had to get our own. I'd have gone back to the room, but Vera told me to stop being a wuss and dragged me over to the buffet. Breakfast looked as bad as I felt.

Carolyn sat over at a table with the Crosswayses, grumbling about the fare — an egg fried solid, a bowl of canned fruit cocktail, and some over-toasted toast with margarine and no jelly. Then she launched into the fact that it was going to be a really rotten Mother's Day, no stop at Tenerife, no decent food because it was all going to the crew downstairs as part of the work stoppage, and no Mother's Day feast and celebration as promised in the brochure.

I fell into a seat and stared squeamishly at some lumpy oatmeal that Vera insisted would make me feel better. Vera said, "I might have known you'd care more about the food and tours you'll be missing than the plight of the poor stewards. You of all people, Carolyn, should know how bad they feel when they know we're upstairs eating gourmet food while they're downstairs eating slop like this and working sixteen or more hours a day. So stop complaining and get with the program. I plan to organize the rest of the crew; they should take heart and walk out with their colleagues."

"And a happy Mother's Day to you too, Vera," Carolyn snapped.

I tried a spoonful of the disgusting oatmeal and gagged. The stuff tasted like sawdust thickened with flour, water, and newspaper shreds. I picked up my coffee, the battery acid variety we had at the downtown command before I took over the coffee-making. If Vera knew that, she'd probably throw me overboard. Bad as it was, I drank it down in one long gulp. Then I went back to the table for more coffee and a couple of pieces of dry toast. Poor Jason. Vera must have been one hell of an awful mother. Imagine having her take care of you when you had stomach flu or ate too many burritos at the Juárez fair and came home barfing.

I met John Killington, Carolyn's computer geek buddy, at the buffet. He took one look at my tray and said, "Good choice. I feel pretty bad myself."

"Rough night?" I asked politely.

"Worse morning," he replied, and walked back with me, interrupted a labor-relations harangue by Vera, and announced morosely, "I discovered a terrible thing on my way down."

Carolyn looked alarmed. "Not another dead person?" she asked.

"No. Why would you think that? The computer room is locked for the duration of the work stoppage. I don't care about the food or the towels. Hell, I sometimes used the same towel and ate takeout pizza for a couple of months at a time when I was an undergraduate, but I never found myself without access to a computer."

Carolyn agreed. "I have columns to send to the syndicate. And there'll be nothing more to write about as long as we're eating crew food."

"*We* have reports to send in to — ah — the Oceanographic Institute," the Crosswayses chimed in.

"Really?" Carolyn gave them a cold look.

"You people make me sick." Vera threw down her paper napkin and stalked off, muttering to herself about third-world wage slaves, while I was trying to figure out why Carolyn was giving the Crosswayses such a disgusted look. They were about as boring as anyone I'd ever met, but the world is full of bores. Carolyn could be one herself, and Vera was obviously ready to compete for the Labor Bore of the Year award.

Meanwhile, I couldn't even imagine how long it would be before I'd be able to stomach anything but coffee and dry toast. If we hit another storm, like the one we must have had last night, I was going straight to Beau and let him take care of me until I got back on solid ground, and I was *never* going on another cruise.

Hartwig and O'Brien

"Patrick, where the hell have you been?" Hartwig demanded.

"Fendin' off the lads an' lassies tryin' to get into the computer room. More people worryin' about that than the sheet an' towel drought. They all want to write home an' tell their loved ones how they've been caught in a dangerous strike at sea. An' you an' Hanna marchin' around like the bloody Black an' Tans with those honkin' big guns in your hands. It doesn't help calm the natives any, you know."

"No one's asking you to carry one if you haven't the guts for it. Did you get the message off?"

"That I did, Bruce, me fine leader.

261

There's panic in Miami this lovely mornin' fer sure."

"Not that one, you ass. The one to Tenerife."

"Niver did you tell me of a message to Tenerife," said Patrick, hiking up the Irish in his accent.

"The hell I didn't. What do you think's going to happen there if we don't dock when we're due in?"

"Didn't think of it at all, at all. What was it you wanted to say to those lads of the Spanish admiralty?"

"Cut the crap, O'Brien. Tell them we've got plague and can't put in to port."

"Right you are," said Patrick, and started to leave.

Hartwig's fists clenched before he reached out and pulled Patrick almost off his feet. "Tell them we have a contagious disease aboard and we're trying to identify it. We'll probably sail on to Casablanca. Tell them that, Patrick, before I knock your stupid Irish tongue right out of your smart Irish mouth."

Patrick's laughter stilled, and he turned to face Hartwig. "You never told me to send a message to Tenerife, and if you take a poke at me, Bruce, you'll have to send your own damned messages. Me, I'll just retire to the bar and let you take care of every little thing you've forgotten to get done."

"Not if you want to collect your share," snarled Hartwig.

30

More Discoveries of an Unfortunate Kind

Carolyn

I had planned to go down to crew quarters to see if I could find Mrs. Gross's emeralds, which would tell me who killed her, but first I dropped by the suite because the filet knife in my pocket was poking my thigh. I wrapped the knife in a pair of panties after tucking a foam rubber triangle taken from my manicure scissors onto the knife tip. Fortunately, the cut hadn't bled through onto my slacks. Then I stuck a Band-Aid onto my leg, stepped back into my slacks, and replaced the knife in the pocket.

It seemed to me that the crew and officers would all be out and about by now, so my raid on crew quarters should be fairly safe, and I'd talked Herkule into lending me his steward room pass card by making him feel guilty about my new lack of access to the good food, not to mention my sympathy for his cause and my need to find out who had killed Mrs. Gross and stolen her emeralds. He even told me the secret safe code so I could look in safes. Of course, he didn't know I planned to search below decks and, if spotted, pretend that I'd come down to complain about the inconvenience of the strike. I just hoped that his card opened doors to all living quarters, and I doubted that crew and officers would have their own safes.

However, before I could start downstairs, I spotted Mr. O'Brien talking to Mr. Hartwig and called out to Mr. O'Brien, hurrying to his side. "Could you tell me when the computer room will be reopened? I don't see any reason to lock it up just because of the strike."

"Better ask Mr. Hartwig here," said O'Brien, and he left without so much as a good-bye.

Puzzled, I turned to Mr. Hartwig. "Oh, my goodness. You're wearing a gun, too!" I exclaimed.

"I'm the chief security officer on board, ma'am, and we've got a touchy situation here. It's my duty to see that the passengers are protected from the crew, if that becomes necessary."

"Oh." Hadn't Miss Fredriksen claimed she was protecting the crew from the passengers? Well, whatever. I did feel the need to add, "I think we'd all be safer with no guns around. Guns are very dangerous."

"Only in inexperienced and unreliable hands, ma'am. Now you asked about the computer room. We feel that the labor dispute is more likely to be settled quickly if no word of it gets out. The line is sensitive to bad publicity. Unfortunately, if we leave the computer room open, passengers might e-mail home, and —"

"Of course. I see your point, although it's very inconvenient to me. As you probably know, I'm supposed to be sending columns to New York."

"Then you'll have to accept my apologies, ma'am. I'd like to order Mr. O'Brien to accommodate you, but we can't afford to play favorites."

"Yes, well I do hope that all the fuss over the work stoppage isn't keeping you from investigating the death of Mrs. Gross. Have you any clues as to who might have murdered her?"

"Her injuries could well have been

caused by a fall downstairs. Elderly ladies have brittle bones. However, I'm also looking into the more upsetting possibility."

"If she fell downstairs, how did she end up in the freezer?" I asked sharply.

"It's a very strange case," he admitted, "and I've heard rumors that she went to the spa the morning of her disappearance. I have to look into that when I have time."

Mr. Hartwig went away after giving me one of his amazingly sweet smiles and telling me that I was a very caring woman to feel more anxiety about Mrs. Gross's death than my own inconvenience brought on by the stewards' strike. What a strange man. I didn't know what to make of him, but I did hate seeing those guns.

When I glanced at my watch, I realized that, having eaten breakfast so late and then spent time securing my leg from my knife, bamboozling Herkule, and talking to the two officers, lunch had already started, and we had been instructed to show up promptly at noon. God only knew what they'd feed us and why it had to be eaten immediately. But I now knew why Herkule had offered to describe his meals to me and the chef had been so apologetic and helpful.

267

Well, I'd just have to visit crew quarters after lunch, but I'd really like to have e-mailed Jason to tell him what had happened and how disappointing my Mother's Day was proving to be, in no small way due to his mother's horrible treatment of me.

The line in the dining hall was very short by the time I arrived and grabbed a cup of soup, a sandwich, and a bowl of Jell-O with a squirt of what I glumly imagined to be some canned nondairy product. Luz had saved a seat for me and was waving, so I was going to have to sit with Vera again. In fact, our usual tablemates, in their usual seats, except for Greg Marshand and the doctor, had gathered. Commander Levinson looked terrible. You'd think a Navy officer with many years at sea would have weathered the storm better than that.

I was feeling a lot healthier myself, even considering the boring packaged meat I spied when I lifted the slice of white bread on top of my sandwich. And the leaf of lettuce was wilted. Randolph Barber caught it in the lens of his video camera. Luz, with her doctor and the cereal king absent, moved over beside me. "Where have you been?" she asked.

I shrugged. "Talking to people."

"Listen, you shouldn't go running off without me. There's been another death."

I stopped contemplating the tomato soup in my cup, canned probably, and the two cellophane-wrapped crackers beside it, and turned to Luz.

"Barney went back to his cabin and found Greg dead in bed."

"Poor fellow," said Barney. "We've been playing golf together for ten years. I never expected to have to bury him. He's younger than I am, and his wife's gone, no children worth mentioning. They never come to see him, which isn't to say that he much cared. They're a quarrelsome lot, Greg included."

"But what happened to him?" I asked.

"Beau says maybe his heart, but he can't tell for sure," Luz replied. "He's wondering about those pills they passed out last night. Everyone woke up feeling so crappy."

I winced at the language, but I didn't complain. Why get into a quarrel with my friend when we now had two corpses?

"Thing is, the pills are evidently all gone. Beau asked Patek what they were, and Patek was very vague; he said medications the ship stored for force-something-or-other winds, and they'd all been passed out last night."

"Why weren't they in Beau's office instead of the chief steward's care?" I asked.

"Beau wanted to know the same thing, but Patek said they were the same sort of pills they keep behind the desk downstairs in case any of the old ladies start feeling like they might puke. Only stronger."

"Well, I didn't take mine," said Commander Levinson. "Beau can have that one if you remember what you did with it, Luz."

"My goodness, are we thinking that the stewards tried to poison us?" I asked. "Herkule would never do that."

"It's on the floor with the broken glass from the bowl I knocked off," said Luz. "I'll have to give it to Beau."

"You might consider sweeping up the glass as well," said Vera, "or are you waiting for the stewards to do it?"

I gave my mother-in-law a look and said, "I'll do it. Just consider it my contribution to friendly labor relations." Then I put my spoon down. "This *is* a fake whipped-cream substitute. Really, I consider this the last straw."

31

Carolyn Goes Missing

Hartwig and O'Brien

Patrick was almost enjoying himself when he searched out Hartwig to tell him Tenerife had been notified that the *Bountiful Feast* wouldn't be docking that day. "I said we're afraid we've got Legionnaires' disease among the passengers."

"I thought that came from bad air-conditioning. Are you sure it's contagious?"

"How the hell would I know, Bruce? They probably won't know either. But I was looking through people's e-mails in the computer room, and guess what I found?" Hartwig muttered something sarcastic about pornography, and Patrick laughed and retorted, "Nothing so innocuous, me boyo. It seems Mrs. Blue has been sending out e-mails to your state department, not to mention your embassy and consulate in Morocco. She told them that Mrs. Gross has gone missing and they need to find out what happened to her."

"That interfering bitch!" muttered Hartwig. "I'm going to have to do something about that."

"No problem," said Patrick gaily. "I'll just send off an e-mail to all of them saying, 'Re: Correspondence from Mrs. Carolyn Blue. Mrs. Gross found. Thanks for your attention.' No need to mention *how* Mrs. Gross was found."

"You do that," Hartwig agreed, and walked off.

Carolyn

Should I check out the spa first or go directly to the crew quarters? I wondered, and decided I'd better go downstairs while the crew and officers were still gorging themselves on wonderful food that *I* should have been eating. I'd been putting off the search because the prospect made me nervous, but I had a perfect alibi as long as I wasn't caught in someone's room. I didn't know what I'd say about that. Maybe the truth, which wouldn't be popular, accusing someone of killing Mrs. Gross and stealing her emeralds, but at least I'd be identifying myself as a public-spirited person instead of a thief.

So I took the elevator down — happily no one was on it — and strolled along the corridors checking out doors, which were, I was happy to discover, conveniently labeled: STEWARDS' DORMITORY. WAITERS' DORMITORY. (Lots of those.) KITCHEN WORKERS' DORMITORY. (No wonder these people were striking. Not only did they work awful hours, but they had to sleep in dormitories.) WOMENS' DORMITORY. (Ah. I turned a corner and found the officers' quarters. One for each.) MR. FRODER. MISS FREDRIKSEN. (I wondered where the captain slept. In fact, I wondered where the captain was. I hadn't seen him today. Maybe up on the bridge, steering the ship away from Tenerife.) Unmarked door. MR. PATEK. MR. HARTWIG.

Suddenly there was an arm around my neck and a hand over my mouth as someone with a white sleeve dragged me backward. Weren't they even going to give me a chance to say why I was here? The arm kept tightening until I couldn't breathe, and although the hand came away from my mouth, I couldn't speak either, and I was dragged through the unmarked door, still unable to see who had grabbed me. My lungs burned, and I saw red light behind my eyelids. Then a cell phone rang. A voice muttered, as I was losing consciousness, "I'll have to take care of you later." Then, nothing.

Jason

The plane got in early. I found a cab without even waiting to see if my bag had made it to Tenerife with the plane, and the driver understood that I wanted to go to the port. Fortunately, I'd picked up some Spanish since moving to El Paso. What he didn't understand was that his driving was the worst, the most dangerous I'd ever been subjected to. I couldn't even complain. I had to get there before Carolyn's boat left. The driver took me straight to the dock reserved for the *Bountiful Feast*; he evidently took passengers there every time it docked. But there was no cruise ship in sight. My God! It had left without me.

There were people loitering around the dock, and I said to them. "Where is it? Why did it leave early?" Non-communication ensued until someone produced an English speaker to whom I could ask my questions and be understood. By then I was more disheartened than frantic — sure I was stuck on this benighted island, peopled by vehicular madmen, while my wife sailed away to a city beset by rioting religious fanatics.

"Ship no come in," said the English speaker. I just stared at him. "No *es* here. No come to Tenerife."

"It's the *Bountiful Feast*," I explained. "It should have been here hours ago, but it's not time for it to leave yet. Maybe it's at another dock."

"No come," insisted the man. He wore a white suit, a straw hat, and a mustache that looked waxed and yet bedraggled. "Come. Come with me."

I shook my head. "I have to find my wife's ship. *Mi esposa.*"

"*Si, su esposa.* On *Bountiful Feast. Si?* Come with me." So I went, thinking he was taking me to the boat. But no, he took me to a building and explained something to a fellow in uniform, a man who nodded and nodded, seemingly half asleep.

"*Bountiful Feast* never come here," said the officer at last. "Not today. Should come, yes. But not come."

"Why not?" I asked wearily.

He shrugged, smiled. "Maybe get lost."

"That's ridiculous. Has there been a storm that might have driven them off their course?"

"No storm here. No storm on radio. Very strange. But not here. Maybe tomorrow. Yes? Maybe some mixed up. Go to Casablanca. Not leave Las Palmas. Who knows? Very strange."

"Can you radio Las Palmas?" I asked. If they were coming in tomorrow, I'd have to find a place to spend the night.

"Sure, Yankee," said the officer cheerfully. "I radio." He went off, and I sank into a chair to wait. And worry.

He came back frowning. "Las Palmas say ship leave yesterday, come here today. But they no come. Very strange."

"Can't you radio the ship?"

"Sure, but they no answer. I radio. No answer."

"My God, could they have sunk?" The thought of Carolyn drowning was too much to bear. "I'll call the cruise line. I have their number."

"Sure," he said, but he wouldn't let me use his phone.

32

A Knife in Time

Carolyn

I woke up in the dark, neck aching, throat burning, sprawled on an uncarpeted floor, with my hands secured to what — a pipe? And secured with what? Because I have long fingers, I was able to bend them and probe my bonds. Plastic. A handcuff-like thing. Perhaps similar to the device Luz had used to capture the Barbary ape on Gibraltar. Too bad I wasn't a protected species. If so, someone would have had to free me. Then I recalled vaguely the voice saying, "I'll have to come back for you," or something like that. How long ago had that been? What did he plan to do with me when he got back? And who *was* he? A crewmember? An officer? The murderer?

Panic-stricken, heart thundering in my

ears, I managed to force myself into a sitting position, which pushed the tip of my little filet knife against my leg, although, strangely, I didn't think that I'd been cut. Realizing that I had to get loose before he returned, I saw the knife as my only hope. I might be able to cut the plastic handcuffs and escape. Of course, I might cut my wrists instead. Tears were running down my cheeks by the time I got to my feet, lowered my hands to waist level, and began twisting my body in an attempt to make my hands meet my pocket and the knife handle.

Five minutes of effort earned me a cramp on one side of my back, which elicited more tears. I sniffed bravely and tried again, wrapping the non-knife-side leg around the pipe and risking dislocation of my shoulder to get my hands in position. And I had it. Well, at least I could feel the handle beneath my slacks. Drawing a deep breath through my nose because there was tape over my mouth, I felt for the edge of my pocket by dint of crushing the pipe into my chest, forcing the opposite hand down as far as the cuffs would allow, and then bracing it from above with the nearside hand.

Success. With my fingers curled around

the handle, I drew the knife upward — and I heard voices in the hall. Oh heavens! Two men were coming for me. One was Patek. I recognized his strange accent. The other? Maybe the Irishman, who had tried to see what I was up to in the computer room. Had one of them been the man who choked me and dragged me in here? If so, I was doomed. I couldn't even decide whether to push the knife back in place so that they couldn't find it.

If I did that, I might find an opportunity to attack if I were released. But I had the sinking feeling that I'd never be able to push a sharp knife into the flesh of another person, even a small knife and a horrid person. And then there was the sound of one door closing, then a second, and silence. I yanked the knife free, only to find that the panties were still clinging to it. A silky flutter brushed my wrist. Probably the foam tip from my manicure scissors was in place as well. I leaned my head against the pipe and sniffled. Now what?

I had to scrape the protective coverings off the knife, so I raised my hands high over my head and rubbed the knife against the pipe. Success, of a sort. The panties fell on my head and covered one eye, just when my eyes were adjusting to the dark.

All right. Now for the handcuffs. Although I twisted both hands one way and another, chafing my wrists, there seemed to be no way to get the knife between my wrists. I did manage to inflict cuts, and my wrists and hands became wet and sticky. For all I knew, I might be bleeding to death. I couldn't tell in the dark with my panties covering one eye. And every minute that passed brought the return of my captor that much closer.

Pure desperation gave me an idea. I would clamp the knife handle between my teeth, hold my head to one side of the pipe, and saw the handcuffs over the knife. Easier said than done. First, I had to peel the tape off my mouth by rubbing it against the pipe. When I got the handle up to my mouth, I had to move my hands down the handle. Naturally I cut my fingers. If I'd gasped, I'd have dropped the knife, which was now between my teeth. Fortunately, I clenched my teeth in pain rather than gasping. Now I had to hold the knife blade gingerly between my slippery fingers while attempting to reposition it firmly between my teeth. Got it.

I clamped down on that handle as if my life depended on it, which it probably did. Then I positioned my wrists and began to saw. Gingerly at first, lest I knock the knife to the floor, but gingerly didn't seem to do much good, so frustrated and frightened, I pressed the plastic harder against the knife and got in three sweeps before knocking the knife out of my mouth. In its fall, the tip caught my thigh, but by then I was immune to the pain of new cuts and stab wounds.

My last chance was gone. I'd never get the knife up off the floor. Furious with frustration, I yanked the cuffs against the pipe and — flew backward into the door, against which I slid down into a sitting position on the floor, giggling hysterically. If someone heard the thud and came to find out what was happening in the closet, I couldn't have done a thing about it.

I'm not sure how long it took me to calm down. Oh, for a watch that glowed in the dark, something I had always thought very tacky. I removed the panties from my head and used them to wipe off the blood I assumed was seeping everywhere I hurt. Then on my hands and knees, I searched cautiously for the knife, which I found on the other side of the pipe. I wiped that off too, helped myself up by clinging to the pipe, and cautiously slipped the now unsheathed knife into my pocket.

I had to leave. I must have looked a fright, but I had to leave. Hide somewhere. Never let my unidentified attacker find me until the ship docked. I certainly couldn't trust anyone on the crew. Possibly I couldn't trust the passengers. I couldn't go to my suite. He'd know where to find me. I couldn't use the elevators. But no one used the stairs! So I needed stairs and a ladies' room. I needed a place where no men went. The spa! Women only. Robes, showers. And I could ask, while I was there, whether Mrs. Gross had actually gone to the spa the morning she disappeared. Of course, she was already dead. Maybe I should just concentrate on staying alive.

Luckily for me, my attacker hadn't thought to lock the door. I peeked out, saw no one, scanned the corridor, and spotted a lighted sign that said EMERGENCY EXIT. Emergency exits led to stairs, so I ran faster than I had ever run in my life. Well, maybe not any faster than I'd run in Barcelona one dreadful night, but let's say I made good time for a woman who dislikes exercise, such good time that I skidded right past the door when I tried to stop.

Also I was leaving a trail of blood scuffs behind me. I'd obviously walked through my own blood, and crawled through it. I noticed when I glanced down at myself that I had blood all over my clothes. I could faint any moment from blood loss if I didn't get up those stairs to the spa floor. Yanking the door open, praying it didn't have an alarm, I let it close behind me and started to climb. And I got smart.

At the first landing, I turned toward the door, then took my shoes off and tucked them under my arms. When he followed me he'd think I exited here. Then I climbed another flight, after which I *had* to rest. After several more flights and rests, I exited and headed for the spa. No one was in the halls. Where were the people? Had the strikers thrown everyone overboard?

Don't be silly, Carolyn, I told myself. *You're just woozy. That's all.* Of course, the door to the spa was closed and locked. In tears again, I leaned my head against the locked door, and remembered Herkule's master keycard, which worked like a charm — like a gift from heaven, or a gift from Albania. I wiped the blood smudge off the door, whirled in, closed the door, and crumpled to the floor with relief, waiting for a kindly spa lady to come forth and take care of me.

Silence. There was no one here. They

must have joined the strike. So I'd have to take care of myself. Fine. I glanced back at the door, saw a lock handle, and turned it. Safe at last with all the spa's facilities at my disposal.

I luxuriated in a shower. I bundled my bloody clothes, including the shoes, together and stuffed them into a covered wastebasket. With no one on duty, no one would be emptying wastebaskets. I wrapped a towel around my wet hair, donned a spa robe, slipped my feet into spa slippers, and went in search of medical supplies. Yes, yes, yes! The medical cabinet in the hair salon was well stocked. Dabbing and wincing, I saw to my cuts. They were many, but they were not life threatening. I applied Band-Aids that promised to be removable without pain. I fixed myself a cup of herbal tea in the kitchen, a brand known for its soothing properties, and nibbled on some stale ladyfingers coated with chocolate. *Get yourself together,* a less befuddled self told me. *You're free.*

Now I had a decision to make. Should I try to stay here, or — what? I couldn't go back to the suite. He'd find me there, and I'd endanger Luz and Vera. Where could I go? I wandered from room to room trying to decide what to do. And then my time was up. I heard men's voices coming down the hall, stopping at the door.

Wild with terror, I spotted the white capsule, flung up the lid, climbed in, pulling my robe belt behind me, and yanked the lid down. Oh God, were my slippers still on my feet? I could hear the door open, men's voices, one saying, "You think the lass would have come here?" It sounded like the Irishman, and then I heard no more because the capsule turned on and swamped me with warm air and perfumed aromas. I was trapped in supposedly blissful comfort, and they'd hear the blasted machine and capture me.

I trembled with fear; I perspired; I pressed on the ridge between my nostrils because the perfume was triggering my sneeze reflex. If they didn't notice the machine, they'd hear the sneeze. Minutes, hours passed. And I fell asleep.

33

Carolyn, Lost and Found

Patek and Hartwig

"What'd you do with her?" Hartwig demanded, grabbing the chief steward by the arm as he hurried toward the elevator.

Umar Patek whirled on the security chief and retorted, "Get your hands off me, Hartwig. I do nothing with anyone, but I am paged now because stewards are drunk in bar and jump in pool with clothes on. If you did not told them to stop work, they be too busy to drink alcohol, swim in passenger pool, and make sex moves on women from spa, who have stop work, too. Now passengers complain of drunk servants and no service in spa, and Sechrest woman chases me asking what to do."

"Christ," snapped Hartwig. "Maybe she's hiding in the spa."

"Who? Hanna disappears?"

"Not Hanna. She's marching around with her gun, stupid woman. I caught Mrs. Blue in crew quarters trying to get into your room. I dragged her into the closet, but then I was paged about the fight in the kitchen, so I had to handcuff her to a pipe and tape her mouth, the interfering bitch."

"So get her from closet. You want to leave her in freezer? Did not work last time."

"I can't leave her anywhere. She was gone when I got back. Blood all over the place. You should take this more seriously, Patek. Patrick found e-mails from her to the State Department telling them about Mrs. Gross's disappearance, and she must have been down below looking for evidence about who killed Gross, which was you."

"So, was me. Blood everywhere? Maybe someone kill her and throw her overboard. Now I go herd drunk stewards to dormitory."

"We can't count on that. We need to find her. I'll check the spa. If she got loose she may have gone there because I told her I'd heard Mrs. Gross —"

"You should keep mouth shut, but is your problem. I got mine."

Jason

I booked a room in a hotel near the harbor and bought a spyglass from a ship chandler so I could keep an eye on the dock assigned to the missing *Bountiful Feast.* Then I called to report the missing cruise liner to the line's Florida offices and was told that they had no reports of problems on any of their ships, that the *Bountiful Feast* was on schedule and following its itinerary. "You idiot," I shouted, "I'm here, and the ship isn't." They hung up on me.

Thirty-five minutes later, the harbor officer called to tell me that the *Bountiful Feast* had radioed that they thought they had Legionnaires' disease aboard and were awaiting a more definitive diagnosis before soliciting entry to a port that would accept them.

"Accept them? You didn't tell them you'd take them here?"

"Señor Blue, is contagious disease, I think. I have call Santa Cruz hospital to see. Health Department must say yes to coming of ship. Maybe even must consult Madrid."

"Madrid?" I groaned. "Legionnaires' disease kills people. My wife is aboard that ship. You have to get those people into port and into a hospital."

"I will call you when we hear from proper authorities. Have a good day. Is American saying, no?" The port officer hung up. I sprawled on my palm-tree-bedecked bedspread and clapped my hands to my head. I felt a headache coming on.

Luz

"Vera, have you seen Carolyn?" I demanded when we met in the suite before dinner.

"Not since lunch. I think she's avoiding me. Doesn't want to help with the strike. I've talked the women in the spa into joining up, and I've made some headway with the gym people next door."

"Why don't you go after the kitchen help? Then we can all starve to death," I snapped. "Listen, I'm worried about your daughter-in-law. I've looked all over the damn ship, and I can't find her."

"She'll be there for dinner. Even if the

food is nondescript, Carolyn never misses a meal."

So we took the elevator to the dining room. Everyone was grousing because the only main dish was meat loaf. I happen to like meat loaf, but then my mother puts long green chili in hers. This stuff didn't have anything but meat and soggy bread as far as I could tell. I don't consider myself much of a gourmet, but I had to wonder what the crew was getting. It had to be better than this. And Carolyn didn't show up. Beau did, nice guy that he was. He could have eaten with the crew, but he sat down by me and whispered that he'd identified the mystery seasick pill we'd all taken the night before the work stoppage. "It's a powerful sedative. Not much prescribed anymore."

"How did you find that out?" I asked, my interest caught.

"When you handed over the pill, I just looked at pictures in the pharmaceutical desk reference until I found it. Have to keep one in my office. People come in sick and can't tell me the names of their medications. If they have samples, I can usually identify them."

"Cool," I said.

"Not really," Beau responded, frowning.

"This stuff is powerful enough to cause heart failure in someone who has a weak heart, and people don't always realize they have heart problems. I think it probably killed Marshand. If you want to help me, I can do an autopsy. The nurse went on strike when I suggested it."

"Can't you just take a blood sample or something? Autopsies have never been my thing, and helping with one? No way."

Beau sighed and said in that case, he'd send the body to the freezer for later inspection, if and when we got into port, but with two probable murders on board and officers running around with guns while the crew got drunk, he was beginning to wonder how this cruise would end.

"Me, too," I agreed, and told him that Carolyn had disappeared. Beau skipped some soggy-looking bread pudding and went off with me to search the ship again. We planned on top to bottom, but we weren't allowed in crew quarters or the engine room. Froder's assistant said no one was allowed in the engine room, especially women, so I had to hope that meant Carolyn wasn't there. The Viking hotel manager in the guerilla outfit said that, under the circumstances, it might not be safe for passengers in crew quarters. I couldn't figure out why. We were the ones who weren't getting our money's worth from this cruise. Looked like the crew was actually having some fun instead of working their butts off.

Carolyn

When I finally woke up in the capsule, I couldn't believe I'd done that. The machine was off, my body was chilled, and my robe damp with sweat, but I felt totally relaxed. What a wonderful television spokesperson I'd make for the comfort machine. I could imagine myself saying, "In a time of great danger and abject terror, the comfort machine not only calmed and relaxed me, but it also put me to sleep."

I felt around for the safety latch, pushed up the lid, and climbed out into darkness relieved only by the night sky outside the windows of the room. I must have had quite a nap. But obviously if people could get in here looking for me, this wasn't my safe haven. I went to take another shower and find a clean, dry robe. Then I rewrapped my hair in a dry towel, after using the spa's cosmetics to turn my face and neck darker and blacken my eyelashes and eyebrows. To that I added an ugly, dark lipstick, and that was about the best I could do to disguise myself. During my transformation, I decided to impose myself on Owen Griffith, a man who would be fascinated by my plight and might have some creative ideas about how to hide me from my attacker. Had the attacker been one of the men who came in searching for me? I didn't know.

With one last look at the new me, I ventured out into the hall, Herkule's card and lock box code in my bathrobe pocket, and walked boldly, in my bare feet, toward an emergency exit. Fortunately, Owen had told me his cabin number; fortunately, I remembered it; at least I thought I did. I took my time going downstairs, hoping he'd be in his room instead of at one of the various bars, hoping he'd let me in. If he wasn't at home, I'd have to retire to the emergency stairway to wait.

I took a deep breath at his floor and stepped out into the corridor. An older couple came walking toward me, and their mouths dropped open when they caught sight of my outfit. I gave them a cheery smile and said, as I had planned, "The spa's open. No attendants on duty, but I just had a lovely twenty minutes in the comfort machine. You ought to go up if you haven't tried it."

They scurried off, and I continued down the hall to Owen's door, where I knocked softly. No answer. Rats! I knocked harder, and, thank goodness, he opened the door, peering out cautiously.

"It's me," I whispered. "Let me in." I glanced nervously up and down the hall, fearing that the louder knocking might have aroused one or more passengers. Owen was still staring, perhaps surprised to find a dark-skinned lady in a bathrobe at his door. "It's Carolyn," I hissed. "Now will you open the door? Surely a thriller writer like yourself isn't fooled by a little makeup."

Owen blinked and opened the door. "I think it was the bathrobe more than the makeup that threw me off," he said, as I scooted inside.

34

A New Identity

Carolyn

It was such a relief to get out of the corridors and stairways. I fell into Owen's desk chair, where on the desk his laptop was open, the screen chockablock with text. Was he writing a new book? Wait until he heard my adventures; they should give him inspiration. "Could I have a drink?" I asked, wrapping the robe tight around my knees and calves.

Owen opened his bar and studied the contents. "Wine?" he suggested and turned to me. "That's a great costume. Did you rush right from the shower to tell me something fascinating?"

"Women don't come out of the shower wearing this much makeup," I replied. "And I'd like some sort of whiskey. Something with a jolt."

"Good girl." Owen grinned at me approvingly and filled a squat glass with ice cubes over which he poured Scotch. "Are you here to seduce me?" he asked cheerfully. "I'm easy prey in case that's your plan."

I took a sip of the Scotch and sighed. It still tasted like mothballs to me, but lacking a tranquilizer, I felt that I needed it, no matter what it tasted like. "I'm here to ask for sanctuary and advice," I replied, and told him the whole story — being dragged into the closet, throttled, and handcuffed to the pipe, my kitchen utensil escape, which I illustrated by pushing up the terry sleeves of the robe and displaying the palms of my hands and my wrists. I kept the leg wound from the falling knife to myself since I had found no underwear in the spa.

"Bloody hell!" Owen exclaimed. "Where did you get all the plasters, and who was the bloke who —"

"I don't know. He was always behind me. I took the fire stairs up to the spa and cleaned up, hid my bloody clothes, and then had to jump into the comfort machine when someone came looking for me." I had to explain the comfort machine, and Owen thought it was hilarious that I'd fallen asleep in it while people were prowling around in search of me. "Then I disguised myself as best I could and came here in the robe, which was all I could find to wear. I can't go back to my suite because that's the first place they'll look."

"You've got that right," he agreed, throwing down the liquor in his own glass and picking up the bottle with a questioning glance at me.

I shook my head. "I need to calm down, not pass out."

Owen poured himself a second drink — he didn't bother with ice — and stared into the liquor between sips, presumably deep in thought. "Righto. Here's what we do," he said at last. "You'll stay here because they won't look for you here, and I'll go out and tell your roommates you're alive. By now, they'll be wondering where you've got to. I'll bring back clothes and whatnot. They'll know what to send. What we need is a wig. And some specs. Wonder where I'd find those? Well, I'll have to suss that out. Will you be all right here on your own while I'm gone on an outfitting rummage? Take the spare bed. You can have a nap."

"As if I could sleep," I retorted. "I slept in the comfort machine. Now I'm all jittery and worked up."

"In that case, I'll just stay and —"

"Please don't go in that direction. I appreciate your help, but I really —"

"Course, love." He put his hand over his heart. "Your virtue is safe with Owen Griffith. On my word of honor as a wild-eyed Welshman."

Not an oath I found reassuring, but I wasn't in a position to be picky.

"So I'm off. Turn on the telly, why don't you? That's good for a bit of calming down, right to the point of stupor. Or pull up the book I'm writing." He waved toward the computer beside me on the desk. "If I didn't lock it up at night, some bastard would have nicked it. That's what happened to all the other computers on board. Now be sure to start at chapter one. You won't want to miss a bloody word." Was my computer gone? I wondered.

Luz

We'd searched the frigging ship from top to bottom and hadn't found Carolyn, and she hadn't come back to the room. Beau and I were worried. Vera insisted Carolyn was probably having a rendezvous with the Welshman, but if she was, I couldn't get his room number so I couldn't check that out. I did get the ombudslady to put through a call to his room for me, but no one answered. Probably out drinking with the crew. The bars were full of them, so we'd gone back to the suite, Beau and I with Vera and Barney, and were playing poker when someone knocked at the door.

Vera got there first and said, "What are *you* doing here? You're not welcome." She tried to close the door in his face, but it was Owen Griffith, and he damn near knocked her over pushing his way in.

I thought she was going to hit him with a lamp, but Barney grabbed her as Owen said, "You want to hear about your daughter-in-law, old lady, or do I need to look for help somewhere else?"

We all calmed down, while Griffith sprawled on the couch and told us the whole story. "She can't stay in your room," said Vera when he was finished. "She's a married woman."

"So where do you want to put her? Back in the bloody comfort machine, whatever the hell that is? Or maybe here where they'll come looking for her? Or maybe they've already been here."

We stared at each other. "Patrick, the Irishman who runs the computer room, asked for her a couple of hours ago," said Beau. "He asked Luz while we were searching, and we said we didn't know where she was. Then Patek, the chief steward, came here to the room. He said he'd heard she was missing and wanted to know if she'd shown up."

"Well, there you go. Next will be Hartwig. My bet is he's the one who dragged her into the closet and handcuffed her. She thought the man was too stocky to be Patek, Froder, or O'Brien. So what would your son rather, Mrs. Blue? A dead wife, or one who has to hide out in my room, where I'm at least able to defend her if I have to? Not that I care what you think. She stays with me. Now, I need some clothes for her and whatever else she'll want, preferably not her own clothes since someone might recognize them. Dark makeup. She'll have to take a shower sometime, and there goes the stuff she plastered on her face in the spa. A wig and glasses would be good. Anyone know where I can get those?"

Barney knew a woman who had a several wigs with her, something about her religion. I said that Carolyn had clothes she'd never worn during the cruise, so no one would recognize them, and I had makeup that I was happy to pass on. I hate wearing makeup and was glad to lend it out, and I knew for a fact that the boutique carried glasses that turned color depending on the light. I'd pick some up tomorrow, but they weren't going on my charge card. "You can pay for them, Vera," I suggested. Beau was worried about the possibility of infection in Carolyn's cuts and promised to slip in with his doctor bag the next morning.

"And how are you going to get back to your room, Mr. Griffith, carrying an armload of women's clothes?" Vera demanded.

Owen produced a bottle from under his jacket. "I'm going to stagger down the halls carrying my Scotch in one hand and the clothes over my arm, telling anyone I see that we're having a costume party tomorrow night in the Grand Salon, men dressed as women, women as men."

Carolyn

I'd read my way to chapter fourteen by the time Owen reeled into the room, waving a bottle, carrying an armload of my clothes, and calling over his shoulder, "Now don't miss the party. And remember: you don't wear the right costume, you don't get in. We're calling it the cross-dresser's ball."

"Are you drunk?" I asked once he'd closed the door.

"Not a bit of it, love. Here's your wardrobe." Under the clothes he held a cosmetic case, all of which went onto the other chair.

"This is a wonderful book," I told him. "As soon as I hang up my clothes — do you have enough room in the closet? — I want to read some more."

"It's two a.m., Carolyn. You've got a nightdress in that pile. Put it on, and go to bed. I promise I won't peek if it makes you feel any better."

"But I'm not tired," I protested. "What I'd really like is to get out of this room. Take a walk out on the deck or something. After all those hours in the closet and the comfort machine, I'm absolutely claustrophobic."

"Or else you're afraid to go to sleep in the same room with me."

"Possibly," I admitted.

"Bloody hell," Owen grumbled.

35

Rescue at Sea

Hartwig

The chief security officer was prowling the deck, sleepless and highly irritated. He didn't doubt that he'd pull off the hijacking and pick up his share of the fifty million in Zurich, maybe more than his share if his confederates didn't get their acts together. He sometimes felt that he had to arrange everything himself, do all the thinking, solve all the problems. And there was something about Patek's attitude. He was an arrogant little wog, or whatever it was the English called people of color. Well, he'd be rid of all four of them soon enough.

Froder would begin moving the ship toward Casablanca tomorrow when the Miami people realized there'd be no dickering about the payoff, not with the explosives aboard. Patek did seem to know his stuff in that area. And the helicopter was arranged for. It would arrive the third day, because the Moroccans wouldn't be paid if they didn't show up, and they knew it. Then he and his colleagues would split up and make their separate ways to Switzerland. Each one had part of the number sequence to the account in Zurich, so they, at least, thought there could be no cheating. Hartwig knew better, but he wasn't planning to scam them as long as they did their parts.

That left the damn Blue woman. They'd all scoured the ship for her without any success. Other than the blood on the floor of the closet, in the corridor, and on the stairs, she seemed to have disappeared at the next emergency door up. O'Brien had put together a heat-seeking gadget to track her down in deserted places. Nothing. Vanished into thin air, the bitch. He should have been getting some sleep, while the damn crew was sleeping off hangovers. Instead, he was out here on deck looking for a fucking food columnist who had got away in a spray of blood — unless someone else got to her in the closet. But why would anyone not part of the hijacking want to kill a food columnist?

Hartwig felt like punching his fist through a wall, but he had himself under control. Stupid displays of frustration wouldn't get him to Zurich and then away from there to live the wealthy life he felt he deserved after years as a mercenary in rat-trap countries and then his fucking, midlife career in cruise-line security. He exited to another deck and went outside. No one around. One more turn and he'd — ah, voices! He moved quietly toward the sound and spotted those two assholes named, so they said, Crosswayses. They were at the rail.

Saviors of the Seas. He'd figured that out early on and run a check on them. They thought he and other crewmembers hadn't seen them dropping flasks down into the water to take samples, fishing up turds, petroleum waste, and chemicals with cries of triumph and slipping them into marked baggies. He'd have had them in the brig at this point if he hadn't planned a better use for the brig. It now held Marbella and the members of the security team, kept gagged and on short rations.

He was congratulating himself on the plight of the captain when he saw the male Crossways lifting a microphone to his mouth. A burst of rage sent Hartwig hurtling toward the couple. He snatched the microphone away and threw it over the rail. "Calling for help? Fool." And he lifted Crossways bodily and tossed him over the rail.

"What are you *doing?*" Bev squealed. "For God's sake, you've —"

"No one's sending any messages off the ship," Hartwig snarled.

"But he was only making — making scientific obser —" Hartwig lifted Bev Crossways next and flung her over, as well, then ran to the door behind the empty bar as her long wail followed her into the sea.

Carolyn

"He — he —" I was stammering, horrified at what I'd seen. Owen and I had been turning a corner during our stroll around the empty deck at the bow of the ship, and I must say that it had been a very refreshing interval. Until we saw the Crosswayses. Since no one was supposed to see me, we ducked under a lifeboat and moved back into the shadow. Then Hartwig accosted the couple. Frankly, his appearance just about sent me into apoplexy, but there was no time for that when I saw what he did.

"Bloody hell," Owen muttered and ran toward the railing. By the time I caught up with him, he had inflated and thrown one life jacket over the rail and was in the process of freeing another. I peered down and heard the Crosswayses calling for help. In the lights of the ship, I could see them splashing about. "Shut up!" Owen called back and dropped the other life jacket.

"Maybe we should try to lower the lifeboat," I suggested. "What if the ship pulls away from them, and they're left bobbing —"

"I don't know how to lower the bloody lifeboat, and neither do you. Here, help me with the rope. We'll have to pull them up."

"Owen, I am not an athletic person. I can't pull a person who is bigger than me all this way —"

"Shut up and help me."

Well, that wasn't very polite, I thought irritably, but since I had to assume that Owen knew what he was doing, I did follow his instructions. He knotted ropes together — I'd never noticed how many there were around. And on a cruise ship — who would have thought? My job was to lower the ropes while he knotted on more. *This will never work,* I thought. The Crosswayses had stopped making a fuss and were paddling about, looking up at the rope as it descended.

Kev seemed to know what to do, because he caught it and tied it to Bev's life jacket. Then he waved to us, and we pulled. Well, I think Owen did most of the pulling, while I thanked Luz in my heart for sending me the rubber gloves that had probably been under the bathroom sink for the stewards when they were still doing bathrooms. I couldn't begin to imagine how terrible my hands would have felt had the cuts on the palms and fingers been exposed to rope.

We actually managed to drag Bev up the side of the *Bountiful Feast* and over the rail, although she was crying when she arrived on deck. What was *she* crying about? I wondered resentfully. If I were caught out here, I'd probably be thrown over with no one to rescue me. We'd all be thrown over.

While I obsessed, Owen lowered the rope to Kev, and the three of us hauled him up. Bev and Owen were breathing hard by then, while I was looking over my shoulder for dangerous people arriving to interfere with our efforts. Seawater pouring off him, Kev leaned against the rail, thanking Owen repeatedly and shaking his hand.

"We're not out of the woods yet," said

Owen sharply. "What do you think Hart-wig's going to do if he sees you alive?"

"I don't know what he thought he was doing when he threw us over. I was only dictating notes," Kev replied plaintively.

"Right." Owen turned to me. "Where do we hide them? Got any ideas?"

"Well, not in your cabin and not in theirs." Then I had a brilliant idea. "Mrs. Gross's cabin. It's empty, and I know where it is. I even have a master keycard."

"The dead woman's cabin?" Bev shuddered. "I don't think I can —"

"She didn't die there," I assured Miss, or possibly Mrs., Crossways. Even sopping wet and in the dark, they did look like siblings. "We don't think she ever got back to her room. She was still wearing the brown dress when she was found in the meat locker."

"I don't know why this is happening to us. We're — we're just adjunct professors at —"

"Horse hockey!" snapped Owen. "You're SOTS. You want to go around targeting cruise lines, you have to expect trouble. Now let's get you to the empty cabin before Hartwig finds out that you didn't drown. Carolyn, stuff the life jackets under the tarp of the lifeboat and take the emer-

309

gency stair down to my room. Here's my card. I hope you've got that master on you. I'll get them into Gross's room."

Because I was afraid to be left on deck by myself and to make the journey to his room alone, I was tempted to tell him that I'd left the master card behind. However, if I wanted to think of myself as an adventurer, an idea that had been growing on me lately, I really couldn't do that, so I took his card and handed him the one I'd transferred from my robe pocket to the pocket of my slacks. Then I found myself alone on the deck and realized for the first time that I couldn't possibly reach the lifeboat. Why hadn't Owen seen that? It was hanging over my head. So where was I to hide the life jackets? And there was the rope. It had to be put somewhere, perhaps even unknotted. Not to mention the fact that Hartwig might return any minute — once he got over his fit of temper — to be sure the Crosswayses had drowned, if for nothing else.

I bit my lip and looked hopelessly at the rescue implements that had been left in my care. Then it struck me. I'd just return the life jackets to their places. I pulled the caps on the blowing tubes and stepped on both jackets until the air leaked out, but then I couldn't figure out how to secure them to their places at the rail. Therefore, I carefully positioned them in such a way that they looked natural.

The rope was another matter. The knots were wet. Everyone knows wet knots are impossible to get loose. So I simply heaved the whole, heavy lifeline over the rail and hoped that it would sink as fast as possible.

36

Desperate Strategies

Jason

I woke up abruptly in the middle of the night in a strange room with the uneasy feeling that I'd forgotten something important. What? I'd bullied the port authorities in Tenerife and called the cruise line without learning anything useful relating to the whereabouts and condition of my wife. What if she was one of those who had Legionnaires' disease? The very thought was so daunting that I got up and plugged my computer into the telephone jack to search the Internet for information on the disease. What I found was not reassuring, but there was no mention of outbreaks on cruise ships.

Then I checked my e-mail since I was up and online, finding the usual scientific communications, which I didn't bother to answer. However, it did occur to me that Carolyn must have had e-mail service on the ship, because that column on bonbons had come out so promptly and been passed on to me. What if she'd e-mailed me in the hope that I'd check my inbox? I went back over the list but found nothing from Carolyn. Although under ordinary circumstances I would never dream of reading my wife's mail, I did know how to access the accounts at home, even Carolyn's personal account.

These were not ordinary circumstances. I logged into her account, checked her inbox, and found nothing about the cruise from friends she might have e-mailed. There was, however, one alarming communication from her contact at the syndicate, asking why she had sent no more columns after the first three. The e-mail ended, "Hope you're not sick, Carolyn. Everyone knows how those stomach viruses race through cruise populations. Take care of yourself," and so forth. I would have welcomed news of a stomach virus, not that I wished it on my wife, but they were over in a few days. Legionnaires' disease wasn't.

Finally, feeling like an eavesdropper, I pulled up her sent list and scanned for the dates of the cruise. There were six e-mails, three to the syndicate that obviously contained the three columns she'd written and sent. The other three were to the American embassy and consulate in Morocco and the State Department in D.C. Why in the world — well, I had to look. She could have been sending a cry for help to the government. So I clicked on the first one, and the second, and then the third.

A passenger had disappeared after the stop in Tangier, and Carolyn wanted the government to institute a search for her, to harass the Moroccan government on this Mrs. Gross's behalf. Obviously, my wife suspected foul play, as well she might. People kept dying on her trips, and she always felt obligated to find out what had happened. With a sinking heart, I closed the computer and returned to bed. If this Mrs. Gross hadn't disappeared in Tangier, there might be a murderer of women on board, as well as Legionnaires' disease. I couldn't sleep, so I calculated time differences and called Miami again.

"We know nothing about Legionnaires' disease," said the man at the cruise line's corporate offices. "There must be some mistake."

"The ship is missing. If everyone is sick,

it could be drifting aimlessly at sea. Furthermore, my wife sent e-mails to various offices of the State Department several days ago to report that a cruise passenger had gone missing around the time of the port call at Tangier. Has the woman been found? What do you know about that?" I demanded. The news about the State Department connection got me transferred to a vice president named Balsam, who steadfastly denied any knowledge of any of these alleged problems but took my number in Tenerife and promised to call me back.

Am I making progress? I asked myself. I had no idea.

Carolyn

I managed to return safely to Owen's cabin, but I was badly shaken. He'd left his Scotch bottle on the desk, so I poured myself a bit in the squat glass I'd used before and sat down at the desk. Perhaps a few more chapters of his book would calm me down, so I pulled up chapter fifteen, donned my nightgown and the spa robe while I had privacy, and tried to concentrate, but without much luck. My thoughts kept returning to the scene at the rail. If

Owen and I hadn't stumbled into it, two more people would be dead. That would make four — Mrs. Gross, the two Crosswayses, and Mr. Marshand, whose death would not have happened if they hadn't passed out those pills — pills that had nothing to do with seasickness. Quite possibly there hadn't even been a storm. And Mr. Hartwig had been willing to kill two people rather than let them make what he thought were calls to the outside world. Add to that the complaints I'd heard from people who were missing cell phones and who resented the closing of the computer room, and I had to deduce that this was more than a work stoppage.

I was in hiding because someone was possibly ready to kill me. Mrs. Gross was dead of a broken neck, and none of these deaths and attacks profited the stewards that I could see. Presumably, the stewards and those who joined them would want their story told to gain public sympathy and put pressure on the cruise line. When known, the deaths would be counterproductive to any solution of their labor dispute. So who profited? And how? The people carrying guns and resorting to violence for whatever reasons? That was my best guess.

I jerked to attention when the door opened, but it was only Owen, saying, "You'd think people going around trying to cause trouble for powerful corporations would expect trouble in return. Those two are still clueless, can't figure out why anyone would throw them overboard when they're acting in the public interest and all that rot." He picked up the Scotch bottle, eyed the level and my glass with a grin, and said, "Getting a taste for it, are you, love?" Then he poured himself a drink.

"I don't think this has anything to do with stewards unhappy with their work hours," I said abruptly.

"I think you've got that right, love."

"I think the ship has been hijacked," I continued, "and would you please stop calling me *love?* It makes me nervous."

"What would you prefer? *Sweetheart?* That's more American." He tipped his glass up. "Or *honey bunch?* Southern, isn't it? You're from Texas, so —"

"I think we're going to have to take the ship away from them," I interrupted.

"Bloody good idea. Course they've got the guns. How do you plan to do it, oh intrepid lady, mistress of my heart, holder of my deepest admiration?"

I glared at him. "Well, they drugged us. Why don't we drug them back?"

"Which ones?" Owen poured himself the last of the Scotch.

"All of them. The whole crew. That would be the safest thing." Then, much to my astonishment, I yawned. "We can start planning it tomorrow." At last I'd become sleepy. Perhaps it was all the physical effort I expended in pulling the Crosswayses to safety.

"Your wish is my command," said Owen, bowing gallantly. "And now if you'd kindly turn your back, my dear Carolyn, I sleep in the nude and am ready to retire to my lonely bed. That is unless you've had a change of heart about joining me there."

I dove into my own bed and stuck my head under the pillow. Only after the lights were out and Owen was breathing deeply in sleep did I realize that I'd gone to bed still wearing the spa robe, which was bulky and hot under the covers.

Jason

I awoke again after only two hours, and my immediate decision was to call the State Department, so I went online again and got a number — an emergency contact number. Carolyn had used the emergency contact e-mail address. When I got through, I was told that the number was used only for after-hours calls. In no mood to be put off by nitpicking bureaucrats, I told the person at the other end of the line that my wife had reported an American citizen missing in Tangier but received no answer from their after-hours emergency contact person, and now my wife was missing, along with the cruise ship, its passengers, and its crew, lost and unaccounted for somewhere in the Atlantic between Las Palmas de Gran Canaria and Santa Cruz de Tenerife, where I was waiting to board a ship that had not appeared.

"The cruise line insists that there is no problem, while the harbor authorities had a message about Legionnaires' disease aboard," I said angrily. "Don't you think it's your business to investigate immediately the disappearance of a group of American citizens lost at sea and possibly dying?"

The State Department person assured me that he thought it was the business of the department and took down all the relevant information — the name of the ship and line, the dates of the e-mails my wife had sent about the missing woman, the name of the port authority officer to whom I had spoken at Santa Cruz de Tenerife, and last, my name, present place of residence, and telephone number. The official promised to start an investigation immediately. *Which is all I can really ask,* I told myself. *So why don't I believe him?*

37

The Counterconspiracy

Luz

I felt like a frigging ingrate when I woke up. Poor Carolyn was hiding out in another cabin in danger of being killed if she showed her face and too straight-laced to enjoy a little fun on the side while she was with Owen. Not that I, generally speaking, approve of adultery, but her husband *had* sent her off on this rotten cruise by herself because he was more interested in whatever it was he did. And Carolyn took it hard, too. She may have acted like she wanted me to come along with her, but she was really pissed off about the Mother's Day thing. No husband to share it with her, and now no Mother's Day at all. When was it, anyway? Yesterday? Today? Good thing I'd arranged to have flowers sent to my mother before I left.

Meanwhile, Beau was sleeping in Carolyn's bed, looking like a happy man. I sure as hell had to get those sheets changed before she returned to the suite. And Vera and Barney were shacked up in her room because neither of them wanted to stay in the room where Greg died. So we were having all the fun, even if the food had changed from great to slop, and Carolyn — well, I felt guilty, which didn't keep me from giving Beau a poke. He woke up all confused and cute with curly hair in his eyes. "Wake up, Dr. Beau. You're supposed to pay a house call on my friend downstairs."

"Can't I pay a house call on you first, sugah?" he wanted to know, but he got up and dressed and picked up his bag of doctor stuff from the sitting room. We met Vera coming in the door with a boutique bag in her hand, Barney behind her carrying his own bag. They were out early.

Beau left, and Vera handed me the bag. "Here are the glasses Griffith wanted for Carolyn, but I'm not paying for them. I expect to be reimbursed."

Barney produced a black wig with a whole lot of hair. "Courtesy of a fellow

Jew," he said. "She was happy to help. Seriously excited would be more like it. She evidently reads detective fiction and likes a good intrigue. She recommended some California writer to me, Rochelle Krich, who has an orthodox female detective. Maybe you could pass that on to Carolyn, the recommendation. I don't read detective fiction myself."

"Carolyn already knows about her," I answered, taking the glasses out of the bag and trying them on. "She recommended the books to me as an example of good writing and a truly believable amateur sleuth, not that I read detective fiction either. Now true crime, that's another —"

A knock at our door interrupted the conversation, and we all hurried to stow the stuff for Carolyn's disguise out of sight in case it was Hartwig or one of his cronies looking for her. Because it was Owen at the door, we dragged the stuff back out and passed it over. Owen was pleased. "Perfect," he said. "Who'd recognize her with hair like that and silly looking glasses?" He perched them on his own nose, where they looked pretty bizarre, and went over to the sliding door to watch them get darker in the sunlight.

Then he sat down and outlined the attack on the Crosswayses last night and the conclusions he and Carolyn had come to. Of course, Vera objected. She said they were just trying to make the workers look bad and break the strike.

Owen, who's one of the few men I'd seen on the cruise who refused to take any crap at all from Vera, gave her a nasty look and retorted, "You just keep believing that, Granny, but the truth is that the stewards are being used as cover for a hijacking. Herkule told Carolyn that Hartwig had encouraged the walkout. Try to explain that one. So anyway, we're taking back the ship, probably tonight. Where's Beau, anyway?"

When we said he'd gone to minister to Carolyn, Owen said, "Good. She was sleeping when I left, but I could see a red patch spreading out from under a Band-Aid on one of her hands. Shouldn't have let her haul on the rope last night. I forgot all about the cuts. So, do I have any volunteers for the counterconspiracy?"

I said, "I'm in."

Vera glared, not yet convinced, but Barney said, "What you're talking about is mutiny." When Owen started to protest, Barney overrode him. "I'm talking about the people carrying around the guns. If they're not staging a mutiny, where's the captain? No one's seen him or any of the other security men except Hartwig since the night the pills were distributed."

"So you're in?" Owen asked.

"I'm in. You'll need someone to take over the engine room and bridge if they've killed that Italian fella or any of the other officers. I should be able to handle a barge like this, even if I did finish my Navy years as a submariner." He turned to Vera and murmured, "Sorry about that, Vera, but each of us has to do what seems right. If this is what Owen and your daughter-in-law think it is, the crewmembers that went on strike will need all the help they can get, and you're the woman who can provide it. I don't even think that we're at cross-purposes."

"We'll see," she replied.

"Well, I need to catch Beau," said Owen, stuffing the wig into the boutique bag with the glasses. I didn't think that was going to do much for the wig, but what did I know? "I'll keep you up to date," he added and left.

Jason

I awoke in the morning after a few more hours of sleep feeling no more reassured than I'd been when I first went to bed. Most of my ire was directed at the cruise line. Obviously, they were hiding something, but I decided that I should at least check in with the port authority before I called Florida again. And what was the State Department doing? Shuffling paper, I assumed. I ate breakfast in the hotel dining room, which had a palm tree growing through the roof and odd fruits on the menu. Then I stopped by the reception desk to ask that any calls coming in for me be noted and the callers asked to leave messages if I was not available.

Having accomplished those tasks, I walked to the pier and confronted the officer I'd talked to the day before. "Is very strange," the officer said without even greeting me. "We radio your wife ship every two hours all night and get no answer. No reports of sightings. Like it disappear. I have radio to fishing boats and other ships that leave this morning to look. Nothing so far. Legionnaires' disease so bad everyone die maybe. Like plague ships in Middle Ages when our islands first visit by people from Spain and Portugal, no? Very strange."

Plague ships? I thought. *God, but that isn't what I wanted to hear.* I lifted my spyglass and scanned the harbor, hoping against hope that I'd see a cruise ship on the horizon. Instead, I saw a gray vessel in another part of the harbor. "What's that ship?" I asked. "The gray one."

"Oh, American Navy ship in for repair," the officer replied.

"Really?" Was help at hand?

Carolyn

I didn't wake up until someone knocked at the door. Owen was gone, and I felt panicky. Hartwig had come to throw me overboard. He probably had his own master room card, and this room had a balcony and nowhere to hide.

"Carolyn," a voice whispered at the door. I crept over and peeked through the peephole, then breathed a sigh of relief. It was Beau, to whom I opened the door, dragging him in hurriedly. Without even letting me get into my spa robe, he began ripping the Band-Aids off my hands and wrists. The text on the packages had lied. It hurt.

"I don't suppose you brought any breakfast," I said hopefully. "Donuts would be nice." It was just possible that he had something to eat in the medical bag, a snack to tide him through a day of seeing blue-haired lady passengers with minor complaints, but who liked the looks of the handsome doctor.

"No," he replied. "There's a little infection here." He rubbed some cream from the bag onto my hand while I peered inside in search of donuts. I didn't see anything to eat. "Any other cuts?" he asked. I sighed. There was the one above my knee. How embarrassing to have to pull up my nightgown. Even if he was a doctor, he was also Luz's lover. Reluctantly I exposed the cut made by the falling knife. "You may have a scar from that one," he said after he'd torn off the bandage. He wasn't all that gentle in my opinion, but then he was a pathologist. He didn't have to be gentle with dead people.

At that moment, Owen used his card to open the door and catch me with my nightgown hiked up to my thigh. "Ah ha!" he said. "A spot of hanky panky going on?" I pulled the gown hastily over my knees.

"Well, now we've got a problem," Beau drawled. "I can't conduct an examination with a smart-mouthed Welshman in the room an' an overly modest patient, so you head for the bathroom an' close the door, Owen."

"I always did say Americans were a

bunch of bloody puritans," Owen grumbled, but he retired to the bathroom, while Beau put more antibiotic cream on my cuts, more Band-Aids on my skin — his didn't even promise painless removal — and produced a supply of antibiotic pills from which I was to take one every six hours, as a precaution, and because one cut on my hand might be infected already. Just what I needed, gangrene.

Then I put on my robe, Owen exited the bathroom, and we held a countermutiny planning session. According to Owen, Luz and Barney had volunteered. Vera hadn't, which didn't surprise me. I didn't care as long as she kept our plans secret from the enemy, and I trusted her enough for that. Owen then asked Beau if he could provide something that would put the whole crew to sleep, something that could be mixed into their dinner tonight.

"The whole crew?" Beau looked taken aback. "That's a whole lot of people."

"Right. Can you do it?"

"How are you goin' to get it in their food?"

"Carolyn will cajole the chef, won't you, love?"

"Not if you keep calling me *love*," I snapped.

329

"Puritan," he retorted, grinning. "So can you, Beau?"

Beau mulled it over. "It's against my Hippocratic oath," he muttered. "Do no harm — you'all ever heard of that?"

Owen assured him that no one would know he'd been responsible for the abrupt collapse of a whole crew.

"Well, in that case, I reckon I could come up with something, but it would be green, an' it can't be cooked. Cookin' would ruin the effect."

"Carolyn?" Owen asked.

"I can only try," I said modestly. "But I do think the chef and I now have a rapport. I can even think of a culinary vehicle for the knockout medicine — if he has avocados."

"Right," said Owen, "So Carolyn, get into your disguise. Beau, start mixing up enough stuff to put the whole crew under. Meanwhile, I'm going to organize a bridge tournament for tonight. While the crew is passing out, we'll be recruiting help at the tournament."

"I'm a terrible bridge player," I admitted.

"Doesn't matter. Your job will be to convince people to join the counter-mutiny, not to win bridge hands."

"I'll bet Luz doesn't even know how to play," I warned.

"So Barney can give her a few pointers. Or you can, Beau, if you have the time. She'll be your partner, so don't complain, whatever she does."

Beau agreed. "I like bridge, but I always get stuck with the bridge sharks at home. Luz an' I can pretend we have our own biddin' system."

"At least it's not poker," I said gloomily, wondering if Owen would be my partner and tolerant of my erratic bidding. Jason sometimes took offense when I paid more attention to the conversation than the hands. Men are so competitive. "But what about the cross-dressing prom?" I asked Owen.

"I was drunk when I started promoting that. Didn't find many people who were interested anyway, and bridge will be a better theater for whispered conspiracy."

38

A Word with the Chef, Please

Carolyn

I hardly recognized myself. My face was about the color of Luz's, much darker than my usual skin tone. All signs of blond hair had gone undercover with the huge, black wig, which was actually rather becoming. Dramatic. Maybe I'd been too conservative in my hairstyles all these years, although whether I could get my hair to pouf out all the way to my shoulders was another matter. I had the length but not the thickness. The wig felt like real hair. It must have taken the contributions of two or three women to make it.

Of course, eyebrow pencil and mascara took care of the remaining blond hair, and

I was wearing a deep red lipstick that would have looked on my real face as if I were bleeding arterial blood from the lips. The glasses distracted attention from my real eye color, because they seemed to turn dark at the slightest provocation, and I'd fiddled with my real clothes, pairing them in unusual combinations, lavender and green for instance. I had to hope that Demetrios could be convinced it was me, but what if the gunmen, and -woman, took me for a stranger and became nervous?

Owen was off to recruit people for his bridge tournament — people he thought likely to volunteer for the takeover. But what if no one would? I advised myself to keep my attention on my own mission. We each had our parts to play, and mine was in the kitchen, to which I traveled by elevator, although I'd much rather have used the emergency stairs again. Owen cautioned that I wouldn't be able to explain my presence on those stairs if I were caught there. Various people bid me good morning, but not in a particularly cheerful way. It was easy to see that my fellow passengers were becoming irritated with the situation, so maybe we'd have more volunteer rebels than expected, although some of these people were really old. People using walkers and canes probably wouldn't — I stepped off the elevator and headed for the kitchen.

An assistant chef blocked me at the door when I asked to have a word with the chef. He advised me that the chef was in a bad mood and no longer taking complaints from passengers. "But I haven't come to complain," I assured him. "I wanted to tell him that no matter what we're being served now, I'll always remember the wonderful meals I had before the work stoppage. My husband and I like to sit on our balcony and reminisce about the tilapia and the braised duck breast and . . ." While I was going on and on, the assistant was eyeing me dubiously. Didn't he believe me? I really did remember those lovely meals, even if Jason wasn't here to discuss them with me.

"I'll — ah — take you to his office and see if he'll speak to you." The man studied me again with a mixture of hope and anxiety. "He could use some cheering up, but I warn you, if you're really just here to complain, he can be very — ah, very —"

"Temperamental?" I suggested, smiling. "All great chefs are temperamental."

That remark seemed to reassure him, and he went off, while I stood nervously in the glass office, hoping no one would recognize me and report me to Mr. Hartwig. It might well be all over the ship by now that I was "missing."

"Madam?" Demetrios had arrived.

"Quick, close the door," I cried. "Don't you recognize me? I'm Carolyn Blue, but I'm in disguise."

The chef peered at me. "You're supposed to be missing. I heard one of the waiters saying that Hartwig was looking for you."

"He is, and don't, for heaven's sake, tell him you've seen me. He tried to kill me. At least I think it was he. Can I sit down? My legs are wobbling."

"It *is* you," said the chef, amazed, and helped me to a chair.

"Sit in your chair," I ordered, "and keep smiling at me. I'm supposed to be telling you how wonderful your meals were, which is true, but I have a different story to tell you, and I need your help."

Then I filled him in on the whole situation — things that had happened, conclusions we'd reached, the action we wanted to take, and what we wanted of him. "Without you, we can't take back the ship," I said earnestly. "You'll be the hero of the countermutiny, if you agree. Captain

Marbella, if the poor man is still alive, will give you a medal on behalf of the cruise company."

Demetrios had begun to laugh. Was that a good sign? I certainly hoped so. I couldn't think of anything more to say to convince him, and he might have some chef's code of conduct that wouldn't allow him to put a whole crew to sleep. Well, not the chefs or kitchen and wait staff. They'd be working, although —

"Say no more, dear madam. Only you can appreciate what I've suffered these last days since I've been forced to cast the pearls of my art before swine unable to appreciate fine food. I shall be delighted to participate. I hope they all fall over and hit their heads when the medication does its good work. Do you have the blessed powders with you? In what shall I include the magic potion?"

"Well, that's sort of a problem," I admitted. "The doctor is mixing up whatever it is. He said to tell you that it would be liquid, green, tasteless, and couldn't be cooked. I did have an idea, but you may have a better one. How we'll get containers of green liquid to you I'm not sure."

"That is no problem whatever," said the beaming Demetrios. He looked so happy that I feared he might jump up and start to dance with glee, which would look peculiar, even suspicious, to the kitchen staff outside the glass windows. "Where cargo is loaded, there is a large — what would it be called? A sort of dumbwaiter. You can load it there and buzz my office. I shall get your signal and meet the bottles here in the kitchen. I will draw you a diagram showing how to find the apparatus." Which he did, while telling me that he would prepare his famous avocado soup for the wretched crew. "Even when they are all in jail, they will remember their last meal with fondness. It is green. It is not cooked. And it is superb. No one can resist it. They will eat every spoonful and ask for more. And they will be given more if there is more to give. Why take chances that some may not collapse as soon as others?"

Great minds, I thought, *run in the same channels.* Avocado soup was just what had come to me, not that I said so. I understood that Demetrios would want to think that the whole operation was his idea.

"Brilliant!" I exclaimed, and we engaged in a mutual beaming contest. Then I had a thought that had not occurred to me before. "Actually, there are some few foolish people who shudder at the idea of eating an avocado. What shall we do with them?"

Demetrios frowned. "I do not allow such foolish aversions at my table. They will eat the avocado soup, or they will get nothing else to eat. To make sure, their entrée will be steak and French fried potatoes — with ketchup. No peasant would pass up such a lackluster entrée. They *will* eat their soup! That is my final word, and on the *Bountiful Feast*, my word on cuisine is law."

"Of course." I wasn't about to argue with him when he'd agreed to the plan, even relished the thought of his own participation. Maybe Owen and I could subvert some waiter, who would be able to tell us if any of the crew, especially the dangerous ones, had refused the soup.

We parted happily, I toward the door into danger, Demetrios back into his kitchen, clapping his hands and announcing in the jolliest of tones that he had had a brilliant idea. "Avocados," he cried triumphantly. "Bring me avocados." Several workers rushed off in search of avocados, while others gaped at the unusual good humor of their leader. The assistant chef squeezed my hand as he escorted me to the door and called me a miracle worker.

39

Negotiations Pan Out

Jason

I calculated that Mr. Mortimer Balsam, vice president of something at the shipping company, would be on his way home to dinner, unless he was still at work actually doing something to rescue Carolyn and the *Bountiful Feast.* Using the cell phone number Balsam had provided in response to threats of adverse publicity, I went back to the hotel and called him. He was driving in rush-hour traffic and was not pleased to be contacted, probably for a number of reasons. "If you have no news for me, Mr. Balsam," I said, "I'm calling the emergency contact number at the State Department."

"Good lord, man," came Mr. Balsam's voice, blurred by traffic noises and sounding as if it came from thousands of miles away, which it did. "It turns out to be a labor problem. We're negotiating. Should be solved by tomorrow. Then your wife will be sailing into port."

I didn't know whether to believe him. A labor problem? "Which port? Can you guarantee it will be Tenerife? You mentioned Casablanca when we last talked. Or maybe it was some other cruise representative I talked to."

"Does it matter what port as long as she's safe?" he asked. "You have to give us time to solve this. It's not something the State Department can or will even consider getting involved in." He sounded quite pleased with himself, and he might be right about the State Department's unwillingness to get involved. They hadn't left any messages for me after my call to them.

"Not good enough," I snapped. "There's a U.S. Navy ship in port. I'm going to talk to them."

Mr. Balsam laughed, but not very convincingly. "We're not at war, Mr. Blue. We're in touch with the *Bountiful Feast* and expect a resolution any minute. Petitioning the U.S. Navy would be a waste of your time and theirs."

I hung up on him, determined to find

the captain of the USS whatever on the other side of the harbor.

Carolyn

I made my way safely to Owen's cabin, although two different couples asked why they'd never seen me before. *Nosy buggers,* as Owen would say. "Of course, you have," I replied in both instances. "I think we were at adjoining tables at breakfast the morning we made port at Gibraltar. Wasn't that a wonderful tour? I bought a delicious handblown vase and had it sent home. Free shipping. Our guide arranged it." One of the women was envious of my good luck and asked for a description of the vase, but I escaped from the elevator without exposing myself to any further danger.

Owen, Luz, and Barney were huddled in the cabin, swigging bourbon and talking over the passenger list, checking off people who had volunteered, and discussing good prospects to be recruited at the bridge tournament. "No blue-hairs," Luz insisted and waved to me as I poured myself a bourbon and mixed it with Coca-Cola from the refrigerator. They all watched

341

that with looks of distaste, but I didn't think it tasted too bad after my first experimental sip. If Vera knew how much whiskey I'd imbibed since my sojourn in the closet, handcuffed to a pipe, she'd tell Jason I was becoming an alcoholic. Good thing she wouldn't be joining our conspiracy.

I sat on the bed beside Luz and said, "Demetrios has agreed and very enthusiastically. He considers feeding the crew his famous cuisine akin to casting pearls before swine." I passed the diagram of the dumbwaiter apparatus to Owen, who looked at it and passed it to Barney. "That's how we can get the drug to Demetrios. He's going to put it in cold avocado soup, which is green and uncooked."

"Bloody hell. Sounds disgusting!" exclaimed Owen.

"I see just where this is," mused Barney, studying the diagram and instructions. "I can get the stuff from Beau to the dumbwaiter if you people can create a distraction to draw the people with the guns away. A bar fight might do it."

"No fear, Commander," said Owen cheerfully. "I'm your man when it comes to a bar fight. Probably you ladies should —"

"I'm not so bad in a bar fight myself,"

said Luz. "Why don't we go together? I can complain that some ass-wipe — open your eyes, Carolyn. This situation calls for all the nasty language I can come up with."

Reluctantly, I opened my eyes.

"I'll complain about being pinched or something. You can defend my honor, Owen. We knock a few heads, get the brawl started, and leave 'em to it."

"That's my girl," said Owen. "A bloody good plan."

I have to admit that I felt a bit jealous. He hadn't congratulated me on having my way with the chef — well, not having my way — oh, rats. I took another big swig of my bourbon and Coke.

Luz advised me to take it easy on the alcohol. "We need you sober and ready to manipulate at the bridge tournament."

"Since I haven't had anything to eat in days, that may not be possible," I responded tartly. Luz passed me a sandwich from which she'd only taken a few bites. Owen produced a few cookies, and Barney pulled some beef jerky from his pocket, brushed off the lint, and claimed he always carried it to tide him over in emergencies. I put the sandwich away for later and attacked the cookies. In my nervous state, they did me a world of good.

"They've caved," Hartwig murmured to Hanna Fredriksen as they passed each other, one coming from, and one going to the crew dining room for a choice of scallop and walnut salad or truffle lasagna.

Hanna turned right around and took Hartwig's arm, drawing him toward a door that led outside. "What did they say?" she demanded when the two were on deck and away from a circle of grumpy-looking passengers, who had been fed bologna sandwiches and chicken with rice soup at eleven thirty.

"The money goes into our account in Zurich at midnight, confirmation sent by one a.m. from two different sources. We'll be off the ship before noon tomorrow. Pass it on to the others."

"The whole amount?" she asked anxiously.

"Of course. It's that or lose the ship and the passengers. They can't afford to delay any more when tomorrow's the deadline. Either they agree, or boom! They hear about the explosion, after we've left with everything in the ship's vault. That wouldn't be what we'd hoped for, but better than nothing. I think of it as our tip for engineering such a successful voyage."

"Huh!" said Hanna. "I want more than a tip."

"We all do, and we'll be getting both. We're cleaning out the vault tonight. Want to help? Women like jewels. You can have first choice." Hartwig was feeling jovial.

"You and Patek can do that. I'll stay on patrol." She patted her weapon. "I don't want any last-minute slipups."

40

Preparations

Jason

Using my spyglass, I focused on the gray destroyer moored at the far side of the harbor. A group of men in uniforms had gathered on the dock, talking to one another and various civilians. Fearing that the sailors might reboard before I could get to them, I hailed a taxi. After all the money I'd spent thus far, another taxi fare wasn't going to make much difference. I threw some money at the driver on arrival and then tried to appear casual as I sauntered toward the ship and its officers; at least, I hoped they were officers.

"Nice ship," I said, joining them, uninvited. "What kind is it?"

"Destroyer. Arleigh Burke class," said one of them, possibly the oldest of the group, but not that old. "The USS *Morgan Fallwell,* out of Norfolk, Virginia."

"And you're here on leave? Tenerife is a pleasant island."

"I wish," said one of the younger men. "We're in for repairs, and then we're headed for home."

Good, I thought. Then maybe they could take a few days to find the *Bountiful Feast* and rescue my wife. "Have you heard about the missing cruise ship?" They hadn't and didn't seem much interested. "My wife's on it. Supposed to have put into port yesterday and didn't. I'm extremely worried."

"It'll turn up," said one of the younger officers. "Probably got lost." They all laughed.

"They haven't answered a radio call since yesterday when they said they had Legionnaires' disease aboard."

"That's odd," said the older one.

I noticed he had more decorations on his uniform than the others.

"Never heard of that aboard a cruise ship. Usually it's that stomach virus, or the odd rape."

I tried to ignore the mention of rape, but found it hard to do. *My poor wife,* I thought. "And no other ships or fishing

347

boats on their route have seen them. I've called the State Department, but they haven't called back."

"Civilians," said one of the officers disdainfully. "You'll wait a long time to hear from them."

"The cruise line has told me repeatedly that nothing was wrong, but today they said it was just a labor dispute."

"A *labor* dispute?" exclaimed the older man, the one I hoped was the captain. "There are no labor disputes at sea. Even on cruise ships. A labor dispute would be construed as a mutiny."

"Ah. Then I wonder if you might be interested in investigating. I assume the Navy disapproves of mutiny."

"You could say that," was the wry retort.

"The *Bountiful Feast* is American owned. By a company in Miami. I don't know about the registry."

"That won't be American," the presumptive captain assured me. "A labor dispute? No captain would allow that, even a cruise ship captain. Sounds to me like something fishy going on there. But we can't help you. We won't be fit to put to sea until tomorrow." He looked extremely irritated. "Not that we're unseaworthy in any usual sense of the word. But we've been accused twice now, while on duty with the task force monitoring Iraq and again off Morocco, of pollution. They say something illegal is escaping from our waste system."

"Really." That was the only good news I had heard all day. "I happen to be a toxin expert."

"Yeah? Too bad you're not in the Navy. No one here seems to know what's going on."

"I'd be glad to help. No charge. In return, perhaps you could find out where my wife's ship is. Don't you have satellite monitoring and that sort of thing?"

"Not on board," said the captain thoughtfully, "but we could put in a request. Ship lost at sea, sickness on board. They ought to honor it."

"Wonderful," I said. "And now, why don't I take a look at your waste system?"

Carolyn

While Beau mixed up the sleeping potion for the avocado soup, Barney was in Owen's cabin giving Luz and me bridge lessons. "This is a stupid game," said Luz after an hour of lessons. "I'll never learn it,

349

and I don't want to." Barney insisted that all she really had to do was learn the language and the basics. Beau would be her partner and wouldn't criticize any mistakes she made.

Owen was out talking to passengers, looking for likely countermutineers. He dropped back in once to bring me two more sandwiches and a piece of cake. I ate the cake first because helping Luz master even the basics of bridge was a thankless and nerve-wracking task. Owen also brought the news that Vera had convinced the gym employees to join the work stoppage, even though they worked more reasonable hours. Then she had moved on to the waiters.

"If the waiters go out, who will serve the avocado soup?" I exclaimed. "Someone has to stop her before she ruins our whole plan."

Barney laughed heartily. "There's no stopping your mother-in-law. You have to admire her spunk. She has a mind of her own."

"Don't worry about the waiters. I heard the stewards, drunk in the bar, saying the waiters were too afraid of the chef to walk out," said Luz as she stared morosely at a hand of cards. "This is a

crappy hand. I don't have any diamonds."
She threw down the cards in disgust.
"They also said the kitchen workers were
even bigger chickens. They'd never walk
out."

"No diamonds is good, Luz," said
Barney. "Let me show you why. Carolyn,
you play the opposing hands. We'll say Luz
got the bid for four spades."

While I fumbled around trying to play
two hands, I was really paying more attention to the stewards' opinion of the waiters
and chefs. My mother-in-law was a powerful arguer, and a bully to boot, but
Demetrios was a formidable opponent and
the terror of any crewmember that entered
his circle of influence. Maybe Vera would
fail to cause any more trouble for us. Who
cared if the gym attendants went on strike?
They were muscular, but they'd be asleep.
We just had to get the avocado soup made
and served.

Beau knocked at the door and was admitted after inspection through the peephole. "Okay, Barney, the stuff is mixed an'
poured into distilled water bottles. Those
are in my office on a medical cart covered
by some linen towelin', all ready to go. You
want me to help?"

"We have to wait for Owen. He and Luz

are going to start the diversion in the bar. Why don't you take over teaching Luz how to play bridge? Maybe she'll be more cooperative for you."

Beau was delighted and sat down, saying. "First, countin' points."

"I've got that," Luz snarled. "I'm not stupid."

"No one ever said you were, my darlin'. So we'll move on to biddin'."

"Which is a real crock."

"No question," Beau replied amiably. "But necessary. Bear with me, my lovely, brown-skinned beauty."

"Oh, shut up."

He dropped a kiss on her cheek and sat down beside her with his arm around her waist.

Lucky me, I thought. I turned over one of the hands to Barney, and I only had to play the other against two lovebirds. And Jason wasn't here to give me support and a kiss for myself. He didn't even know what was happening here, hadn't sent me a Mother's Day telegram, or any more bonbons. Now I was sorry I'd spurned his gift. Luz had eaten the rest of mine.

Owen turned up a half hour later and went off with Luz to initiate the bar fight. Barney left as well to send the bottles of green knockout liquid up to the chef. That left me. All alone with nothing to do. I took a nap.

Hartwig and Fredriksen

Both Hartwig and Fredriksen received the page warning of a fight in the bar off the Grand Salon. They responded immediately and had to disable a number of crewmembers and several drunken passengers while working their way toward the center of the disturbance, where they'd seen a woman coldcock a muscular gym trainer.

The trainer, once revived, mumbled, "I didn't pinch her butt, I swear, Mr. Hartwig."

"Who was she?" Hanna Fredriksen demanded.

"I don't know," said the man, groaning. "All I saw was the back of her. Then some guy knocked me flat on my back, and I think the woman kicked me in the head."

"I think she was that dress designer from Madrid," muttered Hartwig.

"Come on, Bruce," said Fredriksen, as they hauled dazed men to their feet. "How likely is that?"

41

Early Recruiting

Jason

I got a call late in the afternoon from Captain Wickendon of the USS *Morgan Fallwell.* "Professor, Al Wickendon here. Thought you'd like to know that the satellite center got back to us. They've spotted your wife's ship. Amazing stuff — satellite photography. They could see *Bountiful Feast* written right there on the bow and a few passengers walking on the decks. Didn't seem to be anything wrong with the ship except that they were almost dead in the water and off course if they were coming here."

"Don't you think that sounds ominous, Captain?" I asked anxiously. "Shouldn't you sail out and see what's happening? They may need assistance."

"Couldn't if I wanted to, Mr. Blue. First off, the *Morgan Fallwell*, as I said, isn't seaworthy yet. The Canarians pulled all our filters the way you told them to, but now they're standing around scratching their heads. God knows when they'll decide we can put to sea again without fouling their lousy harbor. Can't expel certain things within the twelve-mile limit, and other stuff not at all."

"Captain, I'm coming down again. Frankly, I'm one of the foremost toxin experts in the country — toxins and how to get rid of them." I found myself in an unusual position, having to force my expertise, without asking compensation for my time, on people who hadn't asked. However, there was Carolyn to consider. "I'll be right down. I won't charge you anything, if that's what's worrying you. Except that if you sail out to check on the *Bountiful Feast*, I'd appreciate sailing with you."

"Oh, I don't know about —"

"If you're leaving a toxin trail in the ocean, it would help if I can do an on-site inspection and some testing."

"Well, I —"

"I'm on my way, Captain." I planned to recruit the captain and his destroyer to rescue Carolyn, with myself aboard, even if

I had to take the whole waste purifying system of the *Morgan Fallwell* apart by myself.

Carolyn

I was amazed. The Grand Salon now held twenty or more tables, presumably suitable for bridge. "Do we have permission to assemble this many people?" I whispered to Owen. I was wearing my wig, war paint, and my red blazer paired with navy slacks and a navy scarf. Very oceanic, I thought, although not an outfit I'd normally put together. I'm as patriotic as the next person, but I'd never consider wearing clothing imprinted with the flag, for instance.

"Sure. I think Hartwig was happy to get so many people in one spot rather than have us all wandering around the ship while the crew ate our food. What'd you think of that dinner?"

"Salmon patties aren't one of my favorites. Certainly not those. They must have come straight from a package of frozen dinners, along with the withered green beans and mushy macaroni and cheese."

At that moment, a woman rushed up to

us and clasped my hand in both of hers. "Here you are! Isn't this exciting? I'm Rebecca."

I knew I'd never met her, although she looked vaguely familiar. But surely I'd have recognized that magnificent red hair.

"I lent you the wig," she whispered. "If you need another, I can lend you this one tomorrow." She patted the red hair. As soon as I get back to California, I'm going to e-mail Rochelle Krich and tell her about our adventure. Maybe she'll want to use it in a book."

I nodded. "I'm sure she'd appreciate that, and I am very grateful for your offer, but I have to ask: Will my wearing your wig make it, ah, non-kosher? I mean, I'm a non-Jewish person."

Rebecca laughed merrily and said, "It's not as if I'm going to eat it, dear, after you return it. Anyway, I gave up keeping kosher when I divorced my first husband. So much dishwashing! I even eat lobster now and then these days." She chuckled as if lobster were a daring escapade, which I suppose it was for her. "But I did love the wigs, so I kept those, and my second husband —" she waved at a portly man shuffling cards impatiently at a nearby table "— Morty, is what we call an ethnic Jew, as

357

opposed to a religious Jew. A much less trying form of Judaism, as you can imagine. Now, is there anything else I can do for you? I do want to play my part. Commander Levinson told us what happened to you. By the way, you look stunning in my wig. You should consider getting one of your own. I'd offer to give you that one, but it's one of Morty's favorites."

"Do you have any expertise in guns or hand-to-hand combat, Rebecca?" asked Owen, absolutely straight-faced.

"Well." She gave it some thought. "I once knocked out a burglar by throwing my jewelry case at his head. I used to play softball as a girl, and my aim is still excellent. And Morty was a boxer in his youth. He still likes to go into the basement and hit that bag that bounces around."

"Bloody good news, that is," Owen exclaimed. "Maybe you and Morty would like to join us in taking the ship away from the hijackers."

"My goodness, let's ask him." She led us over to Morty and asked if he realized that they were on a hijacked ship, and Morty, who had a distinct New York accent, said he'd figured that out, but hadn't wanted to worry her.

Rebecca cried, "You are so sweet. Isn't he sweet?" she asked us.

I agreed that Morty was really sweet. At least he'd accompanied his wife on the cruise instead of leaving her to her fate.

"This is Morty's Mother's Day present to me, and we don't even have children together. I have three with my first husband, but I obtained a *get* and took them with me. Mordecai is horrified at the way we're raising them. Oh, but I forgot. Morty, we've been invited to help take the ship back from the hijackers. I told them about my triumph over the home-invasion person and your boxing. I think it would be so much fun. What a wonderful story to tell at dinner parties."

"How do you plan to manage it?" Morty asked Owen. He didn't even look at me, although it had been my idea. Probably he thought dealing with hijackers was man's work. I ought to report him to Vera.

"As we speak, the whole crew is getting groggy. They'll be lucky to make it to the nearest bed before they pass out," said Owen cheerfully. "We've got the chef and the doctor on our side."

Morty nodded. "Good plan. You can count on us as soon as the tournament is over."

"That was fast," I murmured to Owen as we made our way to our own table. Owen had made up a chart, showing where everyone was to sit and how the winners moved in the second round and so forth. Competitive bridge. He was not going to be happy with me if he thought we'd be winners moving each time to a new table.

42

The Bridge Tournament, Round One

Luz

This is going to be a freaking disaster, I thought as I sat down across from Beau for my first and, I hoped, last evening of bridge. Owen had picked all the people we were supposed to recruit. Our first couple was the Karstroms, Sven and Frieda, from Minneapolis. Sven was so tall he looked like he was standing up when he was actually sitting down at the table shuffling cards. Couldn't wait to get going and beat our asses. Poor Beau. This was going to be a bad evening for him even if we recruited everyone we came across.

"Well, you folks look like you're in good shape," said Beau cheerfully. "I'm Beau, and this is Luz. Do you work out?"

"Yup," said Sven, and pushed the cards across the table for me to cut.

"Aren't you the designer from Madrid?" asked Frieda, studying my clothes.

"No," I responded. No use playing that game when Vera wasn't here to translate for me. Anyway, I was sick of it, and one way or another all the games would be over after tonight. I picked up my cards and put them into suits the way Barney and Beau had taught me. "One spade," I said. "I'm a retired cop."

"Cops are good," said Sven.

"What do you mean?" Frieda demanded. "You can't bid one spade."

"We have our own bidding system," Beau confided. "As a doctor, I always like to see people in such good shape. Able to take care of themselves."

"I own Fit and Feisty," said Frieda proudly, "and Sven is the founder of Man's World. It's a gym and self-defense school. And you two may have your own bidding system, but she can't open the bidding. Sven dealt; he opens."

"One diamond," said Sven.

"Pass," Beau said. "Self-defense? Sounds

interesting. I like hunting myself."

"Yup," said Sven. "Bear is good. In Alaska."

"Three diamonds," said Frieda.

"Three spades," I said. They looked pretty good; I had an ace, a jack, and a bunch of little ones. "You two notice anything strange going on on this boat?" Might as well get to the point. He sounded like a good prospect, and she was one of these skinny women with well-defined muscles in her arms. She certainly had them on display in that sleeveless dress. I'd have been covered with goose bumps wearing that in this air-conditioning.

"The strangest thing I've noticed," said Frieda, "is your bidding."

Mean too, I thought approvingly. These two were probably as good as we'd get on a cruise ship.

"Five diamonds," said Sven. His wife, if she was his wife, glared at him. "Well, you answered," he retorted as if she'd actually made a complaint aloud.

"She made that illegal bid. I just wanted to keep it open." Frieda slapped down her cards. "You didn't have to jump to game."

Sven led the king of spades from Frieda's hand. *Dumb move,* I thought, and put my ace on it. It had to be lucky that I was going to take the first trick. Sven put a two of diamonds on my ace, and Beau threw in the three of spades. I grinned and put my hand out to take my winnings, but Beau gave me a little kick. Not, thank God, in the knee. *Oh, shit,* I thought. *Trumps. I forgot about them. What a crappy game. I should have taken that trick.* Instead, Sven swept in the cards with that big paw of his.

"People walking around with guns on a cruise ship," said Sven. "That's strange." He led the ace of diamonds.

"No one in the gym or spa," agreed Frieda. "Unions, maybe."

"We're not getting into contracting out to cruise ships," said Sven. "You can forget that, Frieda."

They took eleven out of twelve tricks and agreed to throw in with us on the counterhijacking. "So," said Sven, when we'd explained the situation as we saw it, "shouldn't be a problem."

"Only four of them with weapons," agreed his wife thoughtfully. "Hell, Sven and I could take them on our own, couldn't we, big guy."

He nodded. "Bad food. Big price." Then he turned to me. "You didn't have to play so bad. I don't like a scam on me. Don't have to win at bridge to help. Police should be more honest."

I had to laugh. "Honestly, I'm a crappy player," I assured him.

"You can say that again," Frieda agreed. "So when do we go after them? After the tournament? And what if they're not passed out? I just saw that ugly security guy stick his head in here."

Beau didn't like that. Neither did I. If the avocado soup hadn't worked, we were going up against four people with automatic weapons. Maybe we needed a new game plan.

Hartwig

Bruce Hartwig was disgusted with himself by the time he'd finished his steak and fries, followed by a big piece of apple pie with ice cream. He was falling asleep in his chair. He'd only been sleeping in catnaps since they took the boat, but that was no excuse. He'd been known to go for days without sleep in Africa during mercenary contracts. Mow down a bunch of ragtag rebels in the bush and head out in search of more. Lousy working conditions, but good pay.

He sighed and stood up, stretching, and walked out of the dining room briskly to get his blood circulating. He'd better take a look at that bridge tournament. The writer had organized it. Hartwig didn't consider a writer much of a threat, no matter what kind of books the guy wrote, but you never knew who your enemy was. In Africa, the people who employed you had been just as likely to shoot you as anyone. So he looked in. A wimpy-looking bunch, drinking and slapping down cards like there was money on the games. The crew was grumbling because the passengers were still drinking up the liquor. Afraid it might run out.

Hartwig yawned. Tomorrow he and the others would be gone, and the crew and passengers could go after each other. The idea amused him. He spotted the writer, who was talking his head off to some guy who looked to Hartwig like a New York Jew. He'd lived in a Jewish neighborhood when he was a kid. Used to make money pushing the elevator buttons for them on high holy days or whatever. And some of the kids he could bully out of lunch money. But there was one who caught him at it and beat the shit out of him. Never liked Jews after that. Probably some bastard who grew up and immigrated to Israel to beat the shit out of Arabs.

Not that Hartwig liked Arabs, either. He particularly didn't like Patek, and he didn't even know what Patek was. Or O'Brien. O'Brien pissed him off with all that Irish blather and computer gabble no one could understand. Now Froder was more like it. Tough. Not much to say. He figured he could count on Froder in a pinch. Froder would probably have been a Nazi if he'd been old enough to join up. Hartwig had always figured he'd have made a good Nazi, but they might not have let him join. He'd never known who his father was. Bound to be better than his mother, whoever the old man had been. She was as mean as a woman could be. Always pounding on him when she was drunk, until he got big enough to kick her teeth in and take off.

Suddenly he found himself in front of his office and couldn't remember heading there. Well, good thing. He needed a cup of coffee.

43

The Bridge Tournament, Round Two

Carolyn

"Sorry about that," I murmured to Owen as we stayed at our table and the winning couple moved on.

"Carolyn, love. You were perfect. I set it up so we'd get to talk to the likely winners from the next table. Luz did well, too. They lost, and the Barbers are in. Harriet seemed downright bloodthirsty."

"Not surprising. If I were black, and Mr. Hartwig muttered *damn niggers* under his breath when I asked why he was carrying a gun on a cruise trip, I'd be angry, too."

"Randolph seemed more interested in

filming the whole thing," Owen observed, "but if he's willing to use that equipment as a weapon if necessary, he could knock someone right off the boat."

"He'd never endanger his camera. Imagine having to look at everything he shoots when they get home. You know, I think that's the first time I've said the *n-word*. Mr. Hartwig is *not* a nice man. The sooner we have him in the brig, the better."

"Sh-sh," hissed Owen. "Hi, I'm Owen Griffith, and this is my partner, Carolyn. You'd be the Povrays, right?"

"That's us," said a tall, rangy man with white hair and one of those string ties held in place by a gold, horny-toad ornament. I hadn't seen anything like that since I met a drug lord at a Juárez mariachi club.

"This here's Wanda Sue, an' Ah'm Hank."

I estimated that Wanda Sue was a good twenty to twenty-five years younger than Hank, but she still had a sort of leathery, rancher look. Still, maybe hers came from sitting by a pool while he was out admiring his cattle.

Since we were the losers, Owen dealt the cards, while Wanda Sue admired my "tan."

"Oh, I'm just naturally dark-skinned," I said.

"Why, honey, are you a Meskin?"

"Greek," I replied. "Carolyn Metropolis. I'm a chef in New York, and I'm here to get some pointers from my cousin Demetrios, the chef on the ship." I could see that Owen was choking back laughter while I calmly arranged my cards. "Are you fond of Greek food?"

"We-all, no," drawled Wanda Sue. "Ah'm a lover of French food."

"French food is nice," I agreed, and returned Owen's three clubs with a six-club bid. If he wanted to lose, I felt obligated to do my part. I hate those three-club bids. Who ever knows what they mean? Everyone looked taken aback at my six clubs, including Owen.

"Well, hell," said Hank, and bid six hearts. That closed the bidding, except for the doubling and redoubling.

Wanda Sue said, "Hank is so impulsive, an' not just at bridge. We went to this big ole cattle sale before we left, an' he bid enough money to keep me in clothes for a year on the ugliest bull you ever did see."

"That there bull's goin' to make us rich," said Hank, leading from the dummy hand.

"We're already rich, honey," Wanda Sue protested.

"We're gonna need to be richer if you

keep buying them trees an' dawgs an' spores an' the like. Wanda Sue is aiming to grow truffles in Texas. They're somethin' that tastes like dirt an' grows in France."

"Truffles are delicious!" I exclaimed.

"Why, do y'all use truffles in Greek food?" she asked me.

I had no idea, but I gamely said, "They're wonderful in rabbit stew," and had to promise to send her a recipe. Actually, her scheme sounded very interesting to me. She was planting the right kind of trees to nourish truffles in their roots and raising dogs to sniff out truffles that she imported and buried in the ground for training purposes. She wanted the dogs to be ready when she harvested her first truffle crop.

"Takes a hell of a lot of good water to keep those truffle trees goin'," said Hank. "Never goin' to make money in the long run. Still, Ah'm a man who likes to keep mah little lady happy, don't Ah, sugah?"

She giggled and leaned across the table to give him a quick kiss. "Ain't she the sweetest thang?" he exclaimed.

I could have swatted the two of them. *Keep the little woman happy?* For once, I thought of my mother-in-law with affection. If she'd been here, she'd have taken a layer off Mr. Povray's leathery Texas hide. All I could do, being given to polite refutation of outrageous statements, was to say, "You don't know what fresh truffles would bring per pound in the States. No one grows them here."

"Well, why don't you tell me, Miz Metropolis," he said with genial condescension.

"If they're seven hundred Euros a kilo in France, which is a quote I saw on the Internet, they'd be twice that here."

"Well, Ah'll be double-damned," he exclaimed. "But then Ah always did say mah little bride here has a head on her shoulders."

After that the men starting talking about something else, and Wanda Sue told me all about importing large trees from Italy and France along with gardeners to tend them. She herself was running the truffle-dog training program. "They took right to it," she claimed. "Ah'm selling some of mah dawgs in France. Plenty of people just don't like pigs around, so the dawgs are gettin' popular, especially with women who own truffle forests. Pig shit, now that does smell bad, but dawg shit, it just dries up an' hardly smells at all, long as it don't rain. You ever visited one of those pig farms in the Carolinas? Ah went looking at pigs when Ah first started out, but the smell, oh mah —"

"Well, Owen, you got yourself a deal," said Mr. Povray, interrupting not only Wanda Sue and me, but people for tables in every direction. "That's the best offer Ah've had this whole dang cruise."

Owen gave him the eye, and the rancher quieted down, while I realized that my partner had lost any chance of making a reasonable showing at bridge since I inadvertently trumped his trick, but he'd still managed to recruit another counterhijacker.

"Wanda Sue, honey," Mr. Povray whispered. "We are gonna have *some* fun tonight! Don't you worry, Owen, if you need any shootin' done, Ah'm your man. Been shootin' all my life an' then some. Fact is, they say my ma shot a twelve-point buck not five minutes before she went into labor. Ah was born in a deer blind while they was out huntin'."

"Glad to have you aboard, Hank," said Owen. "You too, Wanda Sue. I hear you're a crack shot yourself."

"Well, Ah am, honey. But what are we shootin' at? Not fish, I hope. Bullets do tend to ricochet off water."

Since it was time for the Povrays to move on, having beaten us abysmally, doubled and redoubled, we had to wait until after the tournament to explain our mission to Wanda Sue, but Owen did congratulate me on trumping the only trick he had a chance of taking.

I shrugged. "I can't listen and play bridge at the same time, and Mrs. Povray is a talker."

"She is, and I wasn't being sarcastic, love. Because of you, they set us doubled and redoubled. Hank was, as he put it, 'pleased as a pig in slop.'"

At the end of the tournament, those who hadn't been recruited went off to bed, and the rest of us split into teams to check dormitories for sleeping crew members, hunt down unconscious carriers of guns, see if we could find the captain, tie up those we thought should be tied up, and so forth. We took down all the fancy drapery ties in the Grand Salon just to be sure we were well provided with binding materials.

44

Night Maneuvers

Luz

After two hours of bridge, I felt like going to bed. It was more exhausting than physical training had been at the police academy, but no one, well no one we recruited, was going to bed until we had taken back the ship, and then we'd have to work shifts until we could get some help. As Barney said, he couldn't run a whole damn ship by himself with a couple of landlubbers as crew, and we didn't know who we could trust among the real crew. The idea was to lock them in their dormitories.

Some of the people bitched about ending the tournament after three hours, but Owen and Beau said that was the deal, so they straggled away. With any luck, they'd head off to bed so they didn't get in our way when we went after the four or five conspirators. We couldn't agree about the Irishman because we'd never seen him with a gun. On the other hand, we had seen him whispering with the four who did carry guns: Hartwig, Patek, Froder, and Fredriksen.

I was looking over the recruits, and I'll tell you I wouldn't want to serve on a SWAT team with any of them. Randolph Barber didn't expect to do anything but film the takeover. His wife said she was along to take care of Beau, who was her dancing protégé. Crap. Our raggle-taggle group of bridge players would probably end up against the wall with four automatic weapons pointed at us. Tossed overboard, maybe. Carolyn had told me about Hartwig throwing the Crosswayses over, and then the damned Crosswayses wouldn't even help us take back the ship. Thankless turds thought they had better things to do with their time. When it was my turn to take them food, I didn't do it.

Patrick O'Brien solved the problem we had with him by staggering into the Grand Salon and telling Beau he was sick. Beau said, "You look sick, fella. We better head for my clinic. Luz?" Evidently I was supposed to lead the Irishman off to be treated, though God knows what Beau had in mind for him. Beau made a quick stop beside Owen and said, "Start organizing them into teams. I'll be back in about five minutes." Then he caught up with us.

By the time he opened the clinic, I was holding O'Brien up, while he mumbled, "Don't know what's wrong. I've had five cups of coffee, and I'm still . . ."

Beau had him on the table with his shirt off before he could tell us his symptoms. "Holy, Magnolia!" Beau exclaimed, standing behind O'Brien. "Luz, look at this rash."

I went around to look, but O'Brien's back was smooth and white except for some freckles on his shoulders. Beau nudged me, so I said, "Really awful, man." And to Beau, "Anything we can do for the poor guy?"

"Damn right," said Beau. "Mr. O'Brien, you've got shingles." The Irishman stared at him stupidly. "It's a particularly nasty version of the chicken pox virus. Fortunately, we have anti-virals now. Otherwise, you could experience agonizin' nerve pain for the rest of your life."

O'Brien kept repeating words after Beau. "Rash? Chicken pox? Pain?"

"Here, Luz, rub some of this salve on his rash so he isn't bothered with the typical burnin' itch when that starts up." He handed me something that said *Adult Acne Cream*, and I rubbed it on O'Brien's freckles as Beau prepared the shot, and O'Brien kept mumbling that he didn't like shots; couldn't he take a pill?

"You won't feel a thing," Beau assured him and stabbed him in the arm while O'Brien stared soulfully at me and said I had hands as sweet as the Holy Mother's. Then he keeled over against me. Beau tied his feet to the stirrups at the end of the table with rubber tubing and then his hands to the legs of the table. Made me feel like we were a couple of serial killers planning something really nasty.

On our way back to the Grand Salon, we ran into John Killington, who asked, "What's up, Beau? Wanna get a drink? No crew in the bars. No bartenders either, but the liquor's still there."

"Killington! Carolyn's computer hacker, right? Listen, if you want to get into the computer room, the keycard's probably in the pocket of this guy we tied up in my clinic." Killington's eyes lit up, and Beau passed him a keycard to the clinic. "Just leave him there, an' once you get on a computer, see if you can find any e-mails from any of the people who've been carryin' around the guns. Meanwhile, we're takin' the ship from them."

"No way!" exclaimed Killington. "Hartwig, Patel, Froder, and the tall blonde, right?"

"Patek with a 'k,' an' the woman's name is Hanna Fredriksen, i-k-s-e-n."

"I'm on it," said Killington, and he headed back to the clinic at a trot.

Carolyn

We decided to divide up into two teams since we weren't sure that the hijackers had actually succumbed to the avocado soup. After all, Mr. O'Brien had reeled in, and Mr. Hartwig had been seen peering into the Grand Salon when he should have been unconscious. Our plan was to sneak around the halls, checking on the crew dormitories and locking them up if they were full. If we came upon anyone in the corridors, we would pretend to be singing, reeling drunks, and try to overpower whoever it was by crafty maneuvers and sheer numbers.

When Luz returned, she said that was a stupid idea, and a man with an automatic weapon could kill a whole hell of a bunch of crafty, unarmed people. Since a lot of our volunteers were already somewhat the worse for cocktails consumed at the bridge tables, they disagreed violently; they liked the idea we'd come up with. I thought it was good enough myself.

Barney wanted to head straight for the engine room and Froder, so Luz volunteered to go with him. She whispered to me that Barney might be an old fart, which I thought was a very rude remark, but at least he was military. As a result, Beau went off with one half the volunteers; I left with Owen and the others, and Luz went off with Barney, down to "the bowels of the ship," as he put it.

Luz

First we checked out the dormitory, and Barney said it looked like a whole shift sacked out there, plus a few more. Then we crept into the engine room, which was one noisy place — worse than a frigging rock concert. We found some more crewmen snoozing beside various hunks of machinery, and an officer snoring in a room full of dials. No Froder. "What about his cabin?" I asked. "Carolyn said the officers' names are on their cabins." Barney pointed out that we didn't have a keycard. Those had gone with the two other teams. "Hey, I can kick in a door," I assured him. "I've kicked in a hell of a lot of 'em in my time."

Barney was worried about my knees, but I wanted to finish this before someone got hurt, so I said I'd just take extra meds when it was over. We ran into some of the others on the floor above the engine room. The Barbers were checking crew dormitories, which amounted to opening doors, taking pictures of sleeping waiters and cooks, then shoving wedges under the doors so the sleepers couldn't get out.

They came along with us to Froder's door, where Harriet claimed she could hear snoring. *Good,* I thought, and kicked it in. It took two kicks, but I hadn't lost my touch. Then we all piled inside. The door crashing in woke Froder up, and he kind of mumbled at us. Not a guy to let any grass grow under his golf shoes, Barney grabbed the gun, which was leaning against the bathroom door. Harriet yelled, "Get him, Randolph," and Randolph responded by taking a picture of Froder, who had been trying to get up. Not what Harriet had in mind if her expression was anything to go by.

"Out of the way," Barney yelled, because, as any fool would know, he didn't want to shoot any of us; he wanted a straight shot at Froder. He didn't have any luck, because Harriet, letting out the mother of all pissed-off snorts, grabbed the camera from Randolph and beaned the chief engineer with it. Pre-Harriet, he'd been weaving around, knees bent; post-Harriet, he fell down and went back to sleep. Since she was carrying those drapery cords looped around her neck and draped over really, really big knockers, we tied Froder up and left him in his room, with another wedge under that door. So that was two down — O'Brien and Froder, and I'd been in on both. Kind of fun to get into the action again. And I had Carolyn to thank for that. If it weren't for her, I'd be at home walking my dog and watching TV, which is no life for a cop as good as I'd been.

45

Three to Go

Carolyn

Owen and I and our team checked some dormitories, planted some wedges, checked out some officers' quarters, and couldn't find Hartwig. He was the one we really wanted to get, although I didn't like the head steward, Umar Patek, either. I'd have settled for him. Beau and his gang had gone after Hanna Fredriksen and Patek, whoever got to him first. I could see that Beau was disappointed when Luz elected to go off with Barney. Maybe she was getting ready to dump the good doctor. Actually, I couldn't see her in Atlanta as a doctor's wife, even if Beau was a pathologist. "What about their offices?" I suggested to Owen.

We headed upstairs, ready to sing and reel if we had to, but there wasn't anyone around except a clerk who had collapsed behind the reception counter. Since she'd fallen with her skirt hiked up in an unlady-like manner and some of the men were staring at her, I tiptoed around the counter and made her decent before they tied her up. Wanda Sue found a barman sprawled on a couch clutching an empty bottle, so she and Hank stayed to tie him, while Owen and I went down a hall to peek into Hartwig's office. When the handle to his door turned in my hand, I stepped back and whispered to Owen that we shouldn't go in there without weapons. Owen pointed out that we didn't have any weapons, but that Hartwig undoubtedly had a visitor's chair in his office, with which Owen could hit him if he was awake.

I spotted a fire extinguisher — they were everywhere, after all. We should have gotten one for each person we'd recruited before we started this. So I put my finger to my lips, tiptoed down the corridor, and tried to get it off the wall. It wouldn't come off. Fortunately, the wig lady and her hus-band Morty were with us, and he seemed to know how the stupid things worked, but he didn't hand the extinguisher to me. He took it for himself. Meanwhile, Rebecca had armed herself with a long nail file, and

I had nothing but a half bologna sandwich I'd brought along in case I got hungry. Owen counted down from three, and at one we all burst in the door.

Mr. Hartwig, who had been slumped over his desk, which had coffee spilled everywhere, popped up. Rebecca began to sing "Ninety-Nine Bottles of Beer" while she rushed over to the befuddled Mr. Hartwig and jabbed him with her nail file. Since he was gaping at her, he didn't notice her husband aiming the fire extinguisher at him. Once covered with foam, Hartwig let out a roar and lurched forward.

"Hands up," Owen snarled in a very convincing tough-guy voice. He had Mr. Hartwig's gun pointed at Mr. Hartwig's chest. Mr. Hartwig fell forward onto his desk, seemingly fast asleep once more. I could see all that coffee soaking into his white uniform.

Then we tied him up while Owen held the gun on him and gave directions about square knots, which were hard to tie with slippery, braided drapery cords. I was glad Luz hadn't been here to see our attack on the frightening Mr. Hartwig. She'd have thought us dreadfully amateur in our methods.

Luz

Barney and I were on our way back up to find the others, dragging Froder with us. "Sounds like they're around the corner," I said. God, but I needed to take a pee. "You mind hauling him on down the hall while I stop in the Ladies?" Barney went off, dragging Froder by the drapery cord around his feet, while I ducked inside and took the first open booth. Wouldn't you know? The frigging toilet paper fell off the holder and started to roll. When I bent down to catch it, I spotted someone in a booth a couple of doors away. Looked like she sitting on the floor facing the toilet. Puking, probably.

You couldn't pay me to sit on the floor of a public toilet. I managed to snag the roll, took a couple of yards of paper off it, and used some of the clean stuff. I had a mother who was always lecturing us kids on the dangers of public toilets. Don't sit on the seat. Don't use the first layers of paper. When you flush, run like hell out the door before all the wet germs get to you. Well, my mother usually knew what she was talking about, and I can still get myself away from a flushing toilet faster than anyone my age and most people younger. That's why I never use those rotten self-flushers. Either they don't flush at all, or they catch you by surprise.

These weren't self-flushers, so I got out fast, and guess who I found on the floor a couple of booths away? She hadn't even closed the door. Her legs were so long they folded into the next cubicle, and she was fast asleep, lying half across the john. Maybe the avocado soup hadn't agreed with her. She was lucky she didn't fall in and drown. I hauled her up and out, and she never woke up, but she had vomit all over her camouflage shirt. Lucky again. It smelled, but it didn't show up too much.

Beau met me coming out of the Ladies. "Hey, sugah, you got number four."

"Yeah, who's still missing?"

"Patek," Beau replied. "Not in his cabin, not in his office."

"We-all there, Miz Vallejo," boomed Hank, the rancher type.

He mispronounced my name. All his cowhands were probably my color, and he mispronounced their names, too.

"You get that one all by your own self?"

"Whew!" exclaimed Wanda Sue. "She smells." And the two of them went right to it with the drapery cords and tied up the hotel manager. "You know," said Wanda

Sue, as both teams gathered, "they got a big ole safe back in their office. What if the last one is tryin' to get that open? Ah got my birthday diamonds in there that Hank gave me. No tellin' what all else they have locked up. The ship must keep cash money, don't you think? We should —"

"Say, Carolyn." The computer guy from Silicon Valley was trotting down the hall, waving at Carolyn and Owen. "You guys found the head steward yet? I hacked into a Dell in the computer room and picked up an e-mail in the trash bin — like he thought it was gone for good if he deleted it twice. Most people have no idea how long stuff stays on a hard drive and how easy it is to get it back if you know how."

"So are you going to tell us what you found?" Owen asked irritably. We were all getting pretty tired, Carolyn looking like she'd lost interest in the whole thing and wanted to get to bed.

"Patek e-mailed someone in Morocco named Muhammad," said Killington. "Told him to meet the helicopter and kill everyone on it but Hartwig and him. Said they'd torture the Swiss account number out of Hartwig."

There was a lot of conversation about what helicopter, and who Patek really was

388

if he was e-mailing a Moroccan named Muhammad to double-cross the other hijackers. "Muslim terrorists," was Harriet Barber's guess. Sounded reasonable to me.

After that, the whole crowd headed for the room behind the reception desk with the big safe. Some stayed outside to keep watch in case anyone showed up looking for trouble. The signal was "Ninety-Nine Bottles of Beer." Wanda Sue and Rebecca both insisted on going in since they had jewelry in the safe. Me, I wanted to get back to the suite and rub some chili cream into my knees. I was finding out that I wasn't really up to kicking in doors anymore.

Sure enough, when we burst into the office, there was the head steward, stuffing jewelry and money into bags. We're lucky he didn't shoot us all. The gun was right beside him, and he got his hand on it about the same time Sven got to him, hoisted Patek right over his head, and started whirling him around, gun and all. I think what happened is that frigging little creep couldn't get his finger on the trigger before Sven tossed him into the wall. When the gun hit the wall, it fired and blasted the hell out of this picture of a bunch of flowers in *Bountiful Feast* colors.

One or two of his own bullets turned Patek's foot into a bloody pulp, and hitting the wall knocked him out. No one ever figured out how he stayed awake after the avocado soup, but he sort of slithered down the wall and lit among the glass fragments from the flower picture.

"That was Sven's famous Viking Merry-Go-Round," said his wife, Frieda. "He was a wrestler before he founded the Man's Gym chain. Then we merged that with my Fit and Feisty, Inc."

Owen picked up the gun. "Well, that's all five. Let's stow them in the brig. Would you know where that is, Barney?"

"What are you people *doing?*"

We all whirled around to find Sandy Sechrest, the ombudslady, staring at us. She was wearing a nightgown, a robe, and fuzzy slippers, and her hair was rolled up in those big, pink plastic curlers my older sister used to use before her boyfriend came to call and caught her in them.

"Miss Sechrest, thank goodness you're here," said Carolyn, cutting through the crowd to the door. "We just found Mr. Patek looting the safe."

"But —" Sandy looked at the jewels and money scattered around the door of the safe and the three bags stuffed with them, and I could see that she didn't know what to say.

However, my friend Carolyn did. "We have to get Mr. Patek to the clinic. As you can see, he shot his own foot, not to mention the picture over there. And we have to lock the other hijackers up."

"Hijackers?" echoed Sandy in a wobbly voice.

"Yes, so as the only representative of the cruise line here, could you take responsibility for putting all these things —" Carolyn waved at the loot "— back into the safe?"

Poor Sandy, who had been so excited and in charge when she was seeing that my missing clothes got replaced with stuff about forty times the value of what I lost. Now she looked completely bewildered, but we left her to it.

Sven picked up Patek and went off with Beau and me to the clinic to patch the alleged terrorist up and check on O'Brien, who was awake and shrieking when we got there. He wasn't making much sense, but evidently he thought, because of the stirrups, he was going to be given a gynecological examination, which scared the poor guy shitless. I don't like them myself, but I never make that much fuss if I have to have one. I couldn't resist telling O'Brien he had nothing to worry about, that Beau could get to his vagina through his penis. He fainted.

So that's how we captured the hijackers. There was a surprise waiting for the others in the brig, but I wasn't in on that. Beau told me to stop being a wuss and help him with Patek's foot, which was bleeding like a son of a bitch.

46

Early Morning Discoveries

Carolyn

Barney led us off in triumph to the brig with our prisoners, all of whom were unconscious for one reason or another and had to be transported. With our full contingent together, we were able to carry rather than drag them. Frankly, I'd just as soon have gone to bed, but I felt I had to see the mission through since I'd been the one to suggest it in the first place. Lurking at the back of my mind was the uneasy thought that if I'd been mistaken, if they hadn't hijacked the ship, if, in fact, only a work stoppage had occurred, I and everyone else in our party would be in big trouble.

Consequently, I was reassured to find locked up in the brig five security officers and Captain Marbella. That poor man! His handsome uniform was rumpled and dirty, his hair uncombed; he looked as if he'd lost an appreciable amount of weight, and a stream of Italian was issuing from his mouth. Happily, no one could or would translate it; no doubt it was unfit for respectable ears. However, when he realized that we'd taken back his ship and had every intention of restoring him to his command, I thought he might weep. He called us angels of the seas and embraced those of us he could get his hands on.

I must say, he didn't smell very good, but perhaps his captors hadn't provided baths and deodorant. While our captives were carried into the brig and deposited in the cells just vacated, Captain Marbella spat on them as they passed. Since they were still unconscious, they couldn't take offense. He did notice the absence of Patek and asked, "Where is that traitor, Patek?" Owen explained that the head steward had shot himself in the foot and was being patched up in the clinic.

All the way down to the brig, the men had been mulling over John Killington's report on a helicopter, from which all passengers except Hartwig and Patek were to be killed by Muhammad and his colleagues. They decided that the best marksmen of the group should be sent to the top deck to shoot down this helicopter if it appeared. There were four guns, so Sven and Hank Povray were selected because they were experienced hunters.

Owen told the group that he'd been on fox hunts, but that didn't involve shooting the fox, and he had no dogs to contribute, nor did he think they'd be much use against a helicopter; Owen can be very amusing, which was one of the things I liked about him, as long as he wasn't amusing himself at my expense. No one else volunteered, but it was agreed that Luz, as an ex–police lieutenant, and Beau, another hunter, would make satisfactory volunteers once they finished with Patek's foot. The captain muttered, "Let the swine bleed to death for all I care."

Owen, Barney, and I accompanied Captain Marbella to the bridge, where the ship's course had to be changed and the cruise line radioed about the stewards' mutiny, as the captain called it; the officers' hijacking; and the passengers' "brave and heroic retaking of the ship." How nice to be called brave and heroic, I thought, dragging reluctantly behind the men. I didn't feel the part. I wanted to go to bed. Still, there were things I myself felt a need to do. Find Mrs. Gross's emerald necklace, for instance, so I'd know who killed her. Check on the chef to see if he'd be willing to prepare us a celebration dinner, not to mention something edible for breakfast and lunch.

Barney and the captain did necessary things to the radio and contacted Miami, where cruise line executives were relieved to hear that the ship, whose position and situation they didn't seem clear about, was now back in the hands of the captain, and that the hijackers were in captivity. Then the exchange got peculiar. They also hadn't heard anything about a stewards' strike. They wanted to know at what time we had taken over the ship. When they found out that it was after midnight, they expressed dismay.

I thought I heard a man named Balsam ask if the hijackers had been forced to disarm the explosives. *What explosives?* we all wanted to know. Were we prepared to evacuate the ship if necessary? they asked. *What, in the middle of the Atlantic Ocean?* we wondered. *Who would rescue us?* Miami said they'd have to make arrangements. We were instructed to tell our captives that they would all be tried in third-world countries and hanged if any harm came to the passengers. I mentioned Mrs. Gross and Mr. Marshand, as well as the deadly attempts made on the Crosswayses and me. In that case, if harm came to the remaining passengers, Mr. Balsam amended, they'd all be hanged.

"No telling when we can make any threats," said Owen. "They're all unconscious. We drugged them with avocado soup, and those who were still half conscious, we had to knock out." That upset the executives — more and more had gathered in the Miami offices and introduced themselves as higher and higher people in the chain of command. Finally, after instructing the captain to hold an immediate evacuation drill in case of need, they promised to get back to us with new instructions and strategies for rescue.

I thought the whole thing very peculiar, but I slipped away with Herkule's pass card and began a thorough search of the officers' cabins. Within fifteen minutes, I found the emeralds under the mattress in Umar Patek's cabin. Not only was the man a murderer and a terrorist, but he was greedy, as well. He'd stolen jewelry from a corpse and then attempted to loot the ship's safe. At that moment I didn't care if his foot fell off his ankle.

Next I headed for the kitchen to chat with Demetrios. He'd be so pleased to hear my news and would, I was sure, be delighted to recompense me and all the ladies for the Mother's Day celebration we'd missed. He and I reached the kitchen together, having taken the same elevator up. Demetrios was grumbling about having slept badly and dreamt of people making loud noises in the hall and entering his room. However, his pique was nothing compared to the explosion of fury that ensued when he discovered that not a single employee awaited him in the kitchen. "The soup, Demetrios," I reminded him. "They're all unconscious."

"My cooks don't eat the soup," he rumbled angrily.

"Then they're all locked in." We sat down in his office and had a cup of coffee and croissants while I explained the night's activities. He was, as I expected, pleased, and he began to plan the belated Mother's Day feast immediately, *real* avocado soup, a spicy shrimp pasta, rack of lamb with ratatouille . . . I didn't dare object, but avocado soup made me nervous, and lamb? Well, of course it wasn't going to be Mrs. Gross, but still — Oh well, I'd keep a stiff upper lip and enjoy it no matter what. *Mind over matter, Carolyn,* I told myself. "Might I suggest dessert?" I asked. "Could we have the double chocolate raspberry mousse again?"

"But of course, dear madam," he shouted, embracing me. He might not have been so enthusiastic if he'd known that I planned to have two, one of which I'd pass on to Herkule. My dear steward, even though he'd thought he was on strike, had done his best for me with descriptions of food and keycards that made our mission ever so much easier.

"So now we will go to let my staff out of their dormitories," said Demetrios.

I had to agree; he was being so nice about everything. We headed back to the elevator only to hear the rattle of gunfire high above our heads.

The helicopter, I thought. They were trying to shoot it out of the sky, Luz and Beau among them if they'd finished with Patek's foot. And the terrorists probably had arms aboard their helicopter. If Beau and Luz were killed — I could feel the tears coming to my eyes — who would take care of the wounded? Bad enough that I'd had to help deliver a baby once. I simply could not deal with gunshot wounds.

47

An International Incident

Luz

After we finished with Patek, which was a matter of stopping the bleeding — Beau said he was no orthopedic surgeon, so someone else would have to take care of the rest — other members of the team hauled Patek away. But first they stopped to tell us that Carolyn had discovered Mrs. Gross's emeralds under the head steward's mattress. She had a one-track mind, that woman. She wanted to know who killed Mrs. Gross, and by God she kept looking till she got an answer. Carolyn would have made a great homicide detective except she'd have driven everyone in Crimes Against Persons completely nuts.

Beau and I were asked if we'd be willing to stand guard with two others and the two remaining guns up top in case some helicopter showed up. Sven and the rancher were already up there, probably swapping hunting stories. Beau would fit right in, but the only things I'd ever hunted were criminals and a good score on the departmental shooting tests. Still, I was happy to get out in the sunshine after being indoors so long. We scattered over both sides of the deck, scanning the sky with binoculars, and then sprawled in the shade so we could shoot from cover if the helicopter showed up. I never was quite sure why we were expecting a helicopter or why we were going to try to shoot it down or even if you could do that with these guns.

Still, sure enough the damn thing swooped in an hour or so later. Looked military to me, dull colors and all, but when it got close, I could see the Arabic letters on it. Crap! Maybe they really were terrorists. The damn thing made a hell of a lot of noise as it hovered over the end of the boat, blowing deck chairs down and sending sand and cigarette butts flying from ashtray stands. This was one of the few places aboard people could smoke.

A lot of shouting went on. The guys in

the copter were hanging out the windows looking for someone on the decks and yelling in whatever their language was. The only word I caught was *Hartwig,* which was enough for me. Povray got in the first shot. He just stood up and winged one of the Arabs. I stayed under cover, took aim, and shot a rotor blade off. Then the helicopter slewed over and tried to turn.

I think Beau ran a line of shots along the side, while I tried for the nose, which promptly caught fire. Both the Arabs dived out into the sea and swam around shaking their fists at us. When Sven put some more bullets into the copter, it blew up and fell like a comet, fire and parts spewing everywhere. The Arabs must have had some special deal with their God, because they managed to dodge the flaming debris.

Of course, people began to get off the elevator to gawk at the helicopter sinking into the water. "Now," said Beau, "we have to decide what to do about those two." He was talking about the Arabs.

"Hell," said Povray, pushing his cowboy hat back on his head, "let 'em drown."

Barney disagreed. He'd seen enough to decide that they and their copter belonged to somebody's army. "We have to rescue them," he insisted. "Geneva convention."

"Terrorists," Sven objected. "Probably booby trapped, like those suicide bombers."

"Well, if they are, their bombs won't be any good after being dunked in sea-water."

Barney won the argument, and we hauled them up, took a good look at them before we brought them on board, and when we couldn't see any explosives, they got locked in the brig with the rest of the hijackers. That caused a lot of shouting, so I heard, between the helicopter Arabs and Hartwig.

Jason

My crew and I were in the process of re-assembling the ship's filtering systems, which were clogged in places and had had to be cleared out. Some had been deactivated by placement of the wrong filters. It had been a long, messy, exhausting job carried out by sailors and Tenerife laborers under the direction of Spanish-speaking harbor inspectors and myself. I was also assigned more U.S. Navy sailors, as well as technicians provided by the harbormaster's office, men who, when asked, ran analyses on what was running in the pipes and through the filters. The results were often unexpected.

Frankly, no matter what I'd said to the captain in order to get aboard, this was not work to which I was accustomed. My university labs were clean and filled with equipment that had been purchased rather than slapped together on the spur of the moment to meet unexpected needs. My students spoke at least some version of English. And, for the most part, I expected to work regular hours in clothes that were not soaked and stained with various unpleasant substances. I just hoped that my wife would appreciate these efforts on her behalf. I may have missed Mother's Day, but my intentions had been good.

Just as I was about to give the next set of instructions to my motley team of workers, a sailor popped into the area and informed me that the captain wished to confer immediately. After a skeptical look at my clothes, the man repeated, with reluctance, the word *immediately*. So I went as I was.

"Well, the shit's hit the fan," said Captain Wickendon when his new toxicology expert appeared on the bridge, causing several officers to back away from the smell.

"It certainly has," I agreed. "We've found it in several of your —"

"Not talking about the pollution problem," the captain interrupted, as if all that work was no longer of any interest. "What I need to know is if we can leave port."

"When?" I asked.

"The sooner the better. It seems that we've got an international incident on our hands. Someone on the *Bountiful Feast* shot down a Moroccan military helicopter and took the two pilots prisoner. We have it on satellite photos, and a passing Moroccan fishing boat radioed home that the Americans had — well, you get the idea. We've been detailed to steam out there immediately. Chances are that Morocco is sending a ship as well, or at least a flyover. They've already protested to our state department. So can we sail? I don't care if we trail pollution from here to wherever. We do have coordinates for the cruise ship. I just have to know that we're seaworthy."

"Hmmm," I said in my best professorial manner and with every intention of accompanying the ship. "If we put the Canary Islanders ashore immediately, I think I can direct your crew in the last of the reassembly while you make ready to put out to sea. A half hour to do what has to be done, and it should be safe to leave. As for pollution, the problem may well be solved, but only tests while under way will determine that."

"In other words, you've got to stay aboard," said the captain, eyeing me narrowly.

"No, not if you can wait. Three or four hours might do it."

"Lieutenant Hodgkins, clear off the guys from the island. You want to explain it to them, Professor Blue?"

"As best I can," I replied. "My Spanish may be inadequate to the situation."

"Hodgkins will translate."

"But captain —"

"Let me guess. You don't speak Spanish, either. Don't we have a galley seaman who does?"

I returned to the chaos below deck and ushered the Canarians off the ship while multiple translations went on. I couldn't be sure what they thought was happening. Evidently, the harbormaster kept asking if Spain was at war with the United States and was assured that definitely it was not Spain, but possibly Morocco. They were as anxious to leave as I was to see them go. I wanted the destroyer under way before the captain changed his mind about the necessity of keeping a toxicologist aboard. Also, I did want to run tests to see if I actually fixed their problem. If so, it would make an amusing article for *Chemical and Engineering News.*

Once I got the cleanup under way and could no longer see the harbor of Tenerife in the distance, I took two sailors from the cleanup crew to help with testing of the ship's wake and borrowed clean clothes from the lieutenant. I did not want to greet Carolyn looking like a plumber who had spent hours cleaning out a cesspool. She might refuse to get anywhere near me.

48

A Mother's Day
to Remember

Carolyn

We were having our delayed Mother's Day
feast as a midafternoon meal, which would
be served as soon as the chef could produce
it. Staggering crewmembers were reap-
pearing at their posts, groggy but helpful.
The lifeboat drill ordered by the captain
had been performed while we were awaiting
the feast, leaving us time to shower and
dress up in our best clothes. Luz looked absolutely gorgeous in her boutique dress,
and she wasn't even a mother. I was pre-
sentable by comparison, but certainly not
gorgeous, and Vera was really grumpy.

The noisy events of the night had awakened her repeatedly. She had no interest

whatever in our daring exploits, and she warned me that if I attempted to have the stewards and the spa and gym attendants arrested for mutiny, I would become persona non grata in her eyes. *When have I ever been anything else?* I thought bitterly. I had every intention of telling Jason every single thing she'd done to me. Never, never would I go on another vacation with my mother-in-law.

In fact, I didn't even sit with her at dinner. Barney did, faithful man that he was, but Luz, Beau, Owen, and I sat at the captain's table, guests of honor for our counterattack against evil. If he'd had medals on hand, I'm sure Captain Marbella would have pinned them to our chests.

The avocado soup was superb, especially after Demetrios appeared and took the first bowl to prove that it was safe to eat. We all laughed heartily and applauded him. I must admit that I was very relieved to see him swallow spoonfuls and down a glass of the champagne with the soup. And the spicy shrimp pasta that followed was very tasty accompanied by a lovely white wine. But the lamb! Oh, the lamb. Little chops, separated from the racks, pink inside, perfectly glazed outside with lovely lamb gravy inching into the ratatouille. What an absolutely perfect combination paired with a fine, bold red wine.

All through the meal, toasts were drunk to those of us who had participated in the countermutiny, while those who hadn't looked glum. We were a rowdy group — happy, relieved, a bit tipsy, replying to toasts with speeches of our own. I said that this meal made the wait and staying up all night to round up the hijackers well worth it. Owen said he had never expected to get such an exciting book out of this cruise, and we should all look for ourselves on his pages. Luz said she'd discovered that cruising was more fun than she'd expected, and never having gotten to shoot down a helicopter, she was glad she'd come along. Beau said he hoped his medical license wouldn't be suspended for all the undoctorlike things he'd done, but he felt that protecting the lives of the many passengers at risk would excuse him. Barney said sailing on the *Bountiful Feast* was almost as much fun as submarining. Vera didn't say anything because she wasn't asked. But I did, at the end of dinner, get up to explain that I had two double chocolate raspberry mousses in front of me, not because I was any longer binging on desserts as an anti-stress measure, but because I wanted to give one to my sweet steward, Herkule Pipa, who had been so much help in assisting us to retake the ship and who was being taken on as an apprentice chef by Demetrios Kostas el Greco, our own famous executive chef on the *Bountiful Feast.* Herkule was led forward, weeping emotionally, to be presented with his dessert and a modified version of a chef's hat.

That's when the explosion occurred. One chandelier and pieces of the ceiling of the Grand Salon at the other end fell down, fortunately not on those of us who took back the ship.

The captain jumped up and began issuing orders to us and over a telephone, and we were all herded to the emergency stairways and forced to rush to the lifeboat floor. We couldn't go to our rooms for the abominable foam life jackets, but life jackets from the boats and railings were forced into our hands as the boats were swung out, over, and down to deck level. It was terrifying. We had to climb into them as they wobbled over the ocean, while being ordered by shouting crewmembers to blow up our life jackets once the boats hit the water.

I just clung to my seat, closed my eyes,

and prayed. Owen was beside me and shouted, "Maybe it's not too bad. There was only the one explosion."

"So what?" I shouted back. "We won't be able to get back on the *Bountiful Feast* again." The lifeboat slapped into the water, and he suggested that I put on the flimsy little jacket. I was too scared to let go of the seat, so Owen tried to pull my jacket away from me. Naturally, I panicked and pulled back.

"Let go, Carolyn," he ordered, and draped it over my head, completely obscuring my vision of what was happening. For all I knew, the lifeboat was now going down, and the *Bountiful Feast*, as well.

"There," said Owen. "Now, can you fasten the side straps while I get my own jacket on?"

"No," I said. I'd had enough — a horrible night, no sleep, and my lovely dinner sloshing around in my tummy as the miserable little lifeboat, crowded with enough people to sink it, pitched back and forth. "They're all still locked in the brig, aren't they?" I demanded anxiously. "They aren't going to appear at the rail and start shooting at us, are they?"

"No way," said Owen.

"I hope they drown," I muttered, craning

my neck to look for the straps that would keep my lifejacket from washing away in the sea should I be pitched overboard. And how was I to blow up the life jacket? I was so frightened I couldn't get a full breath of air.

"Me too," said Owen supportively. "They probably will drown."

I could hear someone shrieking in another boat that the explosion had been right where her cabin was. "All of our data will be destroyed, Kev," she screamed.

"Holy crap," said Luz, who was in our boat. "If she's right, there goes the only decent wardrobe I ever owned."

Oh my. I had to feel sorry for Luz. She'd looked so amazing in those clothes. I glanced up at the *Bountiful Feast*, looming beside us, and could see the captain standing bravely at the railing directing the lowering of more lifeboats. That fine man was going down with the ship. "Owen, maybe he could jump, and we could pull him in with us."

"Who?" Owen asked. He was fastening his own straps.

"And what happened to Herkule? He probably didn't even get to taste his mousse. And now he'll drown."

"Actually, love," said Owen, as he started

fastening my straps, "the ship doesn't seem to be sinking. Maybe we jumped a bit too early."

"Wouldn't you know?" I muttered. "Here I am, wet, terrified, bobbing around in a stupid rubber boat, and it wasn't even necessary."

"Oh, my God," cried Frieda from a lifeboat on the other side of ours. "Look at that huge gray boat. It's heading right for us. It's probably the Moroccan navy coming to blow us out of the water."

"Don't panic, love," said Owen and shoved a tube into my mouth. "Now blow. Just in case."

I did. If Morocco was going to sink our lifeboats, I couldn't afford to panic and drown because I hadn't inflated my life jacket.

"That's the USS *Fallwell*. It's an Arleigh Burke–class destroyer," said Barney knowledgeably. People stopped talking to hear what he had to say. "Look at that, Vera. It has two gas turbines and two shafts. Does thirty knots or more."

"Is it coming to rescue us, Barney?" I called. "Maybe we should wave at it, if you're sure it's one of ours."

There's nothing more tasty than a

mousse, and the double chocolate raspberry version we had at a belated Mother's Day feast at sea was not only delicious but very pretty, as well. It was also an eventful mousse. I learned after the event that it was responsible for a "work stoppage" at sea, called by some a mutiny, although not by me.

I also used a serving of this mousse as a "tip" for a steward who helped me and my fellow passengers escape the clutches of the evil hijackers, who kept us from enjoying the many delicious meals we might otherwise have had. I expect that even now that steward is learning to make mousse and other delicious desserts for himself, as I arranged for him to become an apprentice chef.

Needless to say, the cruise, as well as the mousse, was "eventful." I include the mousse recipe for those who don't mind a complicated dessert.

Double Chocolate Raspberry Mousse

Refrigerate tall wine glasses or sundae glasses.

Chocolate Mousse: Heat $1/2$ *cup milk* and $1/2$ *cup cream* until it bubbles. Do not boil. Remove from heat.

In blender, mix until creamy: *2 teaspoons butter; $1/2$ teaspoon instant coffee; 2 eggs; 6 ounces finely chopped semisweet chocolate;* and *2 teaspoons rum or brandy.*

At low speed, drizzle in the hot milk and blend smooth (about 1 minute).

Fill cold glasses a third full and refrigerate.

Raspberry Mousse: Put *4 cups whipped cream* in refrigerator.

Mix *$1^{1}/_{2}$ cups fresh raspberries* and *$1/4$ cup sugar* in a saucepan. Stir over medium heat until mixture turns liquid. Stir in *1 tablespoon unflavored gelatin,* remove from heat, and scrape into large bowl. Cool 5 minutes.

Mix 1 cup chilled whipped cream into raspberry mixture until thoroughly combined. Fold in remaining whipped cream.

Fill next third of chilled glasses with raspberry mousse. (Save any remaining mousse for later use.)

White Chocolate Mousse: Stir *8 ounces imported chopped white chocolate; 1/4 cup whipping cream;* and *2 tablespoons light corn syrup* in saucepan at low heat until chocolate is smooth and melted.

Beat *3/4 cup cream* with electric mixer to firm peaks.

Fold cream into white chocolate mixture in 2 batches.

Divide white chocolate mousse among the glasses. Cover and refrigerate at least 4 hours.

Decorative Toppings: (Optional) Make syrup of *6 tablespoons cream* and *2 tablespoons corn syrup* simmering in heavy saucepan over high heat. Reduce heat to low and stir in until melted and smooth *3 ounces chopped semisweet chocolate.* Cool to room temperature and spoon sauce to cover over each mousse. With or without sauce, garnish with *mint leaves, chocolate curls,* and/or *fresh raspberries.*

Carolyn Blue,
"Have Fork, Will Travel,"
Nashville Register

49

The Rescue of the Bountiful Feast

Jason

The captain called me up on the bridge when they sighted the *Bountiful Feast*, and what I saw were lifeboats, at least ten of them. *My God, what has happened?* I wondered apprehensively.

"We managed to contact the captain. Name's Marbella," Wickendon said. "He says they had an explosion during a Mother's Day dinner."

It's not Mother's Day, I thought. *I missed Mother's Day.*

"They put the passengers into boats immediately. Evidently, the hijackers had warned Miami that if the money didn't go into an account in Zurich and the hijackers didn't get away free, they'd blow up the ship. Well, it seems the passengers took the ship back and put the officers who'd done the hijacking into the ship's brig."

My wife could well have been behind that, I thought. Had she survived the counterattack? Was she in one of the lifeboats? I wished with all my heart that Carolyn would give up becoming entangled in dangerous situations. And where was my mother when all these things had been happening? She had been invited so that there would be someone to watch out for my impulsive wife. And, of course, because of her own health. Good grief. Here my mother had suffered a heart attack, and I had callously sent her out on a dangerous cruise.

"Miami thought with the hijackers detained, they couldn't blow the ship. Obviously, they were wrong." The captain was studying the *Bountiful Feast* through binoculars.

I wished that I had the spyglass I'd bought on Tenerife.

"Appears to be listing a little," said the captain. "Not too much."

"Can't we hurry and get those people off the lifeboats?" I asked, fearful for my wife.

"All in good time. It's not as if we can race up to them and stop on a dime."

They were all waving from the lifeboats. Probably terrified. Carolyn among them, or so I hoped. It was a good half hour before the *Fallwell* could start bringing the passengers aboard two at a time in canvas seats drawn up with ropes and winches, a slow and tedious process, with all these people I didn't know appearing over the side of the destroyer. And finally there was Carolyn, all dressed up, wet but beautiful, tearing herself out of the chair and hurling herself into my arms, where she burst into tears. "What are you doing on a destroyer?" she sobbed.

"Well, I flew out to join you for Mother's Day on Tenerife, but the ship never turned up."

"Oh, Jason." She burrowed into my shoulder and got the lieutenant's shirt wet with tears.

"So I called everyone I could think of. The line. The State Department."

"Those horrible people," said Carolyn. "I e-mailed them, and they never replied."

"And then I found the USS *Fallwell* in the harbor, so I volunteered."

Her head snapped up, and she gasped, "You've joined the Navy?"

"No, sweetheart, I just got aboard by volunteering to help with some pollution problems they were having."

"That's so sweet," she sniffled. "Did you know we were attacked by a Moroccan helicopter after we captured the hijackers? Luz helped shoot them down. They were probably terrorists."

"Luz?" I asked, confused. "Luz Vallejo?" That was the only Luz I knew, and I had no idea why she was on the cruise.

The captain had been talking to one of his men and interrupted to say, "Actually, ma'am, that was two guys in the Moroccan army who got paid to steal a helicopter to pick up your hijackers. We just had a radio message from the Moroccan government apologizing for the mistake and asking if we could turn the thieves over to them for trial."

"They're in the brig," said Carolyn. "With the hijackers. Maybe if you wait awhile, they'll all drown."

"Yes, ma'am," said the captain, "but I don't think your ship is going to sink."

"Well, I'm not getting back aboard. You'll just have to take me along wherever you're going."

"Yes, ma'am, we'll take all of you back to Tenerife."

"Good," said Carolyn. "I was really sorry to miss the *guanche* mummies and the Virgin of Candelaria."

Dear Carolyn, I thought. *How like her to go through a hijacking and whatever part she had in taking the ship back, not to mention the helicopter and the explosion, and then find consolation in the thought that she wouldn't miss some interesting historical site, after all.* Over Carolyn's shoulder, I could see the other passengers appearing on deck, among them my mother and Luz Vallejo.

"Well, Jason," said my mother, "I think you should know that your wife has been sleeping with a Welsh crime writer."

Carolyn whirled out of my arms and said, "That's a nasty lie, Vera, and you know it. You're the one who's been sleeping around. With Commander Levinson, not that he isn't a nice man, but having sex in the room next to mine? I was really embarrassed."

"Mother?" I stared in shock.

"Sorry about that, lad," said a short, burly man with clipped white hair, "but my intentions are honorable. I consider your mother the best woman I've met since my late wife died. Women of principle, both of them."

"That's Commander Bernard Levinson," said Carolyn politely. "U.S. Navy Submarine Corps, retired. Commander, my husband, Jason Blue."

I found myself shaking the hand of the stranger with whom my mother had evidently been sleeping, which came as a great surprise. I'd have assumed that her feminist principles would have kept her uninvolved after her divorce from my father over thirty years ago, not to mention the fact that she was now over seventy, not an age at which I'd expect to find her engaging in a fling.

"And I'm Owen Griffith, the accused adulterer," said a fellow with uncombed, black hair. "I wish I could say your mother was right, but your wife wasn't having any of it. Carolyn spent a couple of nights in my room so the hijackers couldn't find her and finish up the job of killing her, but she just wouldn't share a bed, no matter how charming and gallant I was."

"Carolyn was true blue, as always," said Luz Vallejo. "Vera and I were the only ones having sex, but then we're of age and unmarried. Right, Vera?"

I looked down at my wife, who was yawning. "How long since you've had any sleep, sweetheart?" I asked.

"Too long," she admitted. "And all this running down hijackers, and explosions, and being shoved into lifeboats is very tiring. We did have a wonderful Mother's Day dinner." She yawned again. "Once we got the ship back, and the chef didn't have to feed all the good food to the crew. By the way, Captain. You'll want to know that Bruce Hartwig, the chief security officer, is the one who tried to kill the Crosswayses and me. And Umar Patek, the chief steward and probably a terrorist, killed Mrs. Gross and stuck her body in the meat freezer. And hmmm —"

"I wonder if we can borrow a cabin, Captain?" I asked. "Carolyn is asleep on her feet."

"Sure, take mine," the captain offered.

"Don't blame the stewards," Carolyn mumbled over her shoulder. "Hartwig talked them into the work stoppage and then didn't even present their demands to the cruise line."

"I'll keep that in mind, ma'am," said Captain Wickendon. "You have a nice nap now. Help yourself to the bourbon in my desk, Jason."

"It's tasty with Coca-Cola," Carolyn informed me as her head fell against my shoulder. The very thought made me wince, but I knew that Carolyn had never, in all our years of marriage, expressed a liking for whiskey of any kind, much less mixed with Coca-Cola. My wife has very refined tastes in food and drink.

Dessert
Recipe Index

About the Author

Nancy Fairbanks is a pseudonym for Nancy Herndon, who is the author of the Elena Jarvis Mystery series. She has also written historical romances under the name Elizabeth Chadwick. She lives in El Paso, Texas, with her husband, Professor Emeritus of Chemistry at the University of Texas at El Paso and an active researcher. She travels widely and frequently with her husband throughout America and Europe, enjoying new places, interesting people, good food, opera, and scientific conferences.

Visit her Web site at
www.nancyfairbanks.com.

The employees of Thorndike Press hope you have enjoyed this Large Print book. All our Thorndike and Wheeler Large Print titles are designed for easy reading, and all our books are made to last. Other Thorndike Press Large Print books are available at your library, through selected bookstores, or directly from us.

For information about titles, please call:

(800) 223-1244

or visit our Web site at:

www.gale.com/thorndike
www.gale.com/wheeler

To share your comments, please write:

Publisher
Thorndike Press
295 Kennedy Memorial Drive
Waterville, ME   04901